HMS Audax

DAVID O'NEIL

W & B Publishers
USA

W & B Publishers

For information:
W & B Publishers
9001 Ridge Hill Street
Kernersville, NC 27284

www.a-argusbooks.com

ISBN: 9781942981763
Cover art by David O'Neil
Book Cover designed by Dubya

Printed in the United States of America

Chapter One

First Lieutenant John Macklin

The oily waters of the dock glinted in a pattern of colours under the working lights swaying in the fresh breeze off the Solent. The ships were a uniform grey, the outline of their upper-works making stark shapes against the lightening sky.

John Macklin looked at the sky to the east as he walked down the dock, wondering if the forecast of sunny weather would actually happen. As he approached the gangway, the duty Petty Officer stepped forward and recognised him. He saluted "Morning. Sir, Captain is on board. Three new officers have reported in. No men on report."

John returned the salute. "Thank you, Rogers. We can go through the list when the skipper finishes his rounds."

John boarded the destroyer lying alongside the quay, automatically saluting the Sub-Lieutenant standing on deck, and then the quarterdeck aft. Down in his cabin he threw his cap on to the door hook, stripped his wet raincoat off and hung it in in the shower to drip dry.

He took the packet of charts and orders and stepped along to the captain's cabin. He knocked on the door and opened it as he heard the word, "Enter".

"Morning, sir. I have the mail, the charts and the by-hand orders. He placed them on the desk and stood back.

Commander Michael Warrender DSO RN was stocky and fair-haired, thinning on top, his grey eyes seemingly designed to gaze at distant horizons. In fact, he was starting to use reading glasses for close work. He took the package of orders, mail and the new charts and waved to the only other chair in the cabin. "Take a pew, while I run through the awkward bits."

"How was your run ashore?" He said as he flipped through the signals and then opened the orders. "Hello! What have we here?" He picked out the section which obviously contained a matter of interest. He read the instructions carefully, and then he read them again. Looking up, he said. "This will interest you, number one, we have been ordered to collect a seriously important group from Le Havre." He passed the order over to Macklin.

The orders read. *'To Officer i/c HMS Audax: Being in all respects ready for sea, you are to proceed forthwith, with dispatch, to the port of Le Havre. There to collect a party for repatriation to the United Kingdom. Your priority is the safe return of the people nominated regardless of costs.'*

Signed: *J. Howard CBE, DSC, Rear Admiral. Portsmouth.*

Macklin read the order. "That is pretty explicit. We are in all respects ready for sea. That list looks a bit like Debrett to me. I'd better get things started,, since it's 'with all dispatch.'"

"I'll see you on the bridge when we are singled up. Carry on, John."

"Aye, aye sir." John made his way to the bridge. The Cox'n met him there.

"Call all hands. Stations for leaving harbour."

"Aye Aye, sir." The Cox'n clicked on the P/A. "All hands stand by. Stations for leaving harbour." A rush of feet on decks and ladders followed the order.

On the bridge John Macklin gave further orders. "Engines to stand by. Single-up bow and stern ropes."

The calls went out as the Captain reached the bridge.

Macklin reported,. "Ship is ready to cast off and all systems ready for leaving harbour."

"Thank you, Number one. Port engine slow ahead. Starboard engine stand by. Five degrees starboard wheel, Cox'n. Cast off bow line." Then, as the bow swung clear of the vessel moored ahead, "Starboard engine slow ahead. Cast off stern line. Helm amid-ships."

The destroyer moved steadily out along the channel between the moored ships toward the open sea. She gathered speed through the grey waters into the Solent until she was moving at twenty five knots and heading almost due south to the Port of Le Havre.

Further up the channel, the evacuation of Dunkirk was over. *HMS Audax* had been part of that operation, though further down channel, working the port of Dieppe.

In the Captain's day cabin behind the bridge, the skipper sat reading some of the other information he had received with the new orders. The calendar on the bulkhead was crossed off up to the 19th of June 1940, today. Europe was in turmoil already. The French were in disarray.

John Macklin knocked and entered the room. "You called, skipper?"

"I did. Sit!"

John sat on the bunk.

Commander Peter Warrender was reading one of the documents. "I notice here that you know Dr Amy Martin?"

"Who? Doctor Amy Martin?" He thought for a few moments. "Did you say Amy Martin?"

"I certainly did. Why? Do you know her or not?"

"I do recall a gawky girl when I was at Oxford. She was called Amy Martin, I believe. Why do I have to remember the girl in question? I swear I had nothing to do with her fatherless child. So what is up?"

"Dr Amy Martin, PhD, is in charge of the party we are commanded to collect when we reach Le Havre. The spooks think that the Germans may try to infiltrate an agent into the party. Apparently, this female Doctor has assembled a group of people who were left out of the last evacuation collection. They think, if you recognise the lady, there will be less chance of any infiltration."

"I thought the evacuation of Le Havre was over. How the devil am I supposed to know her after four years? She was a year behind me anyway. I only knew her because we were both in the debating society. I do recall she was pretty good at that. But I was reading English and Maths. She was sciences, I think, Physics, Chemistry, I believe."

"Well, you'll soon get to find out. We will be there in about three hours. They should be in the harbour office."

As John made to get up and return to the bridge, Warrender stopped him. "By the way, when we have dropped the party off, we are due to report to Western approaches, Liverpool, for convoy duties."

"That will please most of the crew. At least half of them come from 'oop north'." John grinned. He left the cabin and returned to his post on the bridge.

"Well, Mid, did you lose us while I was away?"

"Fat chance of that, sir. You were only gone for five minutes." The hostilities/only midshipman, Tom Murray, had been left in charge while the first lieutenant was away from the bridge.

John smiled, thinking that Murray would be alright. The h/o tag meant hostilities only – so he was not making a career of the navy. It did mean he would be with the Royal Navy until the war was over. So far\ he had showed the right sort of aptitude and attitude. He also got on with the PO's. The other Middy, Martin Offord, was not so open a character, more difficult to assess. John reserved judgement on him.

He heard Murray check the helmsman, "Watch her head, Jackson." The response was immediate. Reassured that they were all awake and answering to the ship's needs, he strolled over to the bridge wing to check the compass and engine repeaters mounted there. All was in order, so he looked over the side at the water racing past, lifting his eyes to the horizon. There was little to see but the white caps of the waves and the low line of land in view. He guessed at this rate they would be at Le Havre sooner than the three hour prediction given by the Skipper.

Two hours later with the skipper on the bridge, *HMS Audax* entered the French harbour at Le Havre. The quays were mostly empty, so they made their way to the main quay.

"This is a touch and go trip, so just single bow and stern lines, engines on stand-by." John appeared in blue battledress with webbing belt and pistol holster. His .38 Webley revolver, with the lanyard attached, in place at his side. He was carrying a sten gun with a stick magazine in his hand.

"All ready to go, Number One?" The skipper did not sound too worried. "The marines are at the gangway. Do not take any risks."

"Right, sir. I'll be off." John saluted and descended the ladder to the main deck. He crossed the gangway already in place, waiting. Four Marines plus the sergeant were armed and standing by as he stepped on to the quay. They made their way to the Port offices. Several people were on the quay watching the destroyer arrive, but no one made any approach to the ship. At the office a naval officer was waiting.

John saluted him and asked, "Where is the party awaiting collection?"

The naval Commander shrugged his shoulders, "I regret Lieutenant, the English lady and her party have been taken to the police station to await the Germans."

"Have you transport?"

The Commander looked startled. "Of course. I have a truck."

"Take us to the police station please, Sir." John raised the sten-gun. "Sergeant! Send a man to the ship. Tell them I have to collect the party from the police station." He turned to the French Officer. "Your truck Commander?"

"Certainment, Lieutenant. First perhaps..." He pointed to the unloaded Sten gun, the magazine stuck behind John's belt.

John hurriedly clipped the magazine into the gun and cocked it, then set the safety catch.

The Frenchman, now satisfied, led the way to a Citroen truck parked on the quay.

The Marine sergeant returned with the bo'sun and two leading seamen, all armed. "Skipper thought you might need us, sir." The bo'sun gasped.

"Right. All aboard the truck. Load and secure your weapons, safety catches on."

The truck drove up the Rue de Paris to the Police Municipal building on the Rue Jules Lecesne across the road from the Marie.

In the reception area of the police station there was a collection of people, all speaking at the same time, in English and French. John stepped into the throng with the Commander. He called for silence, without result. He called, "Bo'sun!"

The bo'sun raised his call. The shriek of the whistle cut through the noise like a knife through butter. John stepped in immediately. "Doctor Amy Martin, please step forward with your party. "

"Thank goodness!" A female voice said. "My people to the doorway, please. Assemble where that naval officer is standing."

There was a mass movement to the doorway as people sorted themselves out as members of the party and others.

A large French policeman arrived and said something. The Commander translated. "He says, 'You cannot take the English people. They are under arrest, to be held until the Germans arrive'."

John said. "On whose orders?"

"The policeman says. 'Orders of the German high command for the Normandy area'."

John turned to the doctor. "Please get your people onto the truck."

"Of course. Thank you, John. You are a sight for sore eyes."

He turned back to the Commander. "Thanks, Commander. Tell him I took them away by force."

"Of course you did." He spoke rapidly to the policeman, then dashed out to the truck with John. They rode down to the quay and lined the people up to board the *HMS Audax*.

For the first time John really looked at the doctor. He realised that it was the girl he had argued with in the debating society, but not in the same state as he had last seen her. She came over and spoke to him directly, for the first time since they met at the police station.

"Remember me?" She said with a smile.

"I do, and I have to say that, though you have changed, you haven't really. I recognised you straight away."

"Well, I have to say I recognised you also. It has been some time since we were at Oxford. I must say that you came just in time. It was beginning to look as if the French were going to hand us over to the Germans."

John stood back a little and looked Amy in the eye. "Now, why would the Germans ask to have you detained for them specifically?"

"I really have no idea what you are talking about."Amy declared.

John took her by the arm and led her out of the crowd, into the wardroom currently empty. "I have just threatened to shoot the Chief of Police in Le Havre on your behalf. Now why do they want you in particular? What are you a doctor of?"

"Physics! And if I tell you any more, I will have to shoot you." She looked up at him, a small smile on her face.

Baffled, he looked back at her, and then leaned forward and kissed her. After a startled second she kissed him back. His arms went round her, holding her close and she wrapped her arms round his neck. They stood like that for what seemed an eternity. Then they broke apart.

"What brought that on?" Amy asked, a little breathlessly.

A red-faced John admitted, "Ever since we met in debate, I wondered what it would be like to kiss that mouth which, so annoyingly, always had an answer. Now I know." He looked like a schoolboy on the carpet in front of the headmaster.

"Well. Was it worth it?"

For a moment. John was confused. Then he realised what she had said. "It certainly was," he answered enthusiastically.

"You could have done that at any time when we were at Oxford. She stepped forward, "Just in case it doesn't happen again." She grabbed him, brought his head down and kissed him again. As she went to release him he had gathered himself and joined in with enthusiasm, so the release took longer than either expected.

It was the voice of Peter Warrender which broke the spell. "I suppose that means you do recognise Dr Martin then, Number One."

The couple broke apart hurriedly. "We were just completing some unfinished business," the doctor said with an embarrassed giggle. Completely unaffectedly, she took out her handkerchief and cleaned lipstick from John's face.

John hastily introduced his captain. "Amy, this is Commander Peter Warrender, the captain of this ship, and my boss. Skipper, this is Doctor Amy Martin."

The Captain held out his hand and shook Amy by the hand. "How do you do, Doctor. I am pleased we were able to be of assistance. Do you know all of the people in your party?"

"I do not know the French Naval Commander. Otherwise, I know them all."

Warrender looked up at John the question in his eye.

John said, "When I went ashore he was on the quay. He was able to tell me that the doctor and her party had been arrested, and taken to the police station. He also provided the van for us to go to, and return from, the police station. Since he is a naval officer, I invited him to come to England with us."

"Good. Welcome aboard, Doctor. I'll leave you two to renew your acquaintance." He turned and left them alone once more.

John looked at Amy. "If you are not involved at the moment. I would like to renew our acquaintance once we get back to England."

She looked at him, a small smile on her face. She held her hand out and he took it into his. "Agreed. I think it would be interesting. We are different people now, of course. So, yes. Let's see how it works out."

***

For the rest of the trip they saw nothing of each other. On her voyage across the channel the ship was strafed by two Messerschmitt 109's in passing. They kept John pretty busy as a result, until they finally entered Portsmouth harbour and came alongside. He was at the gangway when the passengers went ashore. As Amy came down the gangway, she had a wicked look in her eye as she came to where John was standing. She darted up and kissed him, pushing a piece of paper into his hand. "Call me." She breathed.

The ratings assisting the passengers ashore watched, with obvious approval, at the sight of their Number One getting kissed.

Chapter two

Doctor Martin

The next day was spent getting the ship fuelled and ammunitioned. There were a few other preparations to be done. A period of leave had been granted before the ship sailed to Liverpool for her convoy duties in the North Atlantic. John rang the number he had been given by Amy. The voice at the other end of the telephone was not Amy. It was female, however. "I am calling to speak to Amy Martin," he said.

"Who is calling?" The voice asked.

"My name is John Macklin," he said hopefully.

"Aha! The mysterious Naval Lieutenant. She said to tell you she will be home in Chichester by six this evening."

"Where is home in Chichester?"

"Sorry. I forgot you met in Oxford, didn't you. Home is the Old Mill House. She is fond of claret, by the way. Good luck!"

The voice rang off before he could ask who it was he was talking to.

He went and sorted out the Morgan three wheeler, removing the cover to check the plugs and the oil levels. There was petrol in it already. The tank held ample fuel for the ten mile journey. He put his bag in the car, guessing that he would probably stay in a local pub while he was there. Hopefully, he would be able to spend more than just the evening with Amy. He was still trying to get over the change in her appearance. She had always had an appealing face with lovely dark eyes. But, in the past, she had been like a string bean. Now she was delightfully curved in all the right places, something that he had not failed to notice when she was pressed up against her as they kissed the first and second time. Her hair was now cut short, and framed her face, rather than covering it as it once had, the short tumbled mop topping her five-foot, seven inch figure.

John felt some nervous anticipation as he drove the short distance to Chichester. The picturesque small town, so favoured by the yachting fraternity in peacetime, was not as busy as he had known it in the past. He drove through the centre and sought out the Old Mill House on the banks of the river.

He pulled up outside, relieved to see the figure waiting to greet him. He climbed out of the small car and grabbed the bag with the bottle of claret. "How long have you got?" Amy asked him.

"Three days, if I'm lucky," he said a little breathlessly.

"Did you bring a bag?" She asked.

"It's in the car," he said surprised.

They were walking along the path to the front door. "I'll pop back and get it while you go in and make yourself comfortable.

She was gone before he could protest. So, with a shrug, he continued through the front door where he took off his hat and hung it on the hallstand.

He wandered through to the kitchen. The Aga stove had created a warm cosy zone after the cooler air of the evening. He placed the claret on the worktop and stood with his back to the stove, enjoying the warmth.

Amy appeared, his overnight bag in her hand. "There is a fire on in the lounge where there are places to sit in comfort. I'll join you in a minute.

She disappeared again. He wandered through to the comfortable room overlooking the river. The mill wheel was gone but the garden, mainly lawn sloped down to the dancing waters of the river.

John looked around and removed his uniform jacket and black tie. He slung them across the back of an upright chair and sat back on the long settee, wondering what would happen next, still a little apprehensive, but looking forward to whatever came along.

Amy Martin was as nervous as John. She could see him sitting relaxed through the open door of the lounge. As things were, her experience with men at university had been minimal. Actually zero. Since then, her experience had broadened considerably through contact with her colleagues within the service. Training on the SOE was explicit when dealing with possible interrogation techniques. It had led to experimentation among the trainees especially those who had no previous experience to draw upon.

In her own case, she had discovered a hidden side that she had not been aware of. She was convinced that her guest was not experienced in the relations between men and women, and, since she liked John, she decided to let things take a natural course, rather than take the initiative. Since her mother was coming to dinner that night, perhaps it would clear the air a little.

She walked into the lounge. "Drink?" She managed.

He leapt to his feet and said, "Can I help? What would you like?"

Amy produced the wine and a corkscrew, and passed them on to him. While he did the honours, she asked him about his life since they had last met at Oxford.

"I always intended to join the Navy." He sounded quite shy to her surprise. In his own environment, on board the ship, he was decisive and very much the ship's officer. Here, he was not so sure. "One thing led to another. My mother and father were supportive, so I had no problems there."

"I seem to recall you and a girl, Georgie. I believe were a big item in Oxford. What happened to her?" Amy had been jealous. Georgie Simmonds had been the envy of every other girl of the college with her figure, her skin, and her long blonde hair.

John smiled ruefully. "She was using me as camouflage, and I was daft enough to think she really liked me." He shrugged. "Just goes to show what a fool I was then. She is married to Harry Adams, of the famous butcher's chain of shops. I liked Harry, so I was put out when it all came out. There was a scandal they kept between the few of us involved."

"Scandal?" Amy said surprised.

"Georgie became pregnant. I was supposed to be the reason. Only I was not the man she was after. She tearfully explained that, after a drunken party, she and Harry had accidently fallen into bed together and bingo?"

"Bingo?" Amy giggled.

John laughed. "Something like that."

They were both still laughing when the front door opened and a voice called, "It's only me, darling. I brought one or two things with me."

"Oops, that's mother. She will be with us tonight, off again tomorrow. Do you mind?"

John was relieved. "No, of course not. I'm just a guest remember."

The face that poked around the door was an older version of Amy but with black hair."Hullo, John Macklin, that name is a blast from the past. Nice to meet you after all this time. I'm Amy's mum. You can call me Bella."

"Hello, Bella. Call me John. I am pleased to meet you after all this time."

"Enough, you two. Come on through. We can talk in the kitchen while I get dinner." Amy took charge before things got out of hand.

The evening passed off pretty well, though John discovered that his reputation as a student had been a regular topic of conversation in the Martin household several years ago.

Bella went to bed early after a long day travelling and shopping.

Seated with Amy alone at last, John did not find it awkward. He gathered that Amy had no intention to rush any romantic encounter and, while it was almost inevitable something would happen between them, it was just going to happen naturally, or not at all.

He guessed they would work it out between them.

One common agreement seemed that, whatever did happen, it would not be while Bella was asleep in the third bedroom.

***

They saw Bella off the following morning and, by mutual consent, went walking in the Sussex countryside, conveniently finding a pub, where they stopped for lunch, before returning to the Mill.

John settled down in the comfort of the lounge while Amy prepared something to eat, and the long evening faded into night.

Chapter three

Atlantic

The bow of the destroyer dipped and lifted, bringing a wave of cold water with it as it washed over the forward deck, smashing against 'A' gun before finding its way back through the scuppers to the grey Atlantic Ocean. John wiped the lens of his binoculars and lifted them to scan the area of sea surrounding the ship. The long line of merchantmen stretched against the skyline. The regular wave-motion making them rise into view in turn, and then drop from sight.

Forward, the lead destroyer was plunging and rising, almost disappearing into the cloud of spray she created as she ploughed through the rough sea. The tell-tale from the Asdic flashed with a report of a contact. A light from the lead ship ordered *Audax* to keep contact while the lead destroyer made an attack run. John called to the signalman to acknowledge the order, and spoke to the asdic operator to maintain contact with the submarine, and warning him that *HMS Seraphim* would be dropping charges.

Across the convoy in the far line of ships there was an explosion. A column of smoke and debris rose dark against the bright sky. It was the responsibility of the escorts on the other side of the convoy. Though he felt for the plight of the men from that ship, John ignored it from a practical point of view. His attention was needed on this side of the columns of ships.

He turned to Sub-Lieutenant Fordyce, who was standing watch with him. "Best call the skipper, Jim. Things are getting busy."

He watched Jim Fordyce as he went to the day cabin to arouse the skipper. He was not surprised when the cabin door opened as the Sub raised his hand to knock.

Peter Warrender is looking tired, John thought. It was not unexpected in the circumstances. The U boats had been keeping all of the escorts on the hop ever since they had left Liverpool. They had lost four ships so far. *Counting this morning, make that five,* John thought.

This was their second convoy. In the first one they had made it to Halifax virtually unscathed. The return trip to Liverpool had been a bloodbath. It had seemed at the time that every U boat in the German Navy had congregated to attack their convoy. Twelve ships sunk out of twenty left the escorts reeling. For the *Audax* it was a baptism of fire and the entire crew were on edge. The loss of so many of the ships from what had been a fast convoy had shaken them considerably, especially as the crew were still trying to settle to their task.

The *Seraphim* made a run out to port of the convoy line and dropped a pattern of depth charges. The mountains of yellow-tinged water were impressive, but there was no sign of the U boat, presumably underneath.

John called the Asdic office, "Have you still got the sub?"

"Still got her sir, bearing? 038 degrees sir.

"Bunts!" The signals man responded. "Send to *Seraphim,* 'Sub now bears 038 degrees from us.'"

The clatter of the Aldis signal lamp seemed loud in the morning air.

The swift response from *Seraphim* testified to the efficiency of her crew. As she swung onto a new course, deck-mounted charges were already spilling from her stern while the Y mounts on deck shot others in a widening pattern.

John did not hold out much hope for the success of the attack. He had a healthy respect for the abilities of the U boat commanders they had encountered up to now.

There was no sign of the U boat being killed so the *Seraphim* returned to her place in the line, satisfied that they had perhaps driven it away to a point where it would be hard put to keep track of the convoy. Once again, he did not really believe that the sub had been chased off, but he lived in hopes. They received no more attacks that day, but it did not relieve the tension.

In the wardroom the two sub-lieutenants were arguing about the U boat, and its survival or demise. The Midshipman Tom Murray was listening warily to the argument.

"Have I interrupted something?" John asked.

."We, we... we're working out if we got the U boat or not," Jim Fordyce offered.

"Who has the duty?" John replied.

Owen Jones looked at his watch, and sprang to his feet. "Bugger! I will be late if I don't leave now." He dashed off, grabbing his oilskin hanging dripping in the corner.

"Well, Tom, how are you settling in to life on the ocean wave?" John asked.

"Quite nicely, sir. the beds are a bit lumpy, or maybe it's the sea. I'm not sure yet. Otherwise I am pleased I joined."

The messman came with a bowl of stew for John. It was hot and spicy, and it came with a piece of bread. He tucked in with the appetite of a man who had just spent four hours on watch on a cold and wet bridge.

The Middy sat and watched John eat, waiting until he finished before asking the question that was bothering him. "Sir, are we likely to continue to encounter U boat attacks all the way back across to Liverpool?"

"I'm afraid so. They know we will have ships loaded with provisions of all sorts for delivery to UK, so they will try to stop them coming. That is really what they are there for. I expect we will spend a lot of our time at action stations. Is it worrying you?"

"Not really, though I do get scared. You all seem to keep calm and collected throughout the action. Don't you ever get scared?"

John laughed. "Of course. The thing is, when you have things to do, it helps keep the fear where it belongs, to one side. Normally, during an attack there is no time to be scared. I'm too busy keeping up the pressure on the U boats to worry too much about things."

***

The weather did not improve over the next few days and, though there were three U boat alerts, none resulted in any usable contacts and no other ships were lost.

Cruelly, the convoy was attacked as it approached the port of Liverpool. A torpedo attack came from a submerged U boat from the direction of the Irish Sea. The *Port Arthur* carrying flour and rice, took the full force of the attack and literally exploded over the surrounding sea. Her nearest companions in the next line of ships were coated in flour, and took numerous wounds from the metal debris scattered about the killing zone. Two men died and two others received injuries from the hundreds of small pieces of shrapnel from the shattered freighter. When the air cleared the ship was gone, completely. Of the thirteen man crew, none survived. By the time the nearest escort reached the area the attacker was well clear.

The convoy docked in the port, releasing the much needed cargo to be distributed around the country.

Chapter four

Mavis

John had been given leave when the ship entered the dock for repair. A week which could be spent doing whatever he pleased meant a call to London in hope of contacting Amy.

The number she shared with her colleague was busy when he rang in the first place. He eventually got through to hear that Amy was away at present, though expected back, in two days time.

He made arrangements to stay at the RAC club. His father had enrolled him into the club as a reward for obtaining his degree. The lifetime membership had been useful on several other occasions when he had been stuck in London.

From the club, he rang Amy again and this time he received an answer. Her friend, Marion, was expecting Amy any moment, and she promised to have her contact John as soon as she got in.

Within ten minutes of his replacing the telephone, the steward brought the telephone back to him with a breathless Amy at the other end. "John, Marion has gone off for the weekend, so why not grab your gear and come and join me here. Then we can save time coming and going to two different places.

John did not question the implication in her words. He picked up his gear and called the doorman for a taxi.

Here, was Dolphin Court, west of Sloane Square. John was in a taxi on his way within ten minutes of the call.

Vouched for by Amy in person, he was allowed through the reception area. When Amy closed the door of the apartment behind her, he dropped his bags to the floor, swept her into his arms and kissed her, an action she contributed to with no hesitation.

As he released her, he realised what he had just done without thinking. "I....I am sorry. I just did not ......"

"Sorry? Was it not what you expected?"

"I got carried away. I am not normally so impulsive. It was just that I looked forward to this ......" His voice trailed off as he realised he was digging himself into a hole.

She rescued him. "Was it so bad then?"

"N..No it was great, but...."

"Would you rather we had not kissed?" She was teasing him, but she was still anxious about his answer.

"Of course not. I meant I had been looking forward to doing that while I was away and I just got carried away. I was worried I might have ruined things, in case you didn't feel the same way," he said lamely.

She smiled. "I don't actually make a habit of inviting people I dislike to my private residence,, making sure the coast is clear first."

"I didn't mean that. I'll shut up and we can start again if you like."

"Yes, please." Amy said, slipped into his arms again. She held her head waiting for the kiss which he had finally realised was welcomed.

The rest of the week passed too quickly for both of them, and it seemed that he was leaving far too soon.

***

His train to Liverpool was crowded. Even the first class carriages were full, though there were seats for everyone, which was more than the other passengers could claim. John's memories of the week were still uppermost in his mind. His experience of lovemaking had been limited to amateurish fumbling in the back seat of his father's car. The result had been disappointing to both the girl and John. With Amy it had been incredible. They had just seemed to combine with no real problem. John did not consider that it was unusual, since he had no experience to compare it with. The warm glow of the week stayed with him for the entire journey.

There was an air raid on when the train pulled in, and John was lucky to get a taxi. The driver commented, "I just carry on now, even if there is a raid on. The buggers don't give us much peace anyway, and half the time they are on the other side of town."

He got John to the dock gates without a problem, though John could see that the raids were having an effect on Liverpool. Damaged buildings and blocked off streets were evidence of that. He paid the driver, collected his bag, and made his way to his ship, *HMS Audax* was now alongside the quay, still being worked upon by the dockyard men.

John reported to the captain and was told that this time they would not be leaving with a convoy. New orders specified a rendezvous off the Calf of Man in the Irish Sea, escort for coastal party south. "It seems there is a bit of a panic about getting some experimental gear south as soon as possible. There is talk that the enemy may have found out. We are there to stop them interfering. We take them south, then stand by to escort them into action on the French coast somewhere. I do not know where or when but no chat in the wardroom, please."

"When do we move off?"

"I'm told we will receive a signal."

***

For the next few days John chased up the dockworkers and concentrated on clearing up the mess they left behind. There was time for work to be done on the paintwork, though it was patchwork mainly.

Finally, the orders came through. *HMS Audax* finally got rid of the dock workers, and made its way to the Isle of Man. There, opposite the Calf of Man, they picked up a sleek modern, coastal cargo ship, about three thousand tons. She was named the *Mavis,* and was clean and smart, not to be compared with the scruffy ships on the North Atlantic. Her appearance was matched by her performance. She made an easy 20 knots for most of the way, and the officers on *HMS Audax* got the impression that she was definitely holding back to allow the escort to keep up. Since the destroyer could still raise 36 knots there was little fear of that, but there was no doubt that *Mavis* was a fast, well-found ship

At Milford Haven the mad rush down the Irish Sea ended. The two ships moored in the outer reach of the enclosed waters, far from prying eyes. There the *Mavis* dropped a power boat towing a raft behind it, which raced away across the waters. An opening appeared, a previously unseen panel in *Mavis's* forward side. From it dropped what looked like a torpedo, which shot off after the power boat and her tow. From the bridge of the destroyer it was possible to see that the torpedo matched every twist and turn made by the madly-driven power boat. They could clearly see the wake of both the pursued and the torpedo.

When the torpedo caught the target, there was a brief flash of low-level blue light. At that point the power boat obviously became the recovery craft. It returned to the moored *Mavis,* towing both the target and the torpedo.

On *Audax* John exchanged glances with Peter Warrender. "Now we have some idea of what the panic was about. I wonder how it finds its target."

"I do not think we are supposed to know what we already know." John said quietly. My guess would be that our future is going to be fewer convoys and more cloak and dagger."

Peter replied, "I have a feeling that you are right. I think that, whatever happens, it might be more interesting than the Atlantic."

The Admiral's Barge appeared and came alongside *Audax* in the dark of the evening. It carried a Rear Admiral, his Aide and a WRNS 2nd Officer. The Admiral was Paul Harrington and he was responsible for Special Services. The aide was more efficient than he seemed, and the WRNS officer was drop-dead gorgeous. Her looks belied the fact that she was employed for her brain as much, probably more, than her appearance.

Her presence on the ship lifted moral the moment she stepped aboard.

Peter Warrender looked at John who seemed stunned. A nudge from Peter was all that saved him from being a complete fool. Amy's influence should have been enough to keep his balance, but somehow it wasn't. Their family homes were facing across the Beaulieu River just north of Bucklers Hard. John had known Chloe since he was a boy, at first just as a figure across the river, then when he learned to swim they had met in the river, and on it when both learned to sail. They had been friends ever since, and only lost contact when each went to a different boarding school. But had re-established their friendship at University, where they had shared several courses.

As they saw the Admiral to Peter's cabin, Peter managed to whisper to John. "Do you know the lady?"

John whispered back, "She is my cousin and she has influenced every attempt I've made to find a girl ever since I was fourteen. I thought Amy had done it, now I'm not so sure."

"How?"

"Just look at her. I compare every woman I meet with her and they all fall short."

Peter Warrender smiled widely, understanding John completely.

In the cabin, the Admiral accepted a gin and settled down in the chair. Second Officer Chloe Shepherd, seated herself on the berth. The other three men stood.

Admiral Harrington grunted at the lack of seats. "Forgot how cramped these cabins can be. I'll be brief." He looked at Peter. "Do you know Chloe? John does, of course. My other aide is Michael Jackson. We are here to brief you on your duties."

He sipped the gin and said, "Chloe, have you a copy of the orders there?"

"Yes, Sir." She reached for the brief case she carried, but stopped when the Admiral lifted his finger. "Later. I'm sure you saw something today you have never seen before. You will appreciate that what you saw cannot be allowed to reach enemy ears. There will be other things equally mind-bending in the future. Under no circumstances can they be discussed and I suggest you extend that to members of your crew."

The aide looked at his watch and then the Admiral. The Admiral responded, "Very well, Michael. We will leave Chloe here and collect her after our visit to *Mavis*. She will go through your orders with you, Peter. I presume she will be safe with you. She is John's cousin, I believe." He grinned. "Come on, Michael. The boat awaits. We will stop by in an hour, give you time to catch up on the family news." The two officers left the cabin with Peter to see them off the ship.

Chloe looked at John. "He is always like this. He seems to have a perennial wish to see me carried off by a dashing naval officer."

John grinned. "I reckon you must be spoilt for choice it's great to see you. It's been so long." To his surprise, she stepped forward, slipped her arms round his neck and kissed him on the lips. He took a moment to respond, finding his arms slipping naturally around her slim waist. The kiss did not just stop. It seemed to go on and on. When they finally came up for air, Chloe said, "I have been waiting so long to do that. Ever since we were kids together." She looked anxiously at him. He realised that his arms were still around her waist. "I didn't quite get that. Can we do it again?" He leaned forward and kissed her, accepting the complete cooperation of the other party.

"I have also waited all my life for that to happen," John said seriously. "Thank goodness it has happened at last. Maybe we can get on with our lives now."

"You realise that you have compromised my reputation now. You will have to marry me." Chloe said seriously.

"As a gentleman, I would have it no other way."

Chloe looked hard at him. "You made life difficult for me. We have always been such good friends, and there has been no one else in my life." She blushed. "I'm afraid all the others sort of pale by comparison. You never seemed to see me at all." She shrugged and started sorting papers.

John said, "Did you mean that?"

"What? Did I mean what?"

"What you said about me."

"Yes, I did. Why?"

"Because I always thought exactly the same thing, only the other way round."

Chloe looked confused. "You mean you fancied me?"

"To put it mildly, I have always been besotted with you. But, being me, I could never believe you might feel the same way. I thought Amy Martin would do the trick, but it seems I will have to tell her somehow." There was the sound of feet outside the cabin. "Peter is just coming back, I'll leave you to it." He intended leaving the cabin before Peter came in, but Chloe held him and kissed him again.

Peter came in at that point. He looked at them still in each other's arms. "Thank goodness that's over. Can I be best man, and the first to congratulate you?"

Chloe released John and turned to Peter. She smiled and kissed him. "Thank you, Peter. You allowed it to happen."

Peter looked puzzled, "What did ...?"

Chloe took his arm. "Sort it out later. I have your orders here. She laid out the sheets of a chart and the papers with the orders. Between them, they established the next action set for the ship, to be accomplished over the next three days.

"Wow, you haven't allowed us much time." John said.

"We have no option. The *Dortmund* will be entering the dock at Brest in four days, and *Mavis* must be in position to attack by that time. I presume *Dortmund* will be returning from the Atlantic, and, as she is one of the Pocket Battleships, your presence would not really help *Mavis* if she is spotted by the target. But there are other hazards which you could protect her from: E boats and enemy destroyers."

Chloe stood back and let the two officers get their heads together over the chart. She had been amazed at her audacity, but, looking at John, it was quite evident that her instincts had been correct. Both she and John had been unaware that they shared similar feelings. In each case it had affected their relations with others over the years.

"The Admiral has returned." PO Rogers knocked and reported to the Captain. He was almost immediately followed by the man himself. The Admiral took one look at Chloe and a smile crossed his face. "All tidied up, Chloe?"

"All orders passed and everything arranged, Sir."

"Very good. We will leave you to it, Captain. Good luck. I'll be in touch."

The Captain and his Number One saw the Admiral and his party back into the barge and stood side by side watching the wake disappear as it returned to the shore.

"Now, Sir, I believe I deserve an explanation."

Peter grinned, "All I know is that I left you two alone for five minutes and when I came back you were busy contravening KR's and AI's by kissing a WRNS officer on a King's ship. Anyway, all I did was give you the time to sort things out between you."

Chapter five

Special Operations

The Pocket Battleship was a looming shadow against the horizon. The two Allied ships were approaching from well astern, as the *Dortmund* passed through the boom at the entrance to the Naval Dockyard. *Mavis* stopped and John made out the faint flash of foam as the torpedo entered the water.

The two ships withdrew from the area. A single blip from *Mavis* acknowledged that the torpedo had acquired a target. The speed of the torpedo was controlled after it had passed the boom while it was still open, but did not reach the target until it was entering the dry dock. The explosion, following a flash of light from the base, was a confirmation that the torpedo had hit something at least.

The single Mosquito bomber over the target at that time was able to confirm the hit, and misled the German Navy into thinking it was a bomb from the aircraft, rather than the seeker torpedo. The stern of the *Dortmund* and dry-dock gates had both been seriously damaged.

By dawn, both Allied ships were well on their way back to Portsmouth.

***

Tied up side by side, the two ships rocked with the passing of a cruiser leaving harbour. Lieutenant John

Macklin RN, stepped ashore and strode off along the quay. The weather was cooperating. It was not raining and he had things to do and places to go. The first call was to the admin office, in response to a summons from Operations.

He passed between the sentries at the entrance producing his ID for inspection, and entered the outer office of the operations section. A tall. willowy WRNS 2nd Officer, Chloe, greeted him with a smile and clicked the office intercom to announce his presence to the Admiral

Delighted to see her, John kept cool, still a little unsure, despite the revelations of their last meeting,. He said, "Hullo, Chloe. How's life?"

"Fine thank you. I hear things went quite well with the torpedo trial." The intercom buzzed. "That's your cue. I'll bring the coffee in after you."

John knocked and entered the office, where the Admiral stood behind his desk, stretching his back. He waved to the chair in front of the desk. "Glad to see you survived the trial successfully. Take a pew."

John sat and waited while the Admiral finally rolled his shoulders before seating himself. "We'll hang on until Chloe brings the coffee. Meanwhile how are things personally with you?"

John relaxed and said, "Life is pretty good at the moment, sir. I'm on a good ship with a great skipper, so I don't have any real problems."

Chloe entered at that moment, saving any further social comment while the coffee was being served. After Chloe had finished pouring and assumed her seat beside the desk, the Admiral raised the reason for the meeting.

"As you may have guessed, we have been developing items like the seeker torpedo as fast as we can. Over the past year we have produced several things designed to shorten the war. We were so far behind when we started that, up to now, we have been on the back foot, pushed by an enemy outnumbering us in men and equipped with superior weaponry. That is being addressed as fast as possible. The Spitfires and Hurricanes have made a difference, and, given time, will stop the Luftwaffe in their tracks, I'm sure. Even so, time is the one thing we do not have. The operation at Dunkirk was successful as far as men were concerned. In fact, it was an achievement that the enemy did not expect us to make. Equipment is still short, however."

He leaned forward. "Commander Warrender has been promoted Captain and will take command of a flotilla of escorts. Your promotion to Lieutenant Commander has been approved. You will take over command of *HMS Audax* with immediate effect. From now on, your ship will be part of the test flotilla for experimental equipment." He held up his hand to stop the immediate protest that John was about to make. "Hear me out. We will discuss the matter when I have finished." He paused, sipped his cooling coffee and then continued. "You may be under the impression that this will take the ship out of the firing line and consign it to some obscure safe region where you will be wasted as a fighting unit. So, before I go any further, I would point out that so far you have been placed very much in dangerous waters, and that situation will continue, I am assured.

"The fact is that testing will be done initially in sheltered waters, probably the West Coast and Islands of Scotland.

"However, all the final testing will be carried out in active service conditions, which will require strict security at all times, with skilled observation to monitor the effectiveness of whatever device is being tested. It means you will be carrying scientists at all times, and that is one of the reasons *Audax* was selected. Designed as a flotilla leader, there is extra accommodation built in for the senior officer and his staff. That will be converted whilst you are alongside here, to make accommodation for the two scientists and their four assistants. They travel with you from now on. Your first task will be to fly up to Loch Ewe and do a course to learn about the organisation that is building there as we speak. When you return you will find the two scientists and their staff will have taken their place on the ship. I stress this is an important, essential part of our strategy. Your job will include extreme danger and extreme boredom. If you are up to it, *HMS Audax* will be a name nobody will remember. That is, if we are successful. Meanwhile, we three are the only people allowed to discuss what I have just told you. I know you two are old friends. That should allow you to meet socially without suspicion of anything other than the possible suggestion of a romantic connection." He looked keenly at them both smiled and added. "War can be hell sometimes."

Correctly taking that as dismissal, John rose to his feet as Chloe gathered the cups and coffee pot. He held the door for her and followed her into her outer office.

Chloe put the tray down and unlocked her desk drawer. She removed a document ordering the promotion of Lieutenant John Hervey Macklin RN to the rank of Lieutenant Commander RN. She also found two lapel loops with the two and a half gold rings of his new rank.

She stepped around the desk and faced him with a smile. Reaching up she undid the lapels on the blue battledress jacket and slipped off the loops with two gold rings of his former rank and replaced them with his new rank. "There!" She said, "All done and dusted. She stretched up and kissed him on the lips. "Congratulations, Commander."

"Thanks, Chloe. By the way how is your love life?"

"Charles is wafting about in the clouds in his beloved Spitfire, I am informed. I don't get to see much of him these days. What about you?"

"Do you remember Amy Martin from Uni?"

"The mouse that roared?"

"That's her. Well, she has matured and we were getting to know each other again. She is Doctor Martin now and based in Whitehall somewhere. "Did I understand that we will be going north in three days?"

"I hope so, so you should get back to your ship and start the takeover." She grinned. I'm glad we are working together. I'll send on the travel docs' as soon as they are finalised." She kissed him again, this time lightly on the lips, then turned back to her desk all business once more.

Chapter six

Command

The small aircraft rocked and swayed as they progressed northward. The Percival Proctor was a cabin monoplane designed for the luxury market, but currently used as a communication aircraft by the RAF. The pilot was a small, smiling man whose casual attitude to the gyrations of his aeroplane was both re-assuring and mildly alarming. The weather was not good as far as the midland airfield at Ansty where the plane refuelled. It did improve as they progressed northward. At Glasgow the sun was shining. The green countryside giving way to the mountains of the western highlands was an extension of the surprising number of green areas within the city itself. The final leg of the flight went over and through the mountains, with its glens and snow patches still a reminder of the winter past.

They landed in the flatland alongside Loch Broom. The small town of Ullapool was visible in the distance. Chloe dressed in slacks, rather than the skirt that went with her uniform, clambered out of the aircraft, to be helped down by the cheerful pilot. John followed. Two ratings emptied the luggage locker, and brought their bags to the waiting car.

The Petty Officer who met them was stocky and weather-beaten. He saluted and introduced himself as PO Berry. He drove them to Ullapool and there saw them into the ML lying alongside the quay. The two travellers were seated in the wardroom while the boat left the shelter of the sea loch and out past the entrance to Little Loch Broom, the speed rapidly building as the ML rounded the headlands and turned into Loch Ewe. In the loch there was a Naval presence, including a refuelling point. The travellers were taken ashore and once more by car to the research base in an isolated glen in the hills beside the loch.

There they were greeted by the chief scientist, Professor Edwin Connor PhD, who was in fact an administrator rather than an innovator. His secretary was with him. The visitors were shown to their berths, two side by side rooms in a row of wooden buildings.

They were self-contained with en-suite shower/toilet room, and studio type bed-sitting area. Connor suggested they settle in, then meet for dinner in the mess, further down the row of buildings. They would tackle the briefing the following day.

***

Twenty minutes later there was a knock at the door of John's room and Chloe announced she was ready to go and eat.

John called out for her to come in, and continued dressing. The knot of his tie was being a nuisance. Two hands came round his neck from behind him and he felt a soft bosom against his back. He relaxed and allowed the deft fingers to adjust the knot of his tie for him. When she had finished he felt her slip away with some regret. Then he turned to thank her. To his surprise it was not Chloe it was Amy Martin.

He leaned forward and kissed her, "What ?"...... she put her finger to his lips stopping him from asking.

"Wait until Chloe joins us. I can then say it once, instead of twice."

He nodded and kissed her again."I missed you," he said. It was true. He did miss her. Especially. When he was on his own, though at the moment he also wondered how his relationship with Chloe would survive this encounter.

Then Chloe appeared at the door. He let Amy loose and went to accompany the two important women in his life to the Mess.

Seated with the two women eyeing each other, weighing up the situation with John between them, was not John's idea of fun. "I know you both met at University because I was there as well. I have known Chloe since I was seven. Amy and I crossed debating swords there on several occasions, though we renewed our acquaintance in Le Havre a few months ago and since then have met in London. Chloe has a pilot flying Spitfires, named Charles, to look after her interests. Meanwhile, she is a good friend and currently Aide to an Admiral, who happens to be my current boss."

Amy said, "I am here because you have been nominated for a project my department is running over the next few weeks, possibly months." She sat back looking pleased with herself.

John and Chloe looked at her, surprised. "We are here to do a specialised course for the project we are on at present. I think it could be difficult to shelve the work we are doing currently." Chloe explained.

"Actually, it has been discussed and your people decided that there was no immediate rush as the results of the last tests need to be correlated with previous results and the new developments will take some time to become available. So I think you will be available for my department's project.

"What project do you have in mind?" John asked.

Amy looked around the Mess. The table they were using was not private in the sense that it was in the middle of the dining room. But there were no other occupants close enough to overhear what they were saying. Nonetheless, she leant forward to speak, causing both the others to lean forward in turn. Quietly, she explained.

"When we met in France I was on my way home from an excursion on behalf of my boss. The affair with the collection of Brits and misfits involving the police, which you and your French friend managed to sort out, was unforeseen, but it did help camouflage the real purpose of my French visit. We are now ready for the second part of the operation. The organisation I was tasked to help organise was a secret army able to operate in an occupied country. It was quite obvious that we are not ready to drive the Germans out of France at this time. The formation I am helping organise would be in place to upset and annoy the enemy and, where possible, sabotage their efforts to keep control over the population. Our next task is to get weapons to them, so that they have the ability to inflict great harm. The weapons will include explosives and grenades, as well as rifles, pistols, and machine guns, where possible. The French are recruiting returning soldiers and police personnel, as well as bringing in Boy Scouts as messengers and watchers, though it is still very much at the planning stage.

"My boss managed to obtain an ML. It was damaged at Dunkirk and cast adrift, recovered later by another ML and towed back to Folkestone.

"It had been written off, so my boss grabbed it for undercover operations, and had the boat overhauled and modified. It is lying at Bucklers Hard at present. Your course here will be over in two weeks. You will both be given leave for the following week. When you return home the boat will be on the doorstep, ready loaded. You will need to arrange the rendezvous yourselves.

"A quick trip cross-channel and the boat will be ready for another excursion when needed. It will be part of your command, John, as Captain of *HMS Audax,* from now on, and there will be additions to your crew to man her. Your Admiral, Chloe, will be responsible for all operations, though you will appreciate that my boss is the source of most of them anyway." She stopped and the other two at the table sat silent for a moment, then both started to say something.

John stopped and nodded to Chloe. "You first," he said.

Chloe did not hesitate."Where do I come in? I am not part of the crew of *HMS Audax.?"*

"You speak French and I am not always available to do the deliveries with the ML. You would work in conjunction with me in that capacity. In addition, it will be up to you to organise the loads for delivery, and the places for landings and pickups."

Turning to John, she said, "For security reasons the boat will be kept in the Beaulieu River. Loads can be despatched to the quayside below your house, to be loaded into the boat either alongside, or out at the anchorage if necessary."

"Why?" Said John."Why not load up in the dockyard?"

"The fewer people are aware of this the better," was the blunt reply. "Unfortunately, there are eyes and ears everywhere these days, and the less seen the better."

That seemed to close the conversation. The trio split up to go to their separate cabins to mull over the tasks ahead.

***

Doctor Amy Martin was going south the following day. She and John were able to spend time together alone that evening. She said, "John, I noticed that Chloe and you have a connection?"

"We have been friends since we were kids." John said.

Amy looked at him and grinned. "That has all changed, I suggest."

John looked uncomfortable. "It never occurred to me. I'm sorry...."

Her raised hand stopped him. "John! It's been fun. For me that was all it ever was, a fun interlude. Forget the guilt and get together. You obviously belong with Chloe." She leaned forward and kissed him lingeringly on the lips. "I'm off!" She said. "My carriage awaits. Go get your girl, and good luck. I'll see you on our next excursion." Then she was gone.

***

The next few days were tiring, sweaty and freezing, sometimes all at once. John and Chloe suffered bruises on their bruises, with unarmed combat lessons followed by trekking over the surrounding mountains.

The diving was exciting, using basic re-breather units developed from submarine escape suits.

John was impressed by Chloe's resilience, as she and the other two women on the course not only endured, but enjoyed the challenges.

At the end of the fortnight, the course members gathered together and enjoyed an end-of-course party, while went on until the early hours.

They left the party and Chloe ended up in John's room. There were no words spoken just the urgent removal of clothing and the delight of the long overdue meeting of their two willing bodies.

***

John and Chloe made the train to London, having been dropped off at Mallaig by the ML. They collapsed in the first class carriage, and slept for the entire trip, cuddled together for warmth, as the train's heating system failed before leaving Glasgow. They could have stayed over in London but elected to carry on to their respective homes, separating to their own sides of the river at Beaulieu.

The ML was moored in the middle of the river, no particular overt signs of her proposed activities; the crew members kept themselves to themselves, using the facilities in Portsmouth rather than the local places.

John and Chloe sailed his boat down to the mooring, quietly boarding the ML in the dusk. Chloe in her official capacity, as stand-in for Doctor Martin.

They set off for the shakedown passage into the dark waters of the channel, and for two hours, well out of sight of the land, the boat performed high and low speed manoeuvring with pick-up and drop off in and out of dinghies.

They returned to the mooring before sunrise and quietly made their way back to John's house. His parents were away in the London home maintained by his father whilst he was on business. They spent the rest of the week together, just as they had when they were kids.

John's mother was delighted to see them relaxed and having fun, she had already figured out the situation. Though John pointed out that Chloe had her pilot, Charles, and he had not mentioned his last conversation with Doctor Amy, she just nodded sagely and said privately to John's father. "I always knew that those two were destined to be together. Just mark my words."

John's father of course refrained from commenting, knowing from experience it would make no difference anyway.

***

As the week drew to an end, John and Chloe went out to New Forest in his father's car for a picnic lunch. car. The weather was fine and the sky was patterned with the vapour trails from the fighter planes, Spitfires and Messerschmitts, Hurricanes and Heinkels. The sound of the odd patter of gunfire mixed with the hum of the bees going about their work among the plants. It seemed to highlight the peace and quiet of the summer countryside below.

Chloe lay on her back on the blanket, her red summer dress a splash of colour in the greens of the forest around them. "I could get used to this way of life," she said with a smile. "I have enjoyed this week immensely."

John was leaning against the hamper with a stem of feather-ended grass in his mouth. He bent over and brushed the frond over Chloe's cheek. "You should be eager to get back to the office and the war. I bet Charlie is up there now knocking hell out of some poor Luftwaffe pilot as we speak. Shame on you, girl!"

He flicked away the grass and found himself face to face with his beautiful companion. They kissed. He told himself afterwards there was nothing else to do, and the kiss went on and on. And from that moment the other people in their lives did not matter. There was just the two of them.

When they finally broke apart, John rolled onto his back and they lay side by side, saying nothing, their bodies touching at shoulder and hip. Otherwise they just lay. Until almost inevitably, Chloe rolled over to John and the kiss was renewed, as if she were checking to see if the first kiss was a one of. This time John's arms were around her, holding her close, responding to the contact of her body against his.

Chapter seven

Action

On his return to Portsmouth, John boarded his command and sat down with his new Number One. Lieutenant Ross Sherman RCN was an American, who had crossed the border to join the fight against the Nazi threat. He was tall with wavy blond hair and regular features, slightly disarranged by a broken nose which had been set slightly off line. He had been a volunteer in the RCN from 1938. As an experienced sailor, who had navigated tall ships around Cape Horn, he had been welcomed by the Canadians. His accelerated promotion had been deserved, hence his current rank. He was a good-natured, intelligent officer who had taken over the ship in John's absence with little apparent fuss.

He had only just been advised that the ship had a second unit under command, the ML lying at Beaulieu and he was full of questions as to her use and their intended use of the destroyer.

The team of scientists had arrived and presented their credentials to Sherman before the skipper arrived. They were ensconced in the command suite, now converted for the two lead scientists and their four research assistants. Doctor's Andrews and Barnes were both keen golfers. As soon as they were confident that their equipment had been installed correctly, they disappeared to the golf club, leaving assurances that they would return in plenty of time to greet the captain when he arrived in the evening.

Lieutenant Ross Sherman, having already dealt with everything necessary since he arrived, still had to wait to have his curiosity about the programme satisfied until his Captain, John Macklin, had reported to the Admiral. But as he confided to the CPO, "At least we will find something out when the skipper arrives."

CPO Mickey Rogers shrugged his shoulders, "Maybe, sir. But you know the Navy. You never know!" With this enigmatic comment he departed to chase up some supplies, leaving Ross Sherman wondering how two nations, who spoke the same language, could find it so difficult to communicate.

***

John found that the attachment of the ML to his command a mixed blessing. Whilst the appointment of a crew to the craft was not difficult, the obvious implication, that he would be taking a personal interest in some of its tasks, was worrying. It did mean that his first lieutenant would spend time assuming command in his absence, though, if it were possible, he would also be expected to undertake some of the missions the ML would be tasked with.

Lieutenant Commander John Macklin RN, sat in the office in front of the Admiral's desk. Chloe sat at the right hand of the Admiral with her notebook in front of her. All trace of the woman to whom he had made love the night before they left Scotland and several encores at Beaulieu was gone. The smooth sleek blond was immaculate as usual, not a hair out of place.

It would have been impossible for John to claim that the activities of the occasion had made no impression on him. Personally, he was shocked at his easy acceptance of the incident, despite his last conversation with Amy, and Chloe's involvement with Charles, the RAF pilot.

Though these thoughts flashed though his mind on seeing Chloe, he was able to concentrate on the Admiral who was giving a background to the duties he would expect to be involved with.

"Your Number One was selected for the post in expectation that he would be able to fit in with the unorthodox nature of your duties. If there is any problem, let me know and I will have him replaced immediately. Your liaison will be Chloe. I have arranged for modifications to *Audax* which will take some days, so I suggest you and your Number One visit Beaulieu and get to know the ML. She is a variant of her class and has been in the hands of the boffins for experimental upgrades and modifications. Like all of her ilk she can be fitted across the range of use, from MTB to minelayer. With the power she now generates there is little to catch her when she runs." There was a wistful note in the Admiral's voice that gave John the feeling that the Admiral would rather be John's side of the desk at this point.

John rose to his feet. "I will get together with my Number One, and Lieutenant Cummings on the ML and we'll get a system sorted out."

Chloe rose to her feet also and joined him in the outer office. Both doors were closed and they were alone. She looked at him and smiled. "About the other night, I was as surprised as you undoubtedly were, I will not hold you to any hasty promises. Until now, I was not really anyone's. For me it was right."

She made to say more but John stepped over to her and took her in his arms. "Chloe, you have always been my best friend. Please do not stop. Like you, I would not allow anything to interfere with our friendship. By the way, I enjoyed every moment we were together, and I meant every word that I said. Count on it." He kissed her and stepped back smiling. "I'll be down at the Hard for the next three days, if you get the chance. Come home," He did not see the joy on her face as he left the office.

***

The two officers boarded the ML on a midstream mooring on the river. The 112-ft Fairmile was fitted with an assortment of weaponry. The main-deck gun now fitted was not standard. It was covered with a canvas shroud, to conceal it and to protect it from the elements. It was a Bofors AA gun 40mm, fitted with a self-loading magazine, the two wing MG's were Oerlikon .5's. Both officers were ushered below before they were able to see too much. There they were briefed on the modifications that the boat had been put through.

John said nothing about his previous visit where the Navy alone had been present. He made allowance for the white-coated Commander who briefed them and was cagey about the engines. The Packard engines that were the normal power for this class of boat had been substituted with Napier diesel engines, a version of which was currently being tested for use in aircraft. Apart from the obvious reduction in risk, by using diesel rather than high octane aviation fuel, they actually drove the boat to higher speeds than normally expected. There had been some small modifications to the shaping of the hull, needed for the fitting of the alternate engines. The result of which was to cause an increased stability of the hull when planing at high speed.

The Commander explained that this gave the promise of speeds in excess of 45 knots in reasonable sea conditions.

Both Ross and John were impressed. There was little new to see below decks, but, as the Commander pointed out, how would anyone know that the innocent looking radio equipment was a false-front concealing a high-powered transmitter-receiver, which could create interference sufficient to defeat enemy communications over the immediate area of operation. At present it had a radius of ten miles, though the range was being expanded in the labs ashore, and the extended version would be installed as soon as the bugs were ironed out.

The Commander, whose name John never discovered, pointed out the most up-to-date Asdic, and a device, linked to an attachment on the stubby mast, which produced a warning of approaching ships or aircraft. This he described as a Radio Detection Device. It was new and temperamental, and must not fall into the hands of the enemy. It seemed that the majority of the equipment within the boat fell into this category.

At the end of the tour the anonymous commander disappeared. Lieutenant-in-command, Toby Cummings, RNVR appeared and entertained them to lunch in the wardroom.

"Apart from myself, the crew are mainly made up of technicians. All are also trained seamen, but most have an expertise in one or more of the number of esoteric devices fitted to the boat. It does mean that we have support service for all of the toys given to us to play with." He grinned. "Even our chef is an expert in the preparation of explosive devices for use in sabotage. His expertise is twinned with a touch for cooking which makes simple meals a pleasure to eat."

John looked at him, eyebrow raised.

Toby smiled. "He was sous-chef at the Trocadero before his call up to the Navy.

Having taken the tour, they slipped their mooring and eased down river to the Solent and, in the afternoon sunshine, cruised sedately out into the Channel proper. The murmur of the single diesel made a quiet background to the noise of the sea, and the shrieks of the gulls that accompanied them.

The other engines were started in turn. As the dusk descended the power of all four engines was increased. The speed of the boat rose accordingly. According to the log, their speed through the water increased to forty-eight knots, before John ordered the throttle eased. The stability of the hull was noted and the fact that the engines were not flat out, also.

It was a thoughtful John who ordered the return to the mooring.

***

The following day Chloe appeared and was invited on board the ML.

Given the fact that both John and Ross would at different times be called upon to command the boat in action, they took her to sea to exercise with the crew, and get to know the boat under a range of conditions. For Chloe, despite her previous undercover trip, the cruise was a revelation, and strictly against regulations for WRNS Officers to be permitted on board a serving naval craft, especially in wartime. She wore slacks and had her hair concealed from prying eyes when boarding the boat at the Hard where the ML lay alongside to take on water and fuel.

The outboard dinghy she had used to cross the river was driven by CPO Rogers, and they had boarded by the offside companionway to avoid embarrassment.

Whether the Admiral ever knew or not, John did not know. But it did give Chloe an insight into some of the conditions the boat would meet.

It also introduced Chloe to the crew of the ML. Since their activities would be co-ordinated through her office, and orders would be transmitted by her to the boat, it did no harm for the people to recognize the back-up on whom they depended. In addition, according to Amy, she would be expected to step in to despatch agents and equipment, in Amy's absence.

***

The first operation John commanded involved co-ordination with *Mavis* once more. The torpedo development had progressed to the point where they could let it lie in wait for a target to come along. It would then activate and destroy the ship. Because it would be moving fast the explosive effect would be enhanced by its speed.

All they needed now was a target to experiment on.

The first excursion, into the Solent and thence into the English Channel, was made by the *Mavis* and *HMS Audax*. The ML was still getting modified to use the new torpedo, which required a slightly larger launcher, with a modified butt-cap to accommodate the extra energy developed by the higher-powered motor and the impeller charge that actually launched the torpedo.

The two ships were not actually charged with launching the torpedo on this excursion, though the actual on-the-spot decision was up to John. The captain of the *Mavis* was an RNVR Lieutenant, who was a Doctor of Physics in his spare time. At least that was his way of putting it. Alec Randall was a tousle-haired man five foot nine in his socks, and had been in the RNVR ever since his University days. Qualified as a watch officer, his abilities as a skipper were unchallenged. His other qualifications would normally have kept him in a laboratory for the duration of the war, but his speciality had been development in the field of weaponry, specifically torpedoes. The *Mavis*, a newly constructed super yacht constructed for a Greek millionaire, had been conscripted as a test bed and lab by the Ministry. The convenience of having a trained shipmaster and scientist in the circumstances illustrated that the civil service did not always get things wrong.

Alec Randall was talking to John Macklin, using a version of TBS (Talk between ships.) which was normally only found in US Navy craft.

"That's it. I just follow you for a jaunt out into the Channel, in hopes of sighting a suitable target for my baby."

"That is more or less it. Yes!"

"Is that the best we can do?"

"Until or unless we get intelligence from the DNI (Department of Naval Intelligence), or some other source. Yes! That is it."He switched off and replaced the mike.

As he turned away from the set, he heard a tone from the Echo sounder.

From the Asdic cuddy, the rating on watch called, "Sir, contact 3000 yards off starboard bow, closing."

John swung round and picked up the TBS mike and buzzed Alec on the *Mavis.*

When Alec answered, John said, "How does baby perform underwater?"

"Fine. It makes no difference to baby,"

"I'm pleased to hear it. We have a U boat approaching from ahead, How about you launch and seek?"

"As I speak, baby is off and seeking." Alec sounded cool and collected.

John heard the call from the asdic rating. "Torpedoes in the water, sir."

He pressed the transmit button, "Alec, unless you launched more than one torpedo, there is at least one on its way to us. I suggest evasive action as soon as possible."

He called to the wheelhouse, "Wheel, hard starboard. Increase to full speed ahead."

After 3 long minutes he ordered, "Wheel, amidships. Reduce speed to 20 knots."

The port lookout called, "Torpedo track, 20 yards, passing portside, sir."

As he spoke an explosion occurred ahead of the two ships. The fore section of a submarine reared out of the water. Part of the conning tower, badly shattered at the after section, showed the U with part of the number also visible, though not sufficient to positively identify the shattered boat which slowly slipped beneath the tumbled waters – there were no survivors.

As the noise and the sea subsided, the TBS buzzed in *HMS Audax*. Alec's voice came clearly from the other ship, "I rest my case. Reloading tube."

The Sub on duty logged the sinking and marked the chart for reference. Having done his duty, Jim Fordyce, Sub Lieutenant RNVR leaned against the bridge screen surveying the green/blue waters of the Channel surrounding the two ships. Martin Offord, the middy on watch with him, was using the big glasses to survey the horizon.

Martin was not actually studying the waters toward the French coast. He was using the glasses to cover the fact that he was thinking of other things. The girl he had finally made an approach to, Maddy Ramsey. She was at home when he had arrived home on leave after the Atlantic period. He sighed. Ever since they had attended the local school he had wanted to be friends with her. When he went off to join the navy she had attended his farewell party, and he had at last been able to talk with her.

They had both been shy, but she had kissed him goodbye when he left. She had also written a letter to him, which came while he was on the Atlantic run.

He had written back, but since then, had decided that his letter had been rubbish. When he had received yet another letter from her, it had come as a surprise, and he actually started to think that she was interested in him.

The sight of her at the station when his train rolled in, confirmed that he was not fooling himself. She had to be interested to have waited for the delayed train. He recalled her cold hands when they met. He had taken her into the station buffet to warm up before getting a taxi home. His mother's face was another surprise, as she seemed quite prepared to see Maddy with him when he arrived. He had discovered that the two women had chatted regularly since he left. His mother had been happy that Martin had a girlfriend to come home to, and happier still that it was a local girl that she could relate to.

Martin had been pleased and proud to walk through their home town with Maddy on his arm. It was something that he had imagined, but never really dreamed would happen.

***

He straightened up. Despite his daydreaming, the view through the binoculars had altered. He realised there was one, no two white bow waves being created, by high speed boats racing offshore toward the two British ships. "Two high speed craft approaching on the starboard beam, sir. They look like E boats."

Jim Fordyce swung his head round and lined up his own binoculars. "Looks like you're right, Martin. Well spotted. Call the Captain and advise him." He pressed the buzzer to call the crew to action stations, as he spoke.

The midshipman turned and squawked the voice tube to the Captain's day cabin.

When the Captain answered he said, "Sir, two enemy boats in sight. They appear to be E boats, closing fast."

John acknowledged, and within seconds was on the bridge. "Where away?" He asked, swinging already to search the starboard horizon with his own binoculars.

He studied the two bow waves created by the racing enemy boats. On their present heading both fore and aft 4.7in guns could bear, so he ordered, "Main armament fore and aft, engage when ready." Both guns swing onto the bearing of the approaching boats. The warning buzzer sounded and both guns fired.

With binoculars trained on the targets, both John and Fordyce were able to see the fall of their shells. Both missed, one short the other long. The gun captains adjusted their aim and the next two shots landed near enough to shower the boats with dirty water. The boats immediately started to zigzag to put the gunners aim off. It now became clear that there were three boats as a third E boat came into view, having been hidden by the other two initially.

Both the British ships increased speed at John's order and, as the speed of the ships started to make a difference, the guns continued firing. But the three E boats started to lose ground. The third boat in pursuit suddenly blossomed smoke and flame as it took a shell amidships. Its speed dropped off and it could be seen to start to fold in the middle as the bow and the stern both rose out of the water. There was an explosion on board and suddenly, there was just a cloud of smoke and wreckage, forming a expanding from the water up and out. Then there was nothing to be seen as the cloud dissipated and the scatter of debris fell where once the E boat had been.

Neither of the other boats checked their headlong rush toward the two British ships. John studied the progress of the two enemy boats. He then swung round to check their course ahead. They would have to change course shortly to clear the headland at Cap de la Hague.

There were signs of boats coming out of Cherbourg, so John decided to take on the E boats trailing behind. Accordingly, he picked up the mike for the TBS and spoke to Alec on the *Mavis* "I am going to take out the boats behind us. It looks as if we will be getting trouble from other boats as well so I've decided to clear the decks behind us, we can worry about the others afterwards. So reverse course. Turn to port. I'll go starboard. On my mark. NOW!"

Both ships turned outward away from each other and settled on a course back the way they came.

At their relative speeds the gap narrowed rapidly. Only the forward gun was firing at this angle though the depth charges were being set to minimum settings, if the opportunity occurred. The deck guns on both E boats were firing. Their accuracy was impaired by the tossing and bouncing the boats were subjected to by the increasingly boisterous waves combined with their high speed. Both E boats had fired torpedoes but neither had been effective. As they neared the enemy craft, the forward gun scored a glancing hit on the lead E boat.

It took the antenna away from the roof of the wheelhouse along with half of the port side of the compartment. Since the vessel was still under control, John presumed that there was someone alive still at the wheel. The smaller weapons were now in action, including the Bofors AA gun at full depression. It joined in the action stitching holes across the foredeck of the E boat furthest away, the lowest point of depression aided by the dip of the bows between the wave-crests allowing the gun a better chance of hitting its target.

A second burst of five shots caught the E boat right across the wheelhouse. The shattering effect of a direct hit destroyed its windshield and punched two holes through the armour, smashing the binnacle and the wheel, turning the place into a charnel house from the blood of the three men at their posts, steering and operating the engine room telegraph.

The damaged boat veered away from her companion as the crew attempted to regain control. There were several scars appearing on the armour of the destroyer, which was receiving hits from both enemy boats. The screen of the wheelhouse was starred with bullet marks which had not managed to penetrate the reinforced glass.

The damaged E boat was turning back into the action when it exploded and disintegrated into a shattered mess. The remains of the hull sank rapidly beneath the rising sea.

The surviving E boat was making signs of breaking off the action. But John altered course to allow the aft turret to join the action. The first shell from the after gun took the E boat in the stern and effectively wiped out her engines. She started sinking by the stern. Her forward gun ceased to depress far enough to overcome the angle at which she was sinking. The surviving crew were leaping into the water, giving each other help to avoid the sinking boat.

John launched the jolly boat to help the rescue. They brought all of the survivors aboard and kept them under guard in the wardroom.

Taking a last look at the scene, he ordered the ship turned, to close with the *Mavis* waiting patiently off toward the mainland, where she had located while *Audax* made her attack.

Studying the craft coming out of Cherbourg, John was not sure that a suitable target would be found, and was about to suggest moving on the Brest, to avoid the greater risk of interception by overwhelming force, when the bow of a destroyer appeared, nosing out past the Fort de Chavagnac, into the open waters of the Channel.

As it turned toward the two British ships, it increased speed and the gun mountings swung to and fro before settling in their fore and aft positions, the bows plunging in the worsening weather conditions.

The TBS squawked. John picked up the mike absently, still observing the German destroyer. He heard Alec speak, "I'll release now, torpedo dormant. I am retreating now. Auto capture and trigger set."

John looked across at the *Mavis* as she turned away from the threat of the German ship, and started making her way through the roughening sea.

John acknowledged and replaced the mike. Turning to Ross Sherman, he said, "I think it's time to move out and let the Jerry have the stage, while we see if the boffins have it right."

Sherman turned to PO Jackson, the Quartermaster on the wheel. "Left full rudder, bring her round to north west, we'll adjust from there."

"Left full rudder. Aye, aye, sir."

John called for revs for 30 knots. The rating on the engine room telegraph, repeated the order and operated the handle on the telegraph, then spoke on the voice pipe, "Revs for 30 knots, sir." The repeater on the telegraph rang and the indicator needle moved to meet the other, confirming the order for more speed.

The ship vibrated with the increase in speed and the bows met the rising sea, storm borne, coming in from the Atlantic.

Studying the weather, John called Alec on the *Mavis*. "We will likely become separated in the incoming weather. We'll rendezvous south of Alderney in the Channel Isles, as soon as things calm down a little."

"I'll be making the torpedo active now. It should be worth watching." Alec switched off and John turned to watch the antics of the German destroyer. She was bigger than *Audax* and carried heavier guns, and more of them. But she was still pitching and rolling in the increasing seas. The forward turret on the German ship fired. The shell passed over John's head and fell between the two British ships.

The scene took on a surreal effect as the German ship started to rise in the air. The sound followed. The effect of the torpedo was dramatic and terminal for the destroyer. At the top of its rise in the air the ship broke into two, the keel separating into two distinct pieces.

The forward gun fired again though the shell went straight into the water, directed at the ocean floor.

Ross Sherman joined John, watching the fate of the enemy ship. "I guess I will never really get used to it. I know they are our enemies, but I hate to see a ship destroyed."

"Why on earth did you join the navy, thinking as you do?"

"I may not like it, but I will continue to serve whenever and wherever I can. It is important to remember what we are here for. That does not alter my regret at seeing a beautiful ship destroyed."

John nodded, "I guess I can understand that."

Ross looked sadly at the sinking destroyer. "I saw the Italian fleet at Taranto. They were the most beautiful designs for warships I have seen since the days of sail."

The two men watched the demise of the German ship. The other craft, who had preceded her out of Cherbourg, were at the scene collecting survivors in the disturbed waters.

"What were you doing at Taranto?"

"I was sitting in a 'stringbag'. What you call a Swordfish I believe, deciding whether I would be a birdman or a seaman." He spread his hands out, and nearly fell over as the ship lurched. "As you can see I decided to stay a sailor."

The two men were joined on the bridge by Doctor Mike Andrews. "I left it until you dealt with the enemy ships. I would have come up earlier. Below where we are, its all noise and no vision. That is frustrating and very scary as far as I am concerned.

"Doctor, you are welcome, providing you realise that, when we are in action, this is no place for onlookers."

"Thank you, sir. I will stay for a while now I am here,

The worsening weather was making the motion of the ship uncomfortable. John contacted *Mavis*. "Alec how many more of those whizz-bangs have you got in your back pocket?"

"None that I can use, I'm afraid."

"In that case, it's time to go home. After all, we are only here to test the product. If we have no product there is nothing to test. Form on me and we'll get out of Dodge."

Turning, John said, "Number One. Take us home, please."

"Gladly, sir! Quartermaster, bring her head round to the North East. Pilot! Plot a course for home, please."

Martin Offord blushed. Thrilled to be referred to as pilot and trusted to lay off the course to bring the ship home, he wondered what Maddy would say to that?

The weather ensured that the journey back to Portsmouth, was not to be easy. While both ships were seaworthy the fact was that there were hazards apart from natural ones. An encounter with a section of the hull of a wreck was not anticipated, and not even spotted, until it was under the lee of the ship. The speed through the water of the destroyer caused a swirl making the ship collide with the derelict. It tore a gash in the hull and at the same time pierced the section of the wreck which held the air pocket keeping it afloat. It sank so ceased to be a hazard to shipping, but the damage to *HMS Audax* reduced her speed, and despite running repairs, created considerable delay in her return to Portsmouth.

It also caused a delay in the re-commencement in the exercise interrupted by the action off Cherbourg.

As a result the destroyer was docked for repair while the ML was substituted as escort for the *Mavis* when she returned to sea.

Chapter eight

Looking for trouble

John Macklin found it odd in the rather more restricted space on the bridge of the ML. Toby Cummings was standing between the wheel and the engine telegraphs.

Off in the darkness on the starboard beam, *Mavis* was creating a welter of white water as she smashed into the regular waves, marching one after the other across their path. They were headed once more for the Western Channel.

John had to admit that the diesel engines were performing well and the balance of the boat seemed easier with the substitution of the new engines, allowing the boat to ride the waves better.

The TBS squawked, Cummings picked up the handset.

He listened for a moment then called John over. Passing him the handset, he said crisply, "*Mavis,* sir. Lieutenant Randall,"

John took the mike. "Yes, Alec?"

"According to my information we are just about in place for the first drop. Has your operator any signs of U boats?"

John looked across at Toby Cummings, who was shaking his head. "No signs so far."

"My boffins want to proceed to Lorient, or St Nazaire, both are known bases for the Atlantic wolf packs. If we can get my babies trailing returning subs into their base, we have a good chance of wrecking their facilities, and denying them the use for a considerable period.

John thought about it. "I'll come back to you on that. It will stretch our endurance, especially if we run into trouble. He finished the call and handed the handset back to Cummings. "Let us take a look at the charts, and do a few sums." He nodded to Toby Cummings and led him into the chartroom behind the bridge.

The two men bent over the chart table studying the waters in between their current position and the suggested destination off Quiberon. The two targets were at either side of the notorious bay with 65 miles of dangerous waters between them. The return from the area would be over 400 miles, so they had the endurance. But if they took damage they would be a long way from help without back-up.

John weighed up the situation. The weather was still a factor with the forecast of gales coming in from the Atlantic, so they would be operating on a lee shore. If they had an engine breakdown they would be driven onto the enemy shore. Once they entered the bay they would have to fight their way out to clear the Ushant, so there would be heavier expenditure of fuel than in the outward run from Portsmouth.

He checked with the Asdic operator. There were still no sign of submarines in the area. Stepping onto the bridge once more, he picked up the handset and called *Mavis*. "Alec, batten down and we'll run direct for Ushant. We can adjust our course, at that point. We will have to limit our time in the area. In case you are unaware, there is a big storm coming in from the Atlantic, so we may have a battle the weather to get out of the area."

"I get the message! We'll keep the weather in mind all the time while we are in Biscay."

"Exactly! Things could get rough in more ways than one." John switched off and replaced the handset.

He ducked as a stray sea sent spray across the open bridge. His steward appeared with a dry towel to replace the soaked towel wrapped around his neck to prevent the water getting down the neck of his oilskin jacket.

John stepped into the shelter of the chartroom and gratefully accepted the dry towel, wrapping it firmly in place before venturing out onto the bridge once more.

***

When they reached the area they decided was suitable for their mission, both craft hove-to, and the boffins lowered microphones into the water. They were using passive listening devices so that they did not divulge their presence to the enemy unnecessarily.

Having detected two submarines moving west from Lorient, they had to wait for several hours for two returning submarines to be identified.

On the *Mavis* the chief scientist programmed the weapon. Once the first submarine had passed the two silent ships, the torpedo was launched in its tracker mode. It was then monitored all the way into the harbour, where the submarine was held for inspection prior to insertion into the dry docks for maintenance. Two hours later it entered the dry dock.

Eventually the *Mavis* team were satisfied that all was operating properly. They launched a second tracker after the other U boat and rather than continue in the location for the next twelve hours, they decided they would prefer to decamp to St Nazaire to perform a similar service to the submarine base there.

Before the thought could be put into action, "Torpedo in the water," a voice called from the sonar. John looked at Toby. The action stations buzzer wailed, and boots could be heard all over the ML. Toby shook his head, "Not one of ours, Sir."

"Cox'n on the wheel!" the CPO's voice came over the voice pipe. The lookout on the starboard wing of the bridge called, "*Mavis* taking avoiding action. She is turning to starboard and increasing speed."

"Where is that torpedo?" John called.

Toby Cummings called, "It is targeting the U boat. She is taking evasive action." Toby was listening to the microphones in the water.

"The German torpedo has missed, it's continuing toward the shore. Out of range." He smiled. "They must have mistaken one of their own."

"Can you hear any other subs in the area?"

"I am sweeping the area, but only picking up the original sub. She is circling and making noises, seeking the other sub that shot at her."

"What about the torpedo our people launched? I cannot pick that up."

John lifted the TBS handset. "*Mavis, Mavis.* are you receiving me?"

Alec answered "Alec here, sir."

"What is the situation with the tracker?"

"I am told it is still tracking, our only concern is the fuel for the motor. Hopefully the U boat will stop buggering about and get back on course.

"Can you detect any other subs in the area?"

There was a pause, then Alec came back on the horn. "There was a mini sub in the area, one man saddle over a torpedo. We are collecting him at the moment. He is pretty battered, though I think mainly by the weather rather than any physical cause. We will transfer him over as soon as we get under the lee of the Isle de Groix.

***

Later, the two ships lay in the calmer water in the lee of the island. Rather than use a breeches buoy, the prisoner was transferred in a rubber dinghy, which was launched with a bow and stern rope to keep it tethered during the short crossing.

The prisoner was Italian and small framed. His condition was largely due to exposure. He arrived on board the ML wrapped snugly in blankets and cocooned inside a tarpaulin to keep him dry. Once safely on board the ML, he was bedded down in the sickbay.

The sickberth attendant kept him warm and fed him hot soup, having realised that the man was half starved, as well as exhausted.

The two ships remained in the shelter of the island throughout the night, and since the weather showed no sign of calming down, John decided to chance staying on through the following day.

***

Enrico Tutti was a native of Florence. He had been conscripted into the navy with no particular skills and thus, as an ordinary seaman, was given jobs nobody else wanted. His present situation was a result. As one of the test team for the human torpedoes, he had been launched from a research ship out of Lorient. Testing had been carried out in the Mediterranean by the Italian Navy, but it had been decided to send a team to demonstrate for the German Kriegsmarine. The selection of Lorient was on the basis of it's being a U boat base.

The unfortunate Enrico Tutti, ordinary seaman, had been launched three days earlier. Dressed in his waterproof suit, and supplied with a bottle of water and a packet of sandwiches, he had been launched into the waters of the Bay of Biscay with instructions to use his torpedo to sink a target ship, which had been towed out for the purpose.

Two things had prevented his carrying out of the operation. One was the fact that he had been launched into an eight foot swell, the precursor of the storm currently raging. The second was that Enrico had been violently seasick, and in the urgency of removing his helmet and face mask,(being sick in the facemask was not recommended.) he actually lost the hood. The integrity of his suit being compromised, though it did still offer some protection over the past two days, he had lost heat and was in process of a complete shutdown and death when the U-boat appeared. Unaware of the British ships, his confused mind did not select friend or foe. Merely, that he was there to fire his weapon.

The shock of releasing the torpedo left him with a much more unstable steed to ride upon. He had finally given up hope of survival.

Now he was lying in a soft warm bed, being fed soup and being looked after. Life, Enrico decided, could play tricks, some good some bad, but surely the people looking after him must be on the good side.

When John came into the sick bay, Enrico started to sit up in conditioned reflex when in the presence of an officer. He was gently pushed back down and the officer sat by his bed.

"Do you speak English?" The officer asked.

"Yes, sir. I worked at the Grosvenor House in Park Lane, London, for four years."

John was happy to hear that, as his Italian was basic to say the least."I understand your name is Enrico Tutti, so I will call you Enrico if you don't mind."

"As you wish, Capitano."

"What were you doing out in the bay where we found you?"

"The test for the torpedo. I lost contact. Nobody came to look. They left me to die."

"You fired your torpedo at the U-boat?" John observed.

"Yes, I missed him. They abandoned me. I thought, perhaps revenge. I did not want to be here. I did not want to fight the British. I liked London. I came home on holiday from my job to see my mother. Three days I am in Italy. Then they come for me to serve in the navy. I say 'no', I go back to my job in London. So here I am in navy with little chariot and torpedo." He slumped after the effort, back onto the pillow. As John watched a tear ran down Enrico's cheek. "Why me?" He whispered.

John left him. There was nothing else that Enrico could tell them just now. He understood that the man would recover. With a wry smile he realised that Enrico would be getting back to England quicker than he anticipated.

***

On the bridge once more, John contacted *Mavis* and the two ships returned to the area where they resumed their watch on the submarine, now waiting to enter the dock at Lorient. According to the boffins on board *Mavis* the remote contact with the seeker torpedo was still clear. They were prepared to fire it off as the sub went through the gates.

The fact that the torpedo did not explode was attributed to the interference by Enrico's human torpedo launch, and the chase that had drained it of fuel.

The ML had been fitted with an oversized torpedo tube and it carried a remote-controlled torpedo ready for deployment. The control equipment was in a box on the ward room table. The ML could not control a torpedo at long range. Only on launch could it program the weapon to track and engage. There had not been time to install the long range control equipment prior to sailing. The only advantage they had was that the setting-up could be accomplished by Toby Cummings. There was nearly a day to contemplate the situation as far as John was concerned. It was not until the evening of the following day that the next U-boat was heard and the tracker torpedo launched.

In view of their inability to remotely detonate the torpedo, they had to depend on its detonation on impact with its target, on this occasion the U boat it was tracking. There was no risk that it would run out of fuel as the target's destination was well within its range. Regarding the original torpedo which had not responded to the destruct signal, it was hoped that the explosion of the second might trigger the first. If not, the standard self-destruct should operate 24 hours after the torpedo stopped.

The two ships lay off and waited in quiet mode, passive sonar listening.

As they lay there, there was an explosion from the direction of Lorient. John was unsure whether it was the first or second torpedo which had exploded. Alec Randall was convinced it was the remote-controlled torpedo that had self-destructed, based on the fact that the active signal had disappeared at that point.

It was later discovered that the explosion had demolished the investigation team examining the captured torpedo recovered from the dry dock when they had drained it to service the U-boat.

It had also destroyed the technical workshop and the adjoining building, and punctured a hole in the sail of the U boat, an area that was not part of the pressure hull.

The second torpedo had gone off beneath the stern of the U boat it was tracking. The resultant explosion also blew the port screw off the tanker, currently standing anchored waiting to top up the base fuel tanks.

Subsequent information and photo-reconnaissance indicated that, though the gates of the lock had not been destroyed, they had been distorted .Tugs had to be brought in to shift the tanker, and the loss of the technical team had meant finding technical experts from elsewhere to undertake the specialised maintenance for the U-boats based in Lorient.

As they departed for Portsmouth once more the two ships were able to make fast time with the help of the storm pushing them up channel.

It was with relief that John saw *HMS Audax* alongside the quay, the lighter coloured paint highlighting the location where the damage had been repaired.

***

The report to the Admiral was made personally. The senior scientist from *Mavis* gave his report at the same time. Alec Randall and John Macklin were then de-briefed privately with only Admiral Harrington and Chloe Shepherd present.

In the discussion that followed, it was decided that the full remote-control gear would be fitted to the ML.

With all the other operations being performed along the south coast of England, one of the factors needing important consideration was the integration of effort among the independent operators active at the time.

"Unfortunately, many of the independent operations are ill set up, crossing the lines of others and causing confrontation at pressure points." The Admiral paused. "It seems that everyone and his brother has been allowed to start up secret operations, and the result is that most of them are no longer secret. It also means that many of the contacts in France are actually working for more than one team. This causes conflict of interest in some cases, and gives the game away to the enemy on occasion. There is a move afoot to combine effort under one command, but no one has yet been appointed."

"Where do we stand in that sort of arrangement?" John enquired.

"We don't, since we are official. But we still suffer from the proliferation of independents, which means we have to keep a close eye on all the operators we can monitor."

Chapter Nine

Foreign Parts

Over the next three months the ML spent half its time dropping and picking up agents.

The other half was spent in conjunction with *HMS Audax* and *Mavis* developing the torpedo and the several other odd weapons that had been produced.

In the summer of 1941 *HMS Audax* was cruising through the warm waters of the southern Atlantic.

John came out onto the bridge where the heat was intense. As it was, there was an awning stretched across the open bridge to protect the bridge team from the worst effect of the sun. That combined with the breeze created from their speed, made conditions bearable.

As he settled in his chair John heard the asdic note alter.

"What have we got on the screen he asked the watch officer, Sub Lieutenant Jim Fordyce RNVR.

"It is probably another whale." Fordyce said casually.

Irritated, John said, "I did not ask for your opinion, Mr Fordyce. I asked for the expert operator's opinion."

Fordyce jerked to attention. "Yes, sir." He went to the voice pipe. "What is that signal, Williams?"

"I believe it to be a whale, sir. But since this is the second time we have heard the noise, it should be worth investigating. bearing 357 degrees."

As the ship turned on to the new course the asdic set started sounding in earnest. It became evident that the so-called whale was in fact an enemy submarine. As a result of many hours of exercises and some failure, the crew of the *Audax* was well practised at dealing with U-boats. Applying that practice seemed the sensible thing to do. They ran up the bearing of the submarine, and dropped the first pattern of depth-charges.

Apart from the normal turmoil of water caused by the explosions, there was no result.

There was a buzz from the TBS. Ross Sherman answered it. He called to John. "Skipper, *Mavis* says 'try fuse X18 in one charge in the next drop, set depth at max'."

John turned to CPO Rogers "Pass it on, chief."

"Aye aye, sir." Rogers turned and spoke into his mike. He then turned back and reported. "Next drop, sir."

John nodded and waited. The next drop was made and the bridge party waited for the ensuing explosions.

This time oil came up with the yellow-tinged water,

There was a tense wait until the asdic resumed. The operator reported the submarine still making progress, though at reduced speed.

"Once more, Chief," John ordered.

Rogers spoke into his mike.

Again the bridge team waited.

This time the grey hull of the submarine slid out of the water, almost leaping like a dolphin pursued by a killer whale. The large U on the conning tower could be clearly seen, though the number was half obscured. It slammed level on the surface. Men streamed out of the conning tower and ran to man the gun mounted on the foredeck. Both Oerlikons from either side of the destroyer's bridge opened fire. The men on the submarine deck were mown down before they could get the gun in action.

There was no immediate reaction, then, cautiously, a white sheet was thrust out of the conning tower. It was in the hands of a seaman. John picked up the mike and switching to the loud hailer setting. "You are under my guns. I am ordering you to assemble on deck, the entire crew including all the officers. You have five minutes. I will then sink your vessel with gunfire. A boarding party is on the way.

The launch took a party of marines and Ross Sherman across to the wounded U-boat. It brought the first of the prisoners across to the ship, though there was a scuffle with the German Captain of the submarine, who decided at the last minute to protest. He was stopped by Ross Sherman, who grabbed him before he could do any harm.

The First Lieutenant managed to hold him, until Rogers, who was standing on the deck at that time subdued him with a right hook. With an approving nod, he hauled the semi-conscious officer to his feet and dumped him in the boat with the others.

The damaged U boat settled beneath the surface with little fuss. John was able to see the damage caused by the special depth charge. The twin screws of the sub were now a mangled mess of steel, and the shafts were actually torn out of the stern, causing a fatal wound in the pressure hull.

Back on board Ross Sherman asked John about the U-boat, it being so far south in the Atlantic.

"If you noticed, the boat was bigger than the type we have encountered in the English Channel. It is used as a supply ship for the attack U-boats, who have begun hunting in packs. The Germans call them 'milch kuhe'

(Milk cows). They can carry extra armaments and food to stretch the endurance of the smaller attack craft, and allow them to stay longer at sea."

"Ah, I see. But I still wonder what it was doing here off the coast of Africa?"

"I have to admit it has been bothering me also. Let's take a look at the chart and see what is in the immediate area."

Turning to Fordyce, he said, "Bring us back to our mean course south. You have the bridge. I'll be in my day cabin."

Fordyce turned, gave the order to resume their course, then picked up the mike on the TBS and informed *Mavis* that they would rejoin them shortly. He then strolled with his hands clenched behind him the width of the bridge, looking out over each beam in turn. In command!

He had in the past done several different things, including a walk-on part at the local repertory theatre, though he never had been left in charge. He strolled across the bridge and checked the repeaters to see that the course and revs were as they should be. Then he walked back and lifted his binoculars and did a swift scan around the horizon. He wondered what the receptionist in the Station Hotel in Bournemouth would say if she could see him now. Odd, he had not thought of her for some weeks. They had gone out to the pictures, simply as friends. Both had been at a loose end on her night off. He smiled at himself. He had not even held her hand or tried to kiss her. She had been very pretty, he recalled. He wondered if she was still working at the hotel.

He shrugged, thinking she was probably spoken-for anyway. He had promised to write. Perhaps he would. After all, for the cost of a stamp, he thought he would like to get to know her better. Betty Thomson, that was her name! He was brought back to the present, when the clatter of the cups against the metal dixie could be heard as the rating climbed the ladder to the bridge with the tea. A breath of the steam from the hot drink wafted over the bridge. He accepted the mug gratefully. It did not matter that they were in the tropics. Tradition dictated just as the rum issue was made daily. so the tea came round regularly, wherever the ship happened to be.

When he handed over to his opposite number Sub Lieutenant Owen Jones RNVR, he made sure the Captain's orders were passed on and then went below. He thought for a moment, then sat down and started writing a letter to Betty Thompson at the Station Hotel, Bournemouth.

***

In the day-cabin the two men studied the charts of the African coast.

"We will call into Freetown and drop off the prisoners," John decided. "Now, can you think of any reason why they should be supplying submarines on this coast? If, in fact, they are operating any further south of here, they will be at the limit of their range without any chance of return to Europe without resupply, Therefore the target must be well worth the effort and extremely important to the war, one way or the other."

"South Africa produces gold and diamonds. Both could be the target. But there may be something else that we are not aware of. We could be distracted by the gold and diamonds, and miss something else completely.

"Have we any German speakers on board, I wonder?" John thought aloud.

Ross Sherman answered, "We do." He had recalled looking at the files of the men when he first joined the ship. "I believe Midshipman Murray speaks German. His father was attaché in the embassy in Berlin, from 1929 to 1937. His mother had been killed in a car accident. His father decided that he be educated locally to keep him close to hand. He was taken out of Harrow and placed in the diplomatic school in Berlin, where everyone learned the language as part of the course."

John looked at Ross impressed at his in-depth knowledge of the midshipman's history. "Let us have him up here and see what we can do with some of our prisoners. Perhaps we can get some sort of idea of their itinerary here in the South Atlantic."

***

Tom Murray was tall and slim with fair hair and blue eyes. He was an all-round sportsman; that was, within the limits set by his diplomatic upbringing. He was a decent batsman and fast bowler at cricket. His golf handicap was 9. And he had practiced tennis with Fred Perry, who had regarded him as a decent opponent who could be great if he joined the race for tennis glory, Perry's words not Murray's.

The Midshipman was in the navy because his father had wanted him to be a diplomat. Having lived played and breathed diplomacy for most of his life, Tom had had enough.

He was old enough, and well-educated enough, so he joined the RNVR in 1939. He would be promoted to Sub Lieutenant in three weeks time, all things being equal.

He reported to the Captain as ordered, wondering what he had done wrong.

Ross Sherman opened the day cabin door, and motioned him in. The Captain was leaning over the table studying the chart for the southern African coastline.

When Tom stood to attention in front of the table, he lifted his head and said, "At ease," He then pointed to a paper on the table. "Can you read and understand that."

Tom curiously picked up the sheet and studied it. It was written in German and was an order to patrol a sector of the Atlantic for three weeks of the month.

"Yes, sir. I can translate this quite easily."

"You speak German, I understand?"

"I do, sir," Tom replied.

"I wish to question some of our prisoners, so I will need your help. Do you think you can manage?"

"Of course, sir. I'll be pleased to help in any way I can."

"Good. Number One, bring in the German Ensign." He turned to Tom. He is about your age. So I will leave you two to chat for a short while before I poke my nose in. Will that be all right?"

"Of course, sir. I'll do my best."

Seated at the table, Tom had a pad of paper and a pencil. And as the prisoner was brought in, the captain's steward brought in a tray with tea and biscuits.

The German lad was not as tall as Tom and he had a face scarred with acne. Otherwise he was pale but moved like an athlete. The marine with him remained in the cabin, keeping an eye on the prisoner.

Tom addressed the man in German. He asked his name and place of birth, how old he was and what was he doing in the south Atlantic.

The man answered the first three questions only. I am Helmut Kohn, from Berlin, born 12th June 1922. Serial number 2437896."

"Whereabouts in Berlin do you come from?"

"Potsdam, it's just..."

Tom said, "I know where it is. I used to live there."

Startled, the German looked up at his interrogator sharply.

"We possibly saw each other in passing. I lived in Potsdam for four years, played tennis at the public courts regularly."

"You were the English who helped win the area championship in 1938. I was there. I watched. You are a fine player." Ensign Koln was impressed.

"So here we are, once allies, now through politics, enemies. I am interested in why you should be so far south in the Atlantic. I know normally you operate in mid-Atlantic. You are not an attack boat after all?"

"You are right. We are not an attack boat. This was my first trip. so I am aware that the boat's last trip was to rendezvous off Grand Canaria. This time we came to supply a spe......" The voice ceased as Helmut realised his tongue was running away with him. He shut his mouth firmly. The fact was he had said too much already.

Tom looked at him keenly. "The special sub is in these waters for a reason that you cannot say. Of course, you are too junior to know such things, though you will have heard rumours no doubt. What we call scuttle-butt. I must tell you, if you don't already know, such rumours are seldom true. Far too often things have happened because of mistakes that come about through a word heard out of context."

Helmut Kohl hung his head, ashamed in his own mind for being tricked into admitting as much as he had.

Tom continued to chat as if nothing had happened. "I remember that I used to walk in the gardens. They used to say that, if you watched carefully, you could identify the spies meeting there. Do you know I believe you could? It was sometimes difficult to find a normal person in the park, and the spies of that period were very amateurish. They were mainly army and navy officers who had learned the language, but nothing about the people. So spies stood out. They will all be gone now. The Gestapo will have them.

Helmut spoke out. "Why are you telling me all this?"

"I came into this cabin to hold a conversation with someone who speaks the same language as I do. If we do not converse I am wasting my time and yours, though, if truth be known, you do have time to waste. I did expect to be able to talk man to man about your voyage. After all, we are both sailing men. It seems I was mistaken." He rose to his feet as if to leave the cabin.

Helmut held his hand up. "Please do not go. I will talk with you."

"If you stay too long your friends will believe that you are giving me information."

"They are not my friends. They treat me like dirt. My parents were diplomats like yours, only mine were Austrian. When I joined the navy I became a Lieutenant swiftly because I was quick to grasp the essence of codes. When we were invaded I was transferred to the German navy, and, because of my age, reduced to the rank of Ensign. This posting was punishment for not being German." The anger and frustration was showing clearly now as the young man explained. "Everyone on that ship knew I was there because of my father. Had he not been a strong supporter of Herr Hitler I would have been kicked out of the navy. I am better qualified to run the submarine that that idiot captain. Except I am not German and, since I am not German, I will tell you that the submarine we supplied was equal in size to ours, though it was Japanese. Not German. We encountered it off Windhoek in German South West Africa. It was there, I believe, to sink the round-the-world cruise ship, *Catalina* which left San Francisco two months ago. I believe she will be in range tomorrow."

Tom looked at Kohl in amazement. “But Japan is at war with the Chinese. They have nothing to do with the Americans or the British.”

Helmut sat back with a sigh. “I overheard a conversation between the Captain and a man I recognised as an associate of Dr Goebbels. The Captain had questioned the need for such a long trip with supplies to be given to a Japanese submarine, not an ally, and a dangerous distance away. The sub would be at the limit of its endurance. The risk could not be worth such a loss if things went wrong.

“The prize, the diplomat said, was worth the effort. The *Catalina* is an American cruise-ship full of millionaires.”

Tom reported his findings to the captain who was, like the Midshipman, appalled. He called in Ross Sherman and had Murray tell him of the Ensign’s revelation.

Ross’s reaction was as anticipated, but there was an added reason for his worry. “Skipper, my grandparents are on that ship. They treated themselves to this voyage, and were among the first to book their passage. It was my grandmother’s lifelong ambition to sail around the world. Grandpa promised to do it one day.”

John listened to Ross, working out what they could do. “There can be no excuse for such a dreadful crime.” He looked at his watch. “We can break wireless silence shortly. I want a message to CNO Capetown and to the *Catalina* warning them of the danger. The problem is that the submarine is Japanese and, therefore, technically neutral. The CNO may decide that he cannot interfere, when we really need to get elements of the navy out to stop that submarine.

We are too far away to do anything ourselves, but we can give warning. So signal to CNO in Capetown and advise him of our information. Suggest air patrols also if it can be arranged, if only to try and warn the sub off."

John paused to go over his thoughts and see if he had missed anything, not being able to think of anything he asked, "Can anyone suggest anything I may have missed?"

Neither of the others had anything else to suggest, so the signal to Capetown with the copy to London was sent. The attempt to signal *Catalina* got through on the third try.

To distract himself from the worry about the cruise ship, John considered their task in the scheme of things. His orders were not to be opened until he was off the Cape of Good Hope. That would not be until midnight tomorrow night. Until then, he had no way of knowing what the task in the South Atlantic really entailed. He had the feeling that the protection of a cruise ship full of civilians was not on the agenda.

***

John Macklin was seated with the open orders on his desk in front of him. Ross knocked entered and seated himself on the only other chair in the room.

For a few moments John said nothing. Then with a sigh he spoke, "There is a raider apparently in the area. It seems that the bulk of the naval forces in this area are searching for her. The Commodore has diverted two frigates to contact the *Catalina,* though the Captain of the cruise ship insists that, as a neutral, we have no right to interfere with his legitimate progress through international waters."

Ross looked at John aghast. "Is the man a complete idiot?"

John smiled grimly. "No. he is covering his ass. Technically, he is within his rights to insist that any armed ship keep her distance. To put it bluntly, the presence of warships in a time of war should be a reassurance, though I can see it as a provocation to the other side."

Ross nodded slowly as he thought of the ramifications. "So we can do nothing for them!"

"Exactly, and incidentally, our mission here is to shadow, and find a means of neutralising, the raider currently masquerading as the South African fruit carrier, *Oranjebloom*, armed with two six inch guns and four lighter, possibly four inch guns, mounted two on each side, and one torpedo tube mounted underwater in line with the stem of the ship. Speaking of torpedoes, have 'Torps' go over our remaining torpedo tubes, and the torpedoes themselves. We could need them."

Ross acknowledged the orders. He left John thinking that this was an occasion when he was happy he only had to obey orders.

Chapter ten

Action in the South Atlantic

The towering mountain overlooked the scatter of buildings gathered on her lower slopes and down to the water's edge. John stood on the bridge of *HMS Audax* in the breeze as the ship entered the protection of Table Bay. He turned to Sub Lieutenant Jones. "Call Lieutenant Randall for a conference, please, in my day cabin as soon as I return from the CNO's office."

Seated in his cabin John said to Alec, "Your part could be vital if past history is to be believed. German raiders in the South Atlantic gained a deserved reputation for sheer survival against odds, including, if memory serves, an allied light cruiser, lost after a gun battle with a raider."

Tom Murray had suggested that the Ensign Koln might know something of the ship. Since he was being kept separate from the other prisoners, it would be simple to speak on the subject, as he was currently very bitter about his treatment by the Nazis. He was despatched to get whatever he could from the young man on the subject.

The others discussed general strategy, until Murray returned. The one piece of good news was that the *Catalina* was in Capetown harbour for the next week. She would leaving from there, for Ascension Island and St Helena, on Sunday.

Tom Murray returned, bringing Ensign Koln with him. "Sir, I believe you will want to hear this from source, and, can I get tea for us all?"

"By all means. But hurry, we need to talk to this man, I presume?"

"Oh, he can talk to you. His English is excellent." He blushed as he said it, realising that he could have mentioned it two days ago, though it would not have allowed him to develop the easy relationship he had with the German officer.

John turned to the Ensign, "What have you got to say?"

The German officer looked at the men before him, "I understand that you are seeking the *Oranjebloom*?"

John nodded, "Yes, we are. Do you know her?"

"I know of her. When we were in the base at Brest, I met a colleague from naval college. He had been posted to *Deutschland*, the pocket-battleship. She sailed before he could reach her, so he shipped out on the *Koblenz,* the heavy cruiser. He was boasting of her prowess of how they had killed so many ships on her last cruise, and that they were going to join a raider in the South Atlantic. I laughed and said there were no cruisers in the South Atlantic. He challenged me and said that the *Hippolyte* had just returned and was being replaced with *Koblenz*. It seems they work in concert with whatever raider we have in station there. All the credit goes to the raider. They think it is scarier than people finding there is a great warship just over the horizon. Apart from that, if they keep its presence secret, the British Admiralty are less likely to send a big enough force to deal with a heavy cruiser."

John nodded slowly. "I see.....Well, we will just have to see what we can do about that. Thank you, Mr Kohl, you have been most helpful."

When Kohl had returned to his lonely cell, the others studied the problem they faced.

"My guess is that they are doing what they did in the first war. They have found an island base where they can lay up out of sight. They will have spies in various places through the area of the Southern Ocean. When a juicy target offers, they come out and do the business, then return to the base with the spoils if there are any." Ross had read his history and the idea had merit.

Alec suggested, "If what you say is true, then there should be a history of ships delivering cargoes to such an island base, certainly for quite some time over the past few years. Maintaining a base, in this sort of hostile environment, cannot be done without regular supplies and plenty of them. At least some of the ship losses will be purposely lost for the cargoes they carry. So let us see what the base here in Capetown can tell us about cargoes going on a regular basis to odd destinations."

***

Tom Murray was enjoying the walk through the South African city. The air was brisk not quite cool, but the light breeze carried scents and hints of exotic things that awakened memories of the sea stories of his youth. He carried a letter from the Captain and a bunch of flowers for a lady called Iris Duncan, who worked at the Port Master's office. The letter was the Captain's contribution, the flowers because Tom was calling on a lady at her home. Being properly brought up, Tom knew you should always take flowers when calling on a lady.

He turned up the side street off the main road and started looking for the apartment block where Miss Duncan lived.

It was not difficult to find, the rather raw modern block at odds with the lower level original Dutch architecture of the surrounding houses.

There was a reception desk inside the entrance to the block. The African receptionist insisted on calling Miss Duncan, before she would allow Tom to go up to the fourth floor apartment.

The elevator was smooth and modern. It deposited Tom within three yards of the door of number 42. As he approached, it opened and a figure in a dressing gown with a towel wrapped around her head stood waiting for him.

Flustered by the sight, Tom thrust the flowers at the figure saying, "I am Tom Murray, Miss Duncan. I believe you are expecting me?"

The figure held the towel with one hand and took the flowers with the other. "Yes, Mr Murray. Please come in and excuse the mess. I have just returned from a trip up country."

He followed the woman into the apartment. He could not help noticing her trim figure moving effortlessly within the dressing gown as she preceded him into the lounge. There were clothes scattered around and the scent of some perfume hanging in the air. The lady waved at the settee. "Sit down. I'll be with you in a minute. She disappeared through a door to the right of the room and Tom seated himself on the settee, he moved some of the clothes to one side and found himself holding silky ladies underwear which had been covered by the other clothes on the settee

He looked about with a hunted look. Then he thrust the underclothes under the other clothes at the end of the settee, he still felt embarrassed even though he had nothing to feel guilty for.

He sat silent, still aware of the feel of the silky underwear. He looked at the hand which had held the flimsy garments, desperately trying not to picture them on the lady, and not really succeeding.

Iris Duncan came into the lounge once more, this time fully dressed in smart white blouse, a navy skirt to her knee and black court shoes. Her hair was still not fully dry, but it was cut short in a bob and was lying neatly enough around her face, a face, Tom observed, that he would not forget in a hurry.

"Sorry about this." She said sweeping up the clothes from the settee and turning to take them through to the other room. The underwear slipped from her grasp and Tom stooped to pick the fallen pieces up. Iris almost snatched them from him and dashed through to the other room.

When she returned she said, "Thank you," in a quiet voice. "Would you like a drink or something?"

Tom shook his head. "No, thank you." He took the letter from his pocket and passed it to her. "I was asked to deliver this to you," he said.

She took the envelope cautiously, turning it over in her hands before opening it.

Having read it, she looked at Tom. "Do you know what this is?"

"My guess would be a request for statistics on goods going through Capetown."

"Good guess!" I suppose I really have no option. I cannot deny the Navy access to what is possibly a similar situation to that of the last war. I will see what I can do. Some, though not all, ships give details of their future movements, even though we expect them to. Thank you for the flowers. I presume they are from you."

"Why did you think that?"

She shrugged and lifted the letter. "This is the Government way."

He smiled ruefully. "Penalty of my mother's upbringing, I'm afraid. The words will ever ring in my ear, 'When you visit an attractive lady, take flowers!"

"You consider me attractive?" Iris asked with a small smile.

Tom blushed. "Definitely! Yes."

It was her turn to blush. "Tom Murray, I am old enough to be your big sister at least. But I appreciate the thought."

Tom stood up and looked down on Iris, "Miss, I would just like you to know that the request the Captain has made is very important to the war, and to the people of this area. There is a German raider in this locality. We need to find it. We also need to keep our search as secret as possible. So please only speak to either me, or one of the other officers from my ship."

Iris looked at Tom directly. "This will remain a secret between us. Please tell Captain Macklin that it would make sense if you alone kept in contact with me." She hesitated for a moment. "How old are you, Mr Murray?"

Tom looked surprised, but responded seriously. "I'm 21, Miss Duncan."

"Ah, that is alright then. I am not old enough to be your big sister after all. I also am 21. It would make sense to anyone seeing us together, if we were interested......." Seeing his blank look, she added, "In each other...boyfriend-girlfriend?"

"Oh, yes. I see. He blushed and turned and then turned back. "I should call you Iris, then." He said smiling."

She smiled back. "And I will call you Tom. Come to the office if you are about tomorrow and we can either go out on a date, or you can walk me home, depending on what time you have available. I have nothing planned, so either way could suit me. I should know something by closing time tomorrow. I believe if we are to keep the secret, we must act in public as if our friendship is genuine."

At the door as he turned to say goodbye. She reached up, pulled his head down and kissed him lightly on the lips. She smiled at his confusion and said, "Practice!"

***

Returning to the ship, Tom was still trying to sort out just what had happened. By the time he was at the gangplank he more or less understood that he had been ambushed, albeit for the right reasons, by the best-looking girl he had ever met.

In the Captain's cabin Tom reported to the Captain and Ross Sherman, going over the conversation with Iris Duncan, virtually word for word.

The Captain listened attentively and, when Ross might have said something, the slight shake of John's head stopped him.

When Tom Murray completed his report, John considered for a few moments. "That makes sense. Two young people together. Good. Meet her at the office as she suggest. If there is something immediate to report, take her to the Dundas Hotel. One of us will be there. Tomorrow evening, you can pass the report on. If immediate action is needed, we'll take it from there. Otherwise you and the lady go out on a date. Will you be all right with that? Will it be a problem?"

"Oh, no problem, sir. I'll play my part."

"Good. Well get off now. The First Lieutenant will arrange to clear your duties for the evening."

"Thank you, sir." Tom left the office not knowing whether to be worried or excited. He settled for a bit of both.

It was with some trepidation that Tom was waiting outside the port office at 1700 the following day.

The fact that he was there on business was the last thing on his mind. He was in fact carrying a wrapped box of chocolates for Iris.

When she appeared followed by two other girls he froze for a moment. Then Iris came over to him and reached up and kissed him. He found his arms were around her and both of them were relaxing into the embrace as if it was genuine.

They unwrapped to the accompaniment of comments from the other two girls. Iris coolly turned to them and said, "Carol, Mary, this is Tom. He is mine, so please keep your distance."

She turned back to Tom and took his arm. "Where are we going tonight, Tom?"

As she snuggled up to him he remembered the chocolates and gave her them. Then he said, "Where do you fancy?"

By then they were out of range of the girls, but Iris still stayed hugging his arm close. "Thanks for the chocolates. Shall we get something to eat and go for a walk along the shore?"

***

For Tom the next few days were the best he had experienced in his life. It was with certain trepidation that he reached the end of the information gathering about the movement of ships over the past nine months. At their last official meeting he approached the subject with Iris. Determinedly, he said, "Iris, can we keep getting together whenever I'm here, and write to each other as well."

"Are you asking me to be your girlfriend?"

"Yes. I think I would like to marry you, but I am willing to wait until we know each other better. What I am really scared of is, if you have just been acting all this time. I need to know now. I will be terribly disappointed but I will probably get over it."

For a moment Iris was tempted to string him along, but, looking at him, she realised that if she wanted to keep him, it would be better to be straightforward. She stopped and looked at him. "I have to tell you when we started out I thought what a fun game we were playing. It did not take me long to realise I was not playing. I don't want to let you go. So the answer to your question is 'yes' I want to be your girlfriend and I will write to you. We'll see how it turns out. She stood looking at him defiantly.

Laughing, Tom swept her up into his arms and they kissed and laughed together.

***

At sea later that night, Ross spoke to the Captain. "I guess we have been responsible for young Murray falling in love."

"What do you mean?" He looked across at the midshipman who was looking back at the lights of Capetown through his binoculars.

"The lady, Iris Duncan, and young Murray got friendly while he played his part keeping us informed about ship movements." Ross said.

"Well, that was the best way of keeping what we were really doing under our hats." John thought for a moment. "You mean they started to take it seriously?"

Ross nodded. "They are about the same age, of course. It's not really surprising."

John commented drily, "You are not feeling guilty then?"

Ross looked startled. "Why should I feel guilty? It's just nature taking its course. It will do the lad good. I have the feeling that he has not had a girlfriend up to now."

John looked out over the bow, thinking of Chloe, wondering if they had done the lad a favour. He thought on balance they probably had.

***

The ships started to move more as the Southern Ocean livened up due to a storm 100 miles to the east. The *Mavis* was riding easily, staying just behind the starboard quarter of *HMS Audax.* John had not made any formal plan for dealing with the two German ships, both of which he now realised outgunned his destroyer. Whatever they did, his unit would need a plan and an edge to win any dispute between his ships and the raiders. They had two islands to survey, narrowed down from the information that Iris Duncan had assembled. They would need to scout both. Only then, when they established which was being used, could they make serious arrangements to deal with their opponents.

***

Kommodore Albert Humbert, who commanded the cruiser *Koblenz*, sat in his cabin wondering what he had done to deserve being sent to this arsehole of a place to play pirates with a part time-sailor in a converted banana boat. The fact that Fregattenkapitan Schmidt, captain of the *Oranjebloom,* was homosexual did nothing to improve the relationship between the two captains. The other fact was, he was the personal choice of Vice-admiral Schiller who commanded operations in the Southern Hemisphere. In the opinion of the Kommodore, another shirt-lifter, whose position had been gained by his political status in the Nazi party, and who should never have been allowed to serve in the Kriegsmarine.

His current line of thought was directed to the mooring that they occupied. As far as the raider was concerned there was no problem. Her size and draught slotted into the fjord with no trouble, as did the cruiser. But, although the *Oranjebloom* could swing to face the entrance when leaving the fjord, her length and draught clearing the sides of the fjord without a problem, that option did not apply to the *Koblenz,* whose draught made her just too long in the keel to clear the outcrop of rock extending most of the length of the fjord. She could, of course, reverse out of the mooring, but not with the other ship between her and the sea. Another factor was the sides of the fjord, which towered above both ships. It had occurred to Humbert that he could fire his guns from the mooring, except that he could only direct his fire up the fjord inland, or down, toward the open sea. Either side, his field of fire was obstructed by the walls of the fjord.

The final demerit was, if he did fire his guns in the confines of the fjord, the pressure and shockwaves were likely to bring down the rock walls of the fjord. Admittedly, in that case, possibly clearing his line of fire to some extent on either beam, but with the added complication of trapping his ship within the fjord in the ensuing rockfalls.

The *Oranjebloom* was fitted with a pair of six inch guns taken from a WW1 cruiser. Her gunnery, he admitted grudgingly, was pretty good. So, if the British destroyer which had appeared on the scene came snooping around, the raider should be able to subdue her pretty quickly. The small supply ship sailing with the destroyer would be no trouble and could be useful as a capture.

His thoughts were interrupted by Fregattenkapitan Erich Warner, his second-in-command. They had sailed together since training school in the Baltic, friends and within the cabin, the rank could be discarded.

As the cabin door closed Albert smiled, pulled out the bottom drawer of his desk and produced a bottle of malt whisky, liberated from a captured prize. Nodding to the other chair in the room, he poured two glasses and passed one over to Warner, now seated, hat off and ready to chat.

"What has our Nazi friend suggested this time?" Erich's question followed the first sip of the fine whisky.

"We cannot swap places in the fjord as he would need to challenge any possible target first, and we cannot use the other anchorage because he does not like it. It is gloomy and carries bad memories." He saw the raised eyebrow of his friend and forestalled the question. "The alternative base was used in the last war by raiders, who were all sunk."

Erich sipped his drink again, enjoying the smoky flavour. "They may be barbarians but they surely know how to make a good drink." He thought for a moment, then said, "How about the setting up of guns on the island? Even fixed defences would give us some chance of getting out of here in one piece."

"Can't be done. No guns to start with, and would give-away the fact that we were here."

"So, in essence, unless we are out of here in good time we could be in trouble!"

Humbert nodded, "Precisely!"

Erich indicated the wall of the fjord through the porthole. We have at least got lookouts up, I trust?"

Humbert grinned. "Did you see the ropeways attached to both sides of the fjord?"

"I did, though I am surprised that you got away with it." They both laughed and Albert asked how the link with their agent in Capetown was operating. "Any new information on the two ships sent to catch us?"

"Not really, though he was concerned that one of the midshipmen from the destroyer was friends with one of the girls in the Port Admiral's office."

"Did he say if she was worth the effort?" Albert was vaguely uneasy for some reason.

"In fact he said that she was well worth the effort and their parting was epic."

"Epic?"

"Oh, you know. Kisses and cuddles and promises to write. A sailor's farewell. Could mean 'see you next time' or goodbye and here to the next one. Though it did seem to be genuine, if you know what I mean."

Albert did know, having gone through the same routine several times before he met Lotte. He sighed. Lotte had gone, killed in a raid on Hamburg, one of the first to reach the city. Their house was on the riverbank, a direct hit, from a stray bomb, from a errant aircraft.

He finished his scotch and sat up, all business. "We will have to get to sea as soon as possible. I have a bad feeling about this destroyer. There is something special about it, I'm certain, otherwise they are throwing away the two ships, despite the odds against them, and the Royal Navy do not play those sort of games."

Erich agreed, though he had not felt the unease his friend felt. he knew him well enough to trust his friend's instincts. He did not like the enclosed moorings which seemed to please their companion ship's captain so much.

In fact the man in question was not a fool. He fully understood the position of the cruiser captain, but he had managed to survive nearly a year without the backing of the big ship. He did not fear a destroyer with her puny 4.7" guns, and antiquated fire controls. He was also aware of the cruiser Captain's distaste at having to deal with a homosexual on an equal level. It gave him pleasure to frustrate him when it was in his power to do so. His rank of Fregattenkapitan had been earned, having been serving in U-boats since the Spanish war. He had been rescued from submarines and promoted to captain the raider ship, *Oranjebloom.* So far it had worked out well.

He was strolling back and forth on the bridge of his command, when the request to move came from the other ship,

For some time Schmidt thought about it, then he gave his approval. He had used the wait to assert his authority. Now he gave orders to sail. The ship came to life once more, starting to hoist anchor, and clear the exit from the fjord.

The two German ships sailed away to the area where ships from the Indian Ocean made their approach to the final stretch to Capetown. *HMS Audax,* with her accompanying ship, *Mavis,* sailed into the fjord which had sheltered the two German ships, missing them by eight hours. The ropeway stretched across the fjord was still in place. A party of marines rounded up the lookouts who had been left in place. They were both frail-looking men, conscripted into the navy, and hating every minute they were forced to serve. Because of their lack of ability as seamen, their life on board ship was hell. They had accepted their posts as lookouts with open arms, despite the risk of being left to die there if the ships failed to return.

Interrogation revealed the simple signalling system used to warn or give the all clear to the ships when they returned.

John decided to leave a small party of Marines with the two men and try to catch the two ships when they were back in the anchorage. The lookouts were very forthcoming when they understood that they were now prisoners of war, and that, for them, the war was over. They were able to reveal that there was conflict between the two German captains and that the *Oranjebloom* always entered the mooring last, blocking the other ship within fjord. They also revealed that the cruiser could not turn in the fjord. Apparently there was not enough water depth.

Looking at the walls of the fjord, the gunner said, "That cruiser dare not fire his guns in here. He would bring the whole lot down on top of him and it would probably block in the other ship as well. What we could do is mine the side of the fjord, and block the ships in while they are at their moorings."

John thought otherwise. In conference with Alex, they decided that a torpedo could be left awaiting the return of the two Germans. If it sank the *Oranjebloom,* the cruiser would be locked in. If they stationed a torpedo in the fjord at the far end, it could cripple the cruiser where it sat.

While they were in the vicinity they heard a radio call for help from a ship bound for Capetown, which cut off abruptly.

Leaving the torpedoes in place, *Mavis* landed a team to control the weapons, locating a line of sight spot high in the landward end of the fjord. Both ships then left the immediate area.

***

Sub Lieutenant Martin Offord looked out over the wasteland of shattered rock. His team consisted of three men and a radio. It was his first task as a newly promoted officer, though that was not actually correct. His position, until his return to UK, was acting in the rank. He was qualified and would have been confirmed even in Capetown, but the magic date did not come up until they were off the island, so his acting promotion had been logged and his seniority would commence from that date regardless.

He turned to the Petty Officer with him. "Is all the gear working properly?" The gear was a radio and the control unit for the two torpedoes currently lying on the bottom of the fjord below.

PO Paddy Doyle smiled and replied, "Aye, sir. All the gear has been tested and is in good working order." He did not mind Offord. He was a sensible sort of lad who would grow into his new rank with little real bother.

They had a camouflage net stretching over the tent and the pile of supplies pegged down under a tarpaulin in a depression between the rocks. All four men had been issued with cold weather clothing. The two Marines were there as security for the naval party.

The Marine corporal said, "We should all get under the net, sir. The cruiser's aircraft is making a sweep."

Doyle suddenly started taking off the Arctic coveralls.

"What are you doing, PO?" Offord shouted.

Doyle called back, "They left their men to keep watch. They will expect to see someone in a sailor suit." He got the coveralls off and flung them to the officer. "Take that with you, sir. I'll stay out here and wave.

Offord joined the two Marines under the net, and Doyle waved at the Arado floatplane as it appeared over the high point on the island and zoomed past the tent still in place for the German sailors stationed on the hilltop. The observer waved at Doyle and the plane went off out to sea to rejoin the *Koblenz,* just coming into view on the horizon.

Doyle joined the Sub Lieutenant and the Marines under the net. "I guess we will need to blow the Cruiser as soon as she drops her hook," he commented.

"I was thinking to wait until the *Oranjebloom* was in. That would make sure that the cruiser could not get out."

"I'm bothered that they might send a relief party up here as soon as they come in. I would prefer that they had other things on their mind if we can manage it."

Doyle had a point, Offord had to rethink his plans, and it looked as though they would need to hope that the two ships were close together, returning to their lair.

As the big warship approached they were able to see the raider rapidly catching up to the *Koblenz.*

As Offord watched anxiously the two ships manoeuvred for position before entering the fjord. There was a snow storm building. making things more difficult.

Doyle was watching the clear horizon to the east. "Our two ships in sight, sir, in a hurry from the looks of it. Offord swung round to see what Doyle was referring to.

Both British ships were racing toward the island the bow waves rising high each side as the plunged through the southern ocean swell. They were out of sight of the German ships at present, approaching as they were from the east and the line of the fjord lying north south.

Offord turned back and peered through the snow flurries at the two ships creeping into the fjord, "Doyle, watch me."

As the PO watched, Offord turned the switch for the torpedo allocated to the raider. He then turned the switch for the second torpedo, allocated to the *Koblenz.*

There was not much to see. With the snow flurries and the noise of the engines from the fjord, the explosion was muffled. But it was possible to see the *Oranjebloom* lose power and start to drift across the fjord, finishing up jammed and blocking the way out for the cruiser. The second explosion blew the four propellers of the cruiser into a surreal mix of metal, the steel and brass twisted like pretzels, and punching a hole into the sealed maintenance room at the extreme stern of the ship. The explosion itself drove the ship forward and it struck the side of the fjord, at a point where the bow grounded with the ship at a slight angle, the stern drifting round as if to ground on the other wall of the fjord.

The fjord became a bedlam of noise as loudhailers were used to exchange information. The snow continued to fall reducing visibility. The arrival of *HMS Audax* at the entrance to the fjord was greeted by fire from the *Oranjebloom's* secondary armament. Her main guns could not bear, but the other guns were accurate and the destroyer was hit several times.

John called for torpedoes. The four tubes mounted amidships swung round and lined up on the raider stuck across the fjord.

"Fire two when ready." John ordered.

Two 21-inch torpedoes leaped from the tubes and ran through the entrance of the fjord. One hit the target in the engine room. The explosion broke the back of the ship. The guns stopped firing. The second torpedo was trapped in the wreckage and did not explode immediately. The *Koblenz* was revealed to the destroyer and Kommodore Humbert, furious at being caught in this position because of the stupidity of Fregattenkapitan Schmidt, watched the destroyer manoeuvring to torpedo his ship. He turned to the gunnery officer. "Use the stern mounting and remove that ship." He pointed to the British destroyer.

"Yes, sir!" The gunnery officer replied. "But what about the fjord walls?"

"Just do it." Humbert did not care if the walls fell or not. He was finished in the German Navy. That was certain.

The after-turret rotated slowly. The bearings were not quite in line, following the impact of the grounding, and the shock of the controlled torpedo explosion. As they came to bear on the entrance to the fjord, the eight inch guns fired. The right hand shell hit the rock at the fjord mouth. The left hand gun scored, the shell completely removing the after gun mount on the destroyer, including the gun crew and the crew of the Oerlikon the iron deck beside it. The bridge crew were thrown off their feet with the impact.

The real drama was on the island. The impact of the shell on the wall of the fjord caused a reaction, bringing down a huge slab of rock smashing down on the *Oranjebloom,* crushing the fore end, which separated from the aft section with a tearing creaking noise. Under the weight of the rock, the fore end of the ship sank beneath the roiled water. Whoever was still alive in that part of the ship went down without any chance of survival. The temperature of the water would ensure anyone submerged for more than a few minutes would succumb to hypothermia.

The secondary result of firing the big guns in the enclosed area was a general landslip in the immediate area of the guns themselves. Above the damaged cruiser a large section of the cliff wall detached and fell onto the upper-works destroying the bridge and the gunnery control tower. Pouring rubble through the opened hatches and crushing the crew members on duty on the bridge. The Kommodore himself fell wounded, his arm smashed by the falling rock. He survived, but lost his arm to surgery.

The other survivors were eventually rescued by a neutral cargo ship. *HMS Audax* and *Mavis* being unable to stay on site due to the deteriorating weather.

Offord and his men had struck camp and made their way down to the landing place the rubber dinghies they had arrived in awaited their rescue. Both frail craft made it, sheltered in the lee of the two British ships, for the hectic journey offshore. They brought the two German lookouts with them.

On the bridge of the destroyer, John stood watching the island appear and disappear as the snow squalls opened and closed the visibility. The weather was increasingly worsening. It was common sense to run with the wind and make their way back to Capetown and shelter, to repair the damage and get the injured to hospital.

***

Tom Murray's date for his promotion was rapidly approaching, and he was looking forward to seeing Iris, his girlfriend.

In fact, the looked-for stay at Capetown became a stop on the dash northward. Three days in the dockyard to patch holes in the deck where the aft gun mount had been, and the removal to hospital for the worst injured was just about all the time they had before departure once more.

Tom arrived in time to say goodbye to Iris who was off to England to join the WRNS. Her passage had been booked on one of the ships of the convoy, and they only had a short time together. Tom gave her his mother's address. They had parted all too quickly on the day before the ship completed storing and fuelling. The hammering of the dockyard workers doing repairs was the accompaniment to all the other activities on board at the time.

Iris was prepared to go to England. It was her first journey outside the country and she was excited and worried at the same time.

At least they would not be separated by 6000 miles for the immediate future. Both clung on to that.

With tears and promises to write. they said goodbye on the quay as the boat waiting to take her off to the *Edinburgh Castle* stood by.

HMS Audax sailed the following day, escorting the convoy north to Freetown and thence on to Falmouth.

Ross had managed to see his grandfather and grandmother before they left Capetown. John had spoken to the Captain of the *Catalina* and was re-assured by the fact that the ship had plenty of power in her engines. With a cruising speed of up to 26 knots and a top speed of 29 knots, they had a good chance of evading the submarine.

The convoy and the US ship were in the same waters for some time so John hoped the Japanese sub would be confused by mass of ships in the area. It seemed whatever happened to the Japanese submarine, it did not catch the *Catalina.* Nor was it heard of again.

***

Apart from the weather, the trip to Freetown was without major incident. The convoy suffered the usual delays caused by lack of proper maintenance, despite all the ships being modern and the convoy rated as a 14 knot convoy. Like all ship-owners there were the inevitable corner-cutters, running ships with scratch crews and patchwork repairs where needed. The convoy only lost one day in the initial transit.

The ongoing convoy, despite expecting to run through dangerous waters, included several ships that John Macklin told Ross Sherman were less sound than they should be. He suspected that, in at least two cases, a strong stiff finger could punch a hole in their plates.

"Heaven help them if they come within the circle of influence of an exploding depth charge. I estimate there are two will collapse like a pack of cards. Another pair will lose their stern gear." He pointed to the *Aurora,* a 15,000 ton mixed freighter, currently slipping along with no particular problem. "She was entering the scrapyard last time I saw her, with a broken back. The crack up her side has been welded. Do you see the mark? Heaven help her if we hit a big storm on the way back."

Lieutenant Ross Sherman RCN looked at his captain, stunned by his comments. "Do they realise they are sailing in a coffin ship?"

"Probably, but work is work, and she has survived so far." He shrugged. "With luck she might survive once more. Keep your fingers crossed."

***

Throughout the remainder of the voyage, Ross found himself looking for the *Aurora* every time he came on deck. The weather held fair until they passed north of the Canary Islands. Then it deteriorated and was blowing a force nine gale. The sea built up with the activity generated over two thousand miles of ocean, the waves rising to fifty feet, in long surges, causing the ships of the convoy to lose cohesion and scatter, to allow themselves sea room to fight their own battles in their own way. *Audax* had her own problems. The temporary repairs were beginning to leak water. Over ten years old, the ship was riding the waves well, but rolling in the occasional cross sea did make things uncomfortable. It was this rolling that was putting strain on the repaired areas, causing the leaks.

The storm lasted for four days and the round up of the ships another two. The *Aurora* survived, but both the others that John had pointed out were still missing when the convoy resumed the homeward journey. Extra escorts in the form of two frigates and a corvette joined the two destroyers, with three frigates making the escort up to eight warships, with John in command as the most senior officer. The escort commander from Capetown had left them at Freetown, taking the south bound convoy and the remainder of the escorts that had sailed from Capetown. The second destroyer captain had been junior to John, making John the escort commander for the remainder of the journey home.

Chapter-eleven

Interludes

The two boffins carried by the *Audax*, with their four assistants, had all been working on modifications to the torpedoes and the control gear.

The electronics expert had been able to improve the performance of the radio location gear by increasing the power of the signal giving them a picture of an expanded horizon, admittedly by raising the assembly on the mast. But he had also extended the range in the air to almost fifty miles. He was unsure of the durability of some of the components, so would not guarantee how long the present modifications would work. But he was confident that, once back in Portsmouth, he could locate suitable parts to ensure improved performance over an extended operation period.

It was eight days later that the destroyer finally tied up at Portsmouth. The convoy had made it after a brisk encounter with U-boats off the North Spanish coast.

Of the two missing ships, one had made it to port under its own steam. The other was towed in and, once emptied of its cargo, sent to the wrecker's yard to be broken up.

Tom was happy to see the Edinburgh Castle enter Southampton to offload. He had already been told where his Iris would be stationed for training.

John was able to get home while the repairs to the destroyer were commenced, Chloe was unable to get away so they couldn't spend time together. It did give John time to relax, and he was able to clear the air with Amy. She pointed out that she was happy to be friends, and lovers, but that did not mean an exclusive deal in her case as she did spend time elsewhere and saw no reason to get jealous over relationships, at least up until now. This discussion took place in Amy's bed and could therefore have been awkward. In fact it was not.

For Jim Fordyce, whose first letter had been answered and contact established through, of all people, Jim's mother. Life had become more interesting. Betty Thompson was still working in the hotel in Bournemouth and had contacted his mother, who like, all mothers, was quick to assess the girlfriends of their sons. Luckily, the approval was immediate as Betty's father had, as a plasterer, done work for Mr Fordyce in the past, so Betty was persona grata almost immediately.

When Jim arrived home he was greeted by his mother and ushered into the front room. His mother disappeared murmuring something like 'tea', Jim turned round to find Betty standing there, looking apprehensive.

He was stunned and delighted. His memory had not deceived him. She was as beautiful as he had recalled and his instinctive step forward brought him close enough to take her hands in his. It seemed only natural to kiss her. He leant forward and found her meeting him halfway. The gap between them closed and when the door began to open quietly, mother looked, nodded, and closed the door again.

"I couldn't help it," he said hesitantly.

Betty grinned. "Neither could I. Or didn't you notice?"

He relaxed, still holding her close, smelling the scent of soap or perfume, just a hint, "I really think I need to do that again, just to make sure we know what we are doing."

"Mmm..." Was all the reply he got as they kissed once more.

***

John looked keenly at the Admiral, "On the basis of our conversation so far, I presume we are doing a drop off and pick up."

Back in the office on the quay on Portsmouth the Admiral was discussing operations being set up using the ML

"Right. On this occasion that is exactly what we are doing."

John sat back, considering the forthcoming weeks.

Chloe took up the briefing. "The scheduled modification to the torpedo system on the ML has been undertaken and it is now fully operational. You and the ML are scheduled for a drop-off in one week's time. There will be three agents involved, going in different directions. The chosen site has been deliberately withheld, the reason being that we seem to be suffering from an informer in our camp. We are not even giving out the area of the drop."

John said, "Anyone who knows where the agents are expecting to operate can extrapolate the region of the drop-off. In fact, I suggest that we land a party of Marines at the landing point to clear the area before we land agents.

"In that manner we could possibly get our people ashore safely. The other thing is getting the other agents back. How well do we know the agents we are collecting?"

"Why do you question the agents returning?" Chloe asked.

"One: How is it that the pick-ups go well, but the drop-off have been failing."

"I suppose because the incomers have been betrayed, the pick-ups have not?"

"Tell me. How many of the pick-ups who have returned to their field have been picked up?"

Looking puzzled, Chloe checked her records. "None as far as I can see, they were never any drops that were ambushed."

"Don't you find that odd? Out of all the drop-offs, and pick-ups, some agents have a charmed life. Others are met on arrival. My guess is that the traitors are among the returning agents." He sat back and let the idea percolate.

The Admiral looked at John. "I cannot help thinking that you may have a point there. It is not something that has bothered us here so much, but it does bother the spooks in London. I will see that the notion is looked into when I get back to town."

He turned to Chloe. I'll leave this with you just now. I know you live near the Commander's home. I suggest you get together, and go through the files on the agents we are dropping off. Then I would like you to go through the ones you are picking up. In view of the suggestions from our meeting, I have the feeling that you might find some interesting things. I suggest you do your research at one of your homes. There will be no leaks from there to muddy the waters."

With a nod, the Admiral rose to his feet and picked up his hat. "London calls!" He said with a smile, and left the room.

Alec rose to his feet. "Since I am not involved in the forthcoming activities, I would probably be in the way, so I will leave you two to it." He left the office, a small smile on his face. The remaining pair looked at each other bemused by the rapid exit of their colleagues.

John said, "What was that all about?"

Chloe thought for a moment, then said with a grin, "They think we have a 'thing' going between us."

"Ah, I see. Well let us not disabuse them. If we get packed up now we can be on our way and swimming in the river within an hour at a guess. What do you say?"

Chloe suited action without words and stood gathering the files from her desk and sweeping them into the leather briefcase the Admiral had left on the desk. "I'm ready if you are."

John grabbed his hat and gas mask bag and headed for the door.

They piled into the car allocated to them and John gave the driver Chloe's address.

***

At her house they were greeted by her mother who was delighted to see her and John, whom she had known since he was a boy.

Chloe looked out of the window at the sun-drenched garden with the river flowing past. "

We came down for a swim before going across to John's house to work, so if we change in the boathouse, we can leave our clothes in the boat and row across after the swim. We should be able to join you for lunch tomorrow. John's family are away to London so we will be able to work undisturbed."

"Very well, dear. I'll try and find something nice for lunch." She watched a little forlornly as they went down the garden to the boathouse at the water's edge.

With a sigh she turned away and started thinking about what to give them for lunch tomorrow. Her eyes fell on the book standing half-open on the side table beside the window. Her husband Robert had left it there when he went off to London to work. She was reconciled to the fact that his work was not the only reason he was spending so much time in London. When she had spoken to the telephone number for the accommodation he was using a woman had answered.

Mary Masters was not a fool, though she was at a loss at the moment, unsure how to deal with the matter. Squaring her shoulders she concentrated on the matter at hand. Lunch tomorrow!

***

In the boat house the two friends turned away from each other and stripped off to climb into their swimming costumes. John was ready first and ran straight down to the open end past the Riva motor launch sitting in the cradle within the boathouse. Hurdling the dinghy tied up alongside the small landing stage, he hit the water with a splash, going under then bursting out into the air, spattering water everywhere. His rising body was in time and place to encounter Chloe who managed to head butt him in the solar plexus as she rose in turn to the surface.

John gasped and promptly pushed her head under water in self defence. This led to reprisals and the pair both finished up coughing and spluttering. Laughing, the pair swam back to the boathouse. Untying the dinghy John settled the oars in place and rowed them across the river to the matching boat house on the other side of the water.

Carrying their clothes they walked up to the house, where John found the key and opened the kitchen door.

When both were dried off and dressed once more, Chloe made a pot of coffee and the pair sat and got started on the files they had been given.

***

It was several hours before they finished the entire review of the files. By that time they had reduced the heap to a selection of four files.

John put his hand on them and said, "That is the best I can do, but I find it difficult to decide which of this group I suspect most. I am inclined by instinct to go for Georges Portet. Unfortunately, the other three names all are suspect. Of the two women, I worry about Rosalie Forges, who had a problem with her children that somehow sorted itself out. That is what worries me. With that sort of bother the Germans are not normally very forgiving."

"You think perhaps she is being blackmailed into betraying the others?" Chloe wondered.

"Exactly! It just does not sit right with me."

"Why George?"

"Once more, I have this suspicion that he is more deeply involved than he is saying. I realise it could be that he has other business running parallel with the spy game. I think I would be happier if I knew what that business was."

"Is there such a strong case for the other two?" Chloe asked.

"In a word. No. There is nothing more than a hunch based on the fact that I have decided that I do not like either of them."

"On such flimsy evidence a case is built, and from such a case a life is lost." Chloe smiled to take the sting from her words, knowing that John would not allow his personal feelings to interfere with the apportioning of blame. "Now I suggest we forget about all this and have something to eat. Do you want to go out to eat, or have you anything here we can cook up.

John looked at Chloe keenly, "What about your mother? Does she expect us?"

"No. She is expecting us tomorrow for lunch, so you can relax and either go down to the pub, or stay, and see what I can find in the pantry and fridge. So what will it be?"

John hauled himself up and stretched. "I'll get the wine opened you can cook up some eggs or whatever. We haven't had a real crash-out since we were starting Uni. What do you think?"

Chloe grinned. When they were younger they used to spread the cushions out on the floor and pile up blankets, or latterly sleeping bags, and they would lie down side by side and nibble and talk listen to music, sharing, just as they always had since they were children.

Twenty minutes later, the cushions were down and the twin sleeping bags hauled out of the linen room. The wine was breathing with two stemmed glasses beside the bottle. Chloe walked through from the kitchen in her dressing gown, John heard her and shouted, "I'll be with you in a moment."

She put the plates down beside the wine and slipped off her dressing gown revealing her lace edged nightdress. "I'll be eating yours in a minute."

John appeared in his dressing gown. He slid into his sleeping bag and discarded the dressing gown, revealing the old shirt he slept in at home.

"I do not believe you still have that old shirt." Chloe said, laughing.

"I see you still have that old nightie." John replied. "I always liked it."

"Eat now, talk later," was the short answer. Chloe was hungry.

When they had eaten, and were settled with their wine, they began talking.

Each had a story to tell, and it was with a certain sadness that Chloe related the content of her last letter from Charles, her RAF boyfriend. "It seems he had been forced to bail out of his aircraft, creating a joint problem with his right arm which prevented his immediate return to flying. However the treatment for his shoulder did introduce him to the therapist, a lady named Helen, who has stolen his affection and therefore, dearest Chloe, farewell, adieu, and goodbye."

Chloe told the story calmly enough.

John looked at her as she told him, reached out and pulled her close, hugging her, to let her know that he cared, just as he always did in the past.

"Never really did trust the glamour-boy types. You are well out of that relationship."

Chloe sniffed, just a little. "I confess, though I would never tell anyone else this, I got that letter before we went to Scotland. I was upset because I had no idea that he would do something like that. I really expected that we would be getting engaged when he came home on leave this coming week. As it is, he will be on his honeymoon. How about that?"

John did not have an answer for her, so he just kept cuddling her and neither seemed inclined to break the connection.

***

Waking Saturday, they found themselves firmly locked together still, John's left arm had gone to sleep and he had difficulty straightening it. Chloe rolled away from John and both realised that they were naked having lost their clothing during the night, which had been somewhat more eventful than they had planned.

Chloe started to get up, then realised, thought for a moment, shrugged and stretched herself up, rising to her feet.

John was equally naked and exposed on the floor.

With a small smile, Chloe turned round and looked at John, whilst providing a graphic view of her own body. She then sauntered to the door of the bathroom. Turning once more, she grinned and said "Fancy a shower?" Then turned and went into the bathroom.

John managed to get to his feet as the elegant rear passed through the door. He thought for an instant, shrugged, and followed her into the bathroom to share the shower. Neither felt seriously embarrassed by the situation, perhaps because of the incident in Scotland, or maybe, John thought, because they had been friends so long and had shared secrets for a major part of their lives.

The fact was that neither mentioned the incident and, when they attended her mother's house for lunch, as far as they were concerned, they gave nothing away.

They were not aware of the look Chloe's mother gave them when they walked in together. Her smile might have given away the fact that she was content and accepted that her two favourite young people were clearly on the course she had always expected them to take.

***

After lunch they returned to the four files that they had set aside. There was little progress to be made without further investigation of the suspects. They finished the afternoon with a check-up and clear out of John's 38foot sloop laid-up in the boatyard just downriver from the house.

"We never did get the chance to sail her down to the Med." John said wistfully.

"It was the timing of the long vac that year. Chloe said, "We would have sailed down during that time if the war had not loomed so close."

"If we had believed what Chamberlain was talking about at that time, we would have managed it. As it was between your father and Mr Churchill you were mobilized and as a result so was I. When I volunteered I was still under the impression that someday we would be married. So I decided that, if you were involved, the best thing I could do was get involved myself."

She held up her hand before John could say anything "I know neither of us had said anything, but neither of us had ever looked at anyone else up to that time. We were always so close, I just assumed. It did not take long for me to realise that I was wrong. I know you well enough to know that you would have told me if you had that in mind."

Chapter twelve

Dangerous Waters

The mist made their progress through the gloom slower than John liked, but in these waters it would be dangerous to take chances. Despite the fact that the ML was not deep-keeled, there was always the risk of wreckage or other uncharted obstruction.

Down below in the wardroom the agents all gathered, checking each other's gear and receiving last minute instruction from Amy Martin.

There was bustle and nervousness and perhaps a little justifiable fear in the air as the agents talked among themselves.

For John there was the fact that one of the agents was one of the suspects that he had selected with Chloe. This made him even more wary in his approach to the rendezvous point.

Toby Cummings rose from his place under the hood over the chart table. "Depth level reached. We should drop the hook now."

The splash of the anchor seemed very loud, until John remembered that the background noise that seemed unbroken, was not tinnitus. It was the sea, ever moving, with the wind brushing the surface creating a susurration that made it difficult to isolate other sounds.

"Anchor is fast and holding." Cummings reported.

John ordered, "Secure engines. Quiet in the boat."

At that point the entire boat started to listen.

Toby was amazed and a little amused at the sudden complete cessation of voices and the small noises which made up the sounds of a working boat. It underlined the seriousness of the operation they were involved in. Only now did it really hit him, that when they dropped the agents off, and picked up any waiting, the boat would then return to the comparative safety of Portsmouth. For those agents landing it would be the beginning of a dangerous game of hide and seek. The penalty for failure was death after torture. Not a pleasant prospect, in fact, for Toby, a frightening one.

The squeak of an oar in a rowlock indicated that they had company. The cautious flash of blue light allowed focus on the rowing boat approaching from shore. Toby joined Amy and the departing agents at the sallyport on the starboard side of the boat. The three agents with their bulky equipment bags were crowded up against the armoured bulkhead below the bridge.

The Marine contingent left the boat on the portside without fuss. The six men with blackened faces and their dark overalls blended with the night as the electric outboard engine drove their dinghy shoreward. The returning agents climbed wearily aboard. None were actually injured, though all looked exhausted.

Below in the ward room, Chloe and Sub Lieutenant Jim Fordyce were prepared to greet and do an initial de-brief with the returning agents.

There was a tray of sandwiches and drinks, and an electric water heater for hot drinks.

As the three agents climbed down into the cabin, the third man drew a pistol from his coat and would have shot one of the other agents. The hand of Petty Officer Rogers gripped the gun and peeled it out of the man's hand. The protest that rose on the lips of the disarmed man was stifled by Peter's other hand. The man was eased down onto the bench, as if Rogers was just helping the tired man.

Chloe went to the disarmed man first. She smiled and gave him a steaming mug of tea, seated herself beside him and helped him to take the first sips, all the time whispering quietly to him.

The man calmed down and when she left his side, he made no protest or comment, just buried his face in the tea mug. None of the others had noticed anything. All the action had been behind their backs.

From the shore there came the sound of automatic weapons, short bursts of fire sounding disciplined and controlled, then silence, followed by the sound of a vehicle starting up. The sounds diminished as the vehicle drove off inland. The dinghy with the marines aboard returned with Amy Martin who had gone ashore with the agents.

When she climbed aboard, she reported to John that they had encountered a patrol who had challenged them. The Marines had dealt with the matter, disposing of the bodies on another section of the beach.

With anchor aweigh, the ML left the close proximity of the land and motored quietly out to sea. When they weathered the rocky point projecting like a finger out into the Channel, they were joined by a group of MGB's who had been making life difficult for a German inshore convoy. The combined group increased speed and made for Portsmouth.

In the ML the de-brief went ahead, though the conditions were not the best for the purpose.

Amy Martin came and sat in with Chloe and Jim Fordyce. The man who had drawn his gun was calm now and explained that he had the impression that one of the others with him had betrayed them all.

Chloe asked which person he suspected, but he had not really made his mind up. His reasoning was based on the arrival of the patrol disposed of by the Marines. He had assumed that they were there by arrangement, and that one of his colleagues had betrayed them.

In consultation, Amy recommended that he not be used in France again. She was of the opinion that he had been under pressure too long and should be withdrawn from operations.

None of the three collected agents was on the short list prepared by John and Chloe.

The return to Portsmouth was made without fuss and the agents disposed of to their own section of the service.

***

Seated in the Wardroom of the base quarters, he mentioned to Chloe his conversation with Amy on the last occasion they had been together.

"I seem to have put my foot wrong with Amy somehow," he said, sounding baffled. "I just don't understand what I have done wrong?"

Chloe heard the tale of his suggestion and her rejection and came to a conclusion that she thought John would not like. *Shall I tell him or not?"* she thought.

Their entire friendship through the years had been based on being honest with each other. "John, did it not occur to you that Amy was saying she is a free spirit?" She stopped and let that sink in.

Hesitantly, John replied, "I believe it did. Why?"

"It could be that, though Amy likes you, she has no intention of being with you or any one exclusively. I guess there are others in her life and none of them, including you, will be allowed to occupy her entire life."

Chloe sat back and hoped that she had not gone too far.

John sat contemplating the situation related by Chloe. He did not for one instance believe that her comments were anything but her considered opinion. Their relationship did not allow for lies. It could only have survived this long in an atmosphere of honesty between them.

Chloe sat and allowed the effect of her words to percolate through, in essence watching as John put the pieces together.

He looked up and smiled at her. "I'm an idiot. You did know, didn't you?"

"I've always known," she said quietly. "I also knew that, as soon as you realised, you would tell me. After all, whatever else we may be, or become, we are best friends."

"I am astonished that I could even consider anyone else."

With a grin, she said, "So am I. But then who am I to talk?"

He reached out his hand and took hers. "I cannot believe that I considered anyone else to spend my life with."

She gripped his hand tight. "You do realise that you are asking me to spend my life with you."

"Of course!" He said.

"You also realise that I will hold you to it.?" She said seriously.

"As will I, if you accept."

"Oh, I accept all right. I will not ever let you go willingly."

When her mother and John's parents heard the news, they all smiled quietly and acted as if it had been a foregone conclusion. As far as they were concerned, it always was.

***

Sub-Lieutenant Tom Murray hurried through the throng in Southampton Railway station. He made it to the London train with five minutes to spare. The first class carriage was empty. It was the mid-morning train which explained this unusual situation.

He sat back in the seat, his new cap tipped over his eyes and fell asleep.

When he woke the train was pulling into Waterloo. The station was noisy with the hiss of the steam from several different locomotives leaving and arriving. The platforms were crowded with troops and uniforms everywhere. He walked down to the RTO office and spoke to the Colour Sergeant there.

"Kensington Gardens, sir? Just walk over to the underground. The easiest way is to go to Charing Cross over the other side of the river. The station you would want is Knightsbridge."

"Thank you, Colour Sergeant." Tom returned the salute and made his way to the underground section of the station. He rang the number he had been given, and with some relief he was talking to Iris, having been switched through to her floor.

She sounded happy to hear his voice and, when he said he had a few days off and was staying in the Victory club on the other side of the park, she was delighted.

Her course was a daytime course so it released her at 5.00 pm each week night, and the approaching weekend was free. She had to wear uniform, but she was an acting 3rd officer until she finished her course, which meant that she could be seen in the company of another officer.

He arranged to meet her at the park gates at 5.15 and took a taxi to the club to check in.

They spent all the time she had available together, including the weekend that they spent in Cookham in the country, at a small hotel.

It was there that Iris mentioned his comment when they decided to be boyfriend and girlfriend. "Tom, I know you mentioned that you wanted to marry me. I would just like to say that I would not hold you to that. I do realise..."

She stopped, because Tom had actually put his hand over her mouth.

"When I made that remark I did not really know. It was just instinct talking. I have had time to think things over and I have decided that I have not changed my mind in any way shape or form. I still wish to marry you, though I am willing to wait until this lot is over. Now you can talk." He released her mouth.

She promptly darted forward and kissed him. Startled, he was slow to react, but react he did. When they came up for air, he said, "Well, what have you got to say."

"Yes!"

"Yes! What does that mean?"

"It means 'yes' I will marry you, as and when we decide to."

"I see. You have been planning to trap me all this time, and now the trap has been sprung."

"Exactly, and, as an officer and a gentleman, you cannot now back out."

"True!" He said with a sigh. "So I will just carry on my research into your tickly bits." And ignoring her cry of protest he did just that.

Chapter Thirteen

Spy Games

The repairs and modifications to the destroyer were taking time. John found the operations with the ML were becoming more difficult, as they still had not isolated the traitors or moles in the organisation. The formalised establishment of the SOE, and the increasing part being played by the American OSS, was responsible for the demand for increased activity in the delivery and collection of agents in and out of Europe.

The major problem seemed to be the location of places where successful landings could be made, in addition to the seeking and neutralising double agents and spies in the system.

After the original work carried out by Chloe and John, the actual suspects had been cleared, though their reasoning had been applauded. Since that time little had been said on the subject, though the team were continually on watch for any sign of betrayal from the outgoing and incoming agents they carried. On these trips Amy joined them less and less, which meant that Chloe had to stand in as despatch and retrieval supervisor.

The specialised aspects of the ML operation were set to one side during the spate of setting-up operations as the networks were initiated.

In the briefing for the latest drop John had decided to take the ML himself. It had been the practice to share the command among the qualified officers in the command. Thus Ross, Alec and Toby had all taken command for drops and pick-ups through the preceding months.

The work on the destroyer was near completion. The dockyard had used the opportunity to upgrade and update systems whilst she was undergoing the replacement of the gun turret and major repairs to hull and upper-works.

John realised that the other aspects of the command's duties would once more come to the fore.

Since this drop was to a place they had used before, a section of Marines had been allocated to secure the area in advance.

There were two agents to be delivered, both SOE. The woman was French and dressed in plain, common clothing with a bonnet to place her as a farm woman who could be from any part of the Pas de Calais area.

The other person was a man, middle-aged, wearing a business suit and carrying a small attaché case. He had a raincoat which had seen better days as a disguise, he told John, with a hat folded in its pocket. It was a sort of trilby, and John had to admit the contrast to the natty suit was complete.

Neither was known to him, though the pick-up designated for the return listed two of the people he had carried before, the third being another unknown. All three were coming from different places and expected to meet at the rendezvous point.

Not normally known for jumping at shadows, John was not happy for some reason. He discussed with Chloe his disquiet over this particular operation.

"It could be that this will be your last for some time and you are just a little jumpy about it."

"I confess the idea has occurred to me, but, whatever, I will go ashore with the Marines. I will have the rendezvous under surveillance before they all arrive, just to be on the safe side."

Chloe looked at him. He did not look jumpy. In fact he looked as cool and calm as he ever was. He was checking his personal 9.00 mm automatic as he spoke, automatically checking by feel alone the load in the magazine and the extra round in the chamber. The sten-gun was standing beside his seat on the ward room floor, double magazine in place.

Warrant Officer Ord, in charge of the Marine detachment came in and reported that his men were ready. He passed the tin of blacking over for John to use on his face and hands.

"Take it easy John, and, come back to me." Chloe said and kissed him before the blacking went on.

John said quietly, "Do not follow us until we give the private signal I specified. I do not trust this set-up. If things go pear-shaped after you are ashore, deliver the people to the rendezvous and join up with the Marines. Don't look for me. If I am compromised, I do not want anyone else involved."

As the ML slipped closer to the shore the three rubber boats carrying the Marines, with their electric motors purring quietly, made their way in the shadow of the land, to the small beach in the inlet. Landed, the men made their way to the path along the top of the sand dunes and, staying below the rim, spread out and made their way for the half mile to the set-down, and pick-up point, north along the coast.

John and Ken Ord landed and waited. They could make out the French used by two of the agents awaiting collection. Of the third there was no sign.

As they crouched waiting to receive the reports of the advanced scouts, Chloe landed and appeared with the two agents being sent in. Both were expecting to make their own way, neither of them intending to contact the agents awaiting collection. Over the period of operation involving the Portsmouth command, it had been established for the best results, that agents could communicate, but only if they were operating together.

Groups of agents being distributed to different areas were found to be vulnerable to detection. The main reason being that too many people were involved in the agent distribution. Too many people knew too much about common transport usage and drop off points, where more than one set of agents shared transport facilities. The system had led to a catch-one, catch-all, arrangement which a ruthless enemy found very convenient.

Chloe returned from delivering her two agents, and joined the dinghy waiting for the agents being collected.

Ken Ord had been in the marines for 17 years, at the age of thirty-three, he was the product of operations from China to the horn of Africa. Now, crouched in enemy-held territory once more, his instincts were telling him that there was something wrong. The conversation sounded too glib for a pair of spies waiting for a third from elsewhere.

He signalled his sergeant to take a squad around to the approach from the other direction. Within five minutes one of the squad was back. "Ambush, sir. They are holding a civilian back, probably to arrive on the dot. No sign of force being used. The Sergeant reckons there is a platoon scattered around the rendezvous, he also says the two sitting chatting are under a gun."

Ord turned to John. "I am sending my lads to remove the ambush. We stay and watch."

John shrugged. "It's your decision."

Ord turned to the Marine. "Spread the word. Quietly now!"

The Marine melted into the darkness.

The talk between the two agents stopped suddenly. Both people were brought to the location of John and Ord. They were joined by the third agent, who was not coming quietly.

Robert Lavelle resented being frogmarched along the dunes by Marines with blackened faces.

Once back on board the ML he was brought in front of John and Ken Ord. He was defiant and angry at having his cover blown.

"My cover here has been perfect up to now. You have ruined nearly a year's work." The furious face of the agent was thrust at John Macklin.

Ken Ord, sitting to one side, smiled.

John said, "It says here that you are Robert Lavelle. That you work for SOE, and also OSS. Is that correct?"

"You idiots have cost me endless work and time, setting things up to provide an open channel to the SS and Gestapo HQ in this area." His tirade was stopped at that point when John, whose hand, upheld to stop him raving, turned into a fist threatened to punch Lavelle on the nose.

Silently, John handed the man a piece of paper.

Lavelle took the paper. The heading was Gestapo HQ Paris.(Pas-de-Calais)

It was an order to the SS Generalmajor Horst Keller. Calais.

<u>Subject: Robert Lavelle.</u>

Arrange an escort for the subject and accompany him to the arranged pick-up and drop-off point for British agents. Ensure that the landing party are arrested and sent here for interrogation. The returning agents are now worthless, dispose of them and Lavelle in an appropriate manner. They have served their purpose, as the networks they serviced are now entirely under our control.

The note was signed, Stalheim.

Lavelle dropped the paper on the wardroom table. White-faced he turned and looked at the other two agents, then back at John. "Oh, my God. What have I done?"

John sat back and looked at him. The briefing note which he had explained what was happening. It made clear that, though Lavelle was unaware of it, his entire effort had been leaked to the Germans, who had taken time to identify him, and, for the past three months, used him. They had done so, inspired by the SOE team running a scam within the area. The result had been several non-started operations by the SS and Gestapo in the region. Also, the escape of several most wanted underground fighters who had apparently been missed by arresting teams, by pure luck. The Germans had not suspected they were being manipulated so the scheme had worked so far at least.

John motioned for the other agents to look after Lavelle, who was still looking stunned. He turned to Ken Ord. "How is the clear-up going?"

"The sergeant is just policing the area to make sure there is no sign of the ambush party or the agents." Ken grinned.

The ML was poised ready to leave, the last dinghy was leaving the shore as he spoke.

The two men looked at each other, John nodded. Ken smiled. Their teams had combined to work smoothly together and both acknowledged the fact.

As the dinghy came alongside, the first sign that things may not have gone entirely as they should, became apparent.

Sergeant Beatty RM, slid aboard the ML, and made his way below without delay.

"We have a problem, sir. The boat has been discovered and there are E boats, coming round to cut us off as we make the open channel."

Ord looked at John.

John said, "How do you know, Sergeant?"

"As I was returning from the ambush site, there were two SS men with night glasses discussing us. They had a radio with them, so I let them be and listened to their conversation. When the radio message came through, I heard the orders."

"Did they say anything about the ambush?"

"Only that there was no sign of the platoon of men they expected to see when they arrived. They did report that fact while I was there."

John smiled, "Thank you, Sergeant." As Beatty turned away, John said, "I'll go up to the bridge and have a chat with Toby.

Chloe stood and went out into the short companion way. "Are we in trouble?"

"No more than usual," John said with a grin. "Stay below. I'll call you when it's clear to come up."

He dashed off to the bridge and Chloe returned to the ward room, where she joined Ken Ord with tea and sandwiches. They felt the boat speed up and the motion became more erratic as they cut through the mounting waves. The noise was such that the sound of the E Boats was lost to the people in the cabin. When the guns began, the clatter of the Oerlikons from both sides of the boat joined the bark of the Bofors.

In the cabin with the noise of the guns and the roar of the engines was deafening. By mutual agreement, the Marine and the WRNS officer went to the lobby first, and thence to the bridge. Standing well back out of the way, the whole scene became graphic to the onlookers.

The speed of the ML rose as it made its way past the arm of the headland. To the watchers it seemed that the boat was flying over the water rather than through it. The crashing as the bow met the waves grew more violent, as the waters of the open channel became more active. The watchers found that they had to hang on tight to the bridge rail.

Chloe was glad she was wearing her lifejacket, though the thought of being pitched into the dark waters around them was not something that she welcomed. It was pointless considering going below again. Moving on the pitching deck was too dangerous, so she hung on and watched the drama unfolding in front of her.

She could make out the two E boats attempting to cut them off, their white bow waves very obvious against the dark sea. Also with streams of fire issuing from both boats, they were running abreast like two racing cars in competition. The tracer rounds lit the stream of shot aimed in the general direction of the ML, though none were at the moment, getting close. The portside Oerlikon just beside the watchers opened fire. With the wind ripping the sound away, the noise became a part of the general racket that was this mad dash through the night.

On the fore deck the Bofors added its contribution to the general melee.

Standing as they did behind the Oerlikon, Chloe and Ken Ord could see that the gunner was having just as much trouble aiming as his German opponents. The tracer rounds painted a curved path toward the E boats, but seemed to fall short, until the ML rose to a bigger wave and suddenly the nearside E boat was lit up by a scatter of flashes as the gunfire from the ML found the range. The Bofors on the fore deck was the next to get lucky. The other E boat took a shell in the wheelhouse. Armour worked against them. Having shattered the glass, the tumbling solid round ricochet bounced from the armoured bulkhead to bulkhead, passing through flesh and bone and the woodwork wherever it hit. Without direction, the boat swung wildly off course. The wheelhouse was a nightmare of blood and pieces of body. Nobody had survived. Both of the gunners were hanging in their harnesses. One had broken ribs from the force of the sudden loss of direction. The other was dead anyway his head split almost in two by a shard of glass, from the broken windscreen. The foredeck gunner was crawling, holding the grab rail in the forecabin roof, to try and get into the wheelhouse. The violent pitching of the boat was creating real problems for him and, as he reached for another handhold, he was caught off balance by the action of the boat and thrown through the vacant space where the window had been. His passage past the razor shards of glass still projecting around the edge of the frame created terrible wounds to his unprotected body, which ended up battered and bloody in a crumpled heap in the corner of the space.

Stunned and shocked for a moment he just lay there. Then with agonisingly painful moves, he crawled to the chair anchored to the deck in front of the controls, and dragged himself up reaching for the engine throttles. His fingers caught the lever for the port screw. With a desperate lunge, he managed to grasp both levers and dragged them back reducing the mad speed of the boat which in turn, reduced the wild gyrations of the unattended helm. The gunner was unaware of his success. His final effort had resulted in a rupture of his damaged aorta and he was dead, still draped around the seat of the helmsman, who in turn had been scattered in bits around the wheelhouse.

The surviving E boat continued its mad dash out to sea, in a vain hope of stopping the British boat. Finally, it slowed as the captain realised that the superior speed of the ML put it beyond his own boat's abilities. He was forced to watch it speed away out of danger into the darkness of the channel night.

***

The Calais headquarters of the Gestapo was busy as usual. The office of the counter-intelligence Reichskriminaldirector, Peter Schramm, was occupied with people going in and out with reports and messages.

He sat in his chair and supervised the process of weeding out fact from conjecture, though he still was unaware of the location of the platoon of Waffen SS, sent with the double agent Lavelle. His first assistant was leaning against the wall, chewing a piece of doughnut, looking gloomily at the activity around him.

"When will I be allowed to go and take a look at the scene of the crime?" He said as he looked for and found the final piece of doughnut.

"Klaus, you really should give up your disgusting diet. It not only ruins you body and health, but it does nothing for your diction also. For all our sakes, stop eating before talking."

Klaus Richter ignored the telling off, and repeated the question without the addition of the doughnut. He finished with the words. "So. When?"

Schramm thought for a moment. "Go now, and take that idiot, Schiller, with you. His platoon can help with the search. Report to me as soon as you know anything."

Richter levered his long frame away from the wall. "Got it." He stepped out of the office and shouted, "Schiller, you lazy sod, get on your feet and get that bunch of reprobates moving. We have a job to do for the Reichskriminaldirector and we have no time to piss about. Passing civil service staff shuddered at the coarse tones. That was the reason Richter did it. He resented having to share the HQ with the snooty bunch of local administration staff.

He set off out of the front door of the building. As he turned to see if Schiller had got the message, he stumbled into somebody carrying a stack of files.

He swung round ready to give whoever it was piece of this mind and realised that the woman, crouched gathering her files together, was someone his did not know. She was also very pretty, with a shape which deserved investigation. He dropped to his knee and started to help her gather the files together.

"You can just keep your clumsy hands off my files. If you cannot look where you are going, then your help is probably as useless as your eyesight.

Klaus grinned. "I did apologise already. I was preoccupied."

"You are not the only busy person on this planet. I daresay Mr Churchill is busy too. But he is a gentleman and would look where he was going, unlike your bunch of thugs and layabouts in the Gestapo."

Mary Curtain did not pull any punches. Apart from the current example of loutish behaviour, her next door neighbour had been arrested and assaulted by Gestapo agents, who had humiliated her by strip-searching her in the front hall of the women's apartment block. They were apparently investigating the loss of a toilet roll from the communal ground floor toilet. The fact that men were not permitted to enter the block without special permission appeared immaterial when it came to the Gestapo.

Klaus gathered the remainder of the files and stood up. "Where to?" He said.

"Ground floor, room 8." Mary said tersely.

Klaus passed Schiller as he re-entered the building. "Get your platoon loaded and wait for me in the yard."

Schiller stuttered, "Yes, sir!" and scuttled off.

Mary looked at him warily. Who was this she had been telling off.

She hurried into her new office and made space on her desk for the files she had brought with her. She pointed at the chair beside the desk, for the man to put the files he carried there.

"Thank you for helping me," she said grudgingly.

"Whom am I helping?" Klaus said mildly.

"Oh. I am Mary Curtain, research specialist."

He gave a short bow. "Klaus Richter, detective. Auf Wiedersehen!" He left the office with a brief smile, and without further comment.

Mary Curtain put her collection of files on the desk. She had been unhappy at being shifted to this building, despite the promotion it confirmed.

The news was not all bad. It did remove the ever present threat of sexual harassment embodied by her former boss, Dr. Karl Rittenbach. He had been a man whose hands seemed eternally on the move, touching, groping at every opportunity. The women in the office put up with it, shrugging when she questioned their attitude, it being the way things were. He could make or break them. Work of this kind, protected from the need to find additional work to keep family and body and soul together was hard to come by. So they put up with the casual groping, and the occasional demands for a private session in the office.

When Mary joined the department she was the only qualified psychologist there. Rittenbach was the product of a mail-order qualification. His Doctorate would not have survived a basic examination paper. The only occasion he had trapped Mary in the private office had resulted in his discovery that this was one staff member who did not drop her panties at his request and who owned a strong right arm and accurate fist that targeted the tender part of his anatomy in a most unexpected and painful way.

The tongue lashing he received made it quite clear that any repetition of this conduct coming to her attention would be rewarded with a formal discussion of said conduct in the presence of Professor Heinlein, Chief of Medical research staff.

The announcement of her promotion had been published within the month and her transfer to the Gestapo building had followed almost immediately.

***

Three days later Mary had concluded her inspection of the initial pile of files. A knock came at the office door.

She looked up surprised, "Come in!" She said briskly.

The door opened and Klaus Richter poked his head in. "Just thought I would see if you were settled in okay."

He stepped through the doorway and looked around the office. There were pictures on the wall and the photograph of her brother in his Luftwaffe uniform, goggles round his neck, and a grin on his face.

Mary saw his eyes focus on the picture. "My brother, Rudy. He flies fighters, stationed in France at the moment." She did not know why she bothered explaining. This man was a stranger, and in the Gestapo.

Klaus smiled. "I confess. I called to see you settled in, but I also wondered if I might invite you out for coffee, perhaps lunch?"

Mary was surprised. Whatever she might have expected it was not that, "Is it that time already?" She looked at her watch and noticed that it was almost one o'clock.

"I...I suppose it is time for lunch."

"Good. My timing was right." He stopped as the figure of her former boss appeared at the door.

Not seeing Klaus, who was behind the open door at the time, Rittenbach said, "Ah, I caught you, today, missed you yesterday. I'll take you to lunch."

Mary flushed, angrily. "Doctor Rittenbach, may I introduce my fiancé, Kriminalinspector of the Gestapo, Klaus Richter."

Klaus appeared from behind the door and towered over the Doctor. Mary added sweetly, "We were just going to lunch I'm afraid. Did you say it was the General, Klaus?"

Klaus smiled. "Yes, but it is an exclusive invitation I believe. Though I can ask if the Doctor might join us, if you wish?" He looked at the thoroughly frightened man who stood shaking his head.

"Oh no! I would not dream of intruding into a private party with the General; perhaps some other time, Fraulein Curtain." He beat a hasty retreat, leaving the pair laughing at his discomfort.

"Come. Before there are any more interruptions." Klaus took her arm and steered her out of the office. He checked that she had locked it properly before they left the building.

As they settled in their places in the restaurant, Klaus said, "Flattered though I am, I have never been accused of being engaged to be married after a five minute acquaintance before?"

Mary blushed for the second time that morning. "Sorry, that man was my former boss. He has groped and harassed every woman in the department, at least up to the time I arrived. As the only qualified person in the department I was placed to work directly with him. At his first approach I threatened him with the department chief.

I added that if I saw him make any further assaults on the female staff, I would personally see him punished. He made a try at me at that point. We were in his private office. I punched him in his most tender spot. He squealed like a pig. I was promoted and moved to my present office within the month."

Klaus smiled. "His most tender spot?"

"Right between his legs. I was sitting down at the time."

"Ouch! No wonder he had you transferred. You obviously made an impression. We will check your office out when we get back. Then we will change the lock."

Mary looked at him astonished. "Why on earth would we do that?"

"Weak, nasty, vindictive men tend to get their revenge in crafty ways. Planting evidence is a regular method. The offices in the building all have duplicate keys. As a former member of his department he might legitimately get such a key."

Mary was shocked. But they left matters there and enjoyed a chatty, friendly lunch. When they returned, true to his promise, Klaus joined her in checking up that nothing had been tampered with in the office. A locksmith appeared and replaced the door locks with others that Klaus guaranteed would not be easy to tamper with without leaving evidence. The locksmith gave both sets of keys to her personally.

When the activity was over, she turned to Klaus. "As a stand-in fiancé you have done well. Thank you, Klaus Richter."

"From that lofty position may I be permitted to call upon you. Perhaps for lunch again?"

She smiled. "I can hardly refuse in the circumstances."

Klaus was quick to say, "Oh, please! If I invite you out again, can you promise it is not just because you are grateful."

Mary thought about that for a minute. She realised that she had enjoyed lunch and his company regardless of the circumstances. "In that case, I accept. No strings, just people."

"Done!" He said with a grin.

She reached up and kissed his cheek, "Thanks for everything," she said, and shooed him out of the office.

Chapter fourteen

Manoeuvres

HMS Audax rose to the wave and hesitated before settling down into the trough between the swells. She was alone on a seemingly endless sea, no sign of any man made thing within view.

The waters off the starboard side suddenly roiled and foamed. The conning tower of a submarine appeared, rising until the narrow deck was just clear of the water.

Ross Sherman was studying the horizon intently, seeking the first sign of any watcher.

"Asdic!" He called, "Any visitors?"

"Nothing on the scope, sir."

"All clear, sir," Ross called down to the captain in the motorboat alongside.

"Very well, Number One. Cast off, Bo'sun." The boat set off to the submarine, corkscrewing in the lively sea.

The conning tower had sprouted a bunch of people, mostly looking out all-round for intruders. The captain stood alone waiting for the destroyer's boat to come alongside.

He did not have long to wait. Soon John was scrambling through the hatch of the submarine and, with a flourish of foam, the submarine sank beneath the waves once more.

Below, John felt a little claustrophobic, though he would never admit it. He followed the captain to his cabin, a minute room just down the companion way from the main control room.

"How are the preparations going?" John asked the submariner.

"Lieutenant Commander Peter Wingate DSO RN shrugged. All well so far. The boffin has been busy ever since we left base, but he assures me that we will be ready to test the weapon this afternoon, as planned. I trust your lads are ready to spot the results."

"I seem to be more concerned with technicality these days than real work."

"Can you tell me what this thing is supposed to do?" Wingate asked.

"Actually, no. And I don't mean that if I tell you I have to shoot you. I literally do not know. The boffins I have on board won't tell me a thing, so, like you, I await with bated breath the outcome of this test."

The submarine sailed along steadily, the captain periodically raising the periscope to look around. *HMS Audax* maintained her place two hundred yards more or less behind the submarine. For John that was some reassurance at least.

Eventually, a white-coated scientist came through into the control area. He reported that they were ready to proceed with the test.

The submarine surfaced. The captain and John went up to view proceedings.

The destroyer raced off into the distance putting plenty of space between the submarine and the ship. The white coat appeared with a box of controls and they watched as a model airplane rose from the ship and started to circle. There was disturbance in the water under the bow of the Submarine. A sleek torpedo appeared travelling fast. Shorter than the standard model, it rose out of the water on stubby wings and flew toward the model aircraft in the distance. The torpedo was soon lost from sight. It was not until an explosion occurred in the distant sky, that John realised what he was looking at.

He turned to the scientist writing notes. "Tell me, when will this weapon reach us, for use in battle?"

The man smiled, "In this case, possibly never. The problem we have is the propulsion method. We can drive it out of the water, and we can drive it in the water. The combination of the two is the difficult bit. That unit cost half the price of this submarine. You should therefore not get your hopes up." He turned back to his work.

John looked around the horizon, raised his binoculars and called to Peter Wingate. "There is a periscope in the waters where I am pointed now. I can only presume it is not friendly."

Orders were snapped by Peter. The lookouts all disappeared through the hatch followed by the scientist. John was bundled down, avoiding the boots of the captain with more luck than judgement.

"Dive! Dive! Dive!" The order rang through the boat.

The boat tipped forward at an angle and rapidly descended under water, turning towards the bearing where the periscope had been spotted. The radio officer had warned *HMS Audax* of the sighting and she was working up to speed as the submarine started her dive. In the submarine the control room was quiet. The sound of the sonar now indicating the presence of the other submarine, as well as the approaching destroyer. "How will they know that we are friendly and the other sub is enemy?" John sounded concerned.

"Position first and, once on the plot, they should be able to label each move." Peter said tersely.

John realised that he was in the way in the control room and made his way to the wardroom where he lay down on a bunk and tried to concentrate on a paperback novel left out by one of the submarine's officers.

The periodic shudders and crashes outside the hull did nothing to dispel the feeling of helplessness that John felt, as the activity going on all around him excluded any contribution from his point of view. It was therefore doubly frustrating and not a little frightening; to just lie there and let it all happen, helpless.

***

Once he was back on the destroyer John felt better. The feeling of the wind in his face and the lift of the hull beneath his feet was more natural to him than the confinement of the hull of the submarine. As he thought of the experience, a shudder of revulsion warned him that service in submarines would never rate high on his list of duties.

The U-boat had been found and surprisingly despatched. There was no indication of the observation of the test being broadcast. However, though John felt that their secret had been kept, further testing was cancelled despite the protests of the Senior Scientific officer.

In the arguments for and against, John was forced to point out that the entire operation was subject to his judgement of the security risks. There had been no survivors of the U-boat. Therefore there was no way of knowing whether the enemy had sent a message off prior to the discovery of the U-boat. In the circumstances there was no option as far as John was concerned.

***

In Portsmouth the pace of the war was speeding up. There was an urgency about the dockyard, a feeling that things were happening. John was in the Admiral's office reporting his view of the latest test. "In my opinion the weapon is incredible and the ability to target an object accurately at that range, exciting! But the reaction of the scientist was not as reassuring as I expected. In fact my confidence was not raised by the astonishment that the scientists' staff showed at the accuracy of the trial."

"What are you suggesting?" The Admiral had the reports on his desk. He stirred the paperwork with the letter-opener he was idly playing with as he discussed John's comments on the test.

"We were using a converted seeker torpedo. At least, that was the impression I received. The addition of winglets to the body gave it sufficient lift to rise high enough to take out the remote-control aircraft. My feeling was doubt on two fronts. I do not consider the test was a true one. In fact I would go as far as to suggest that it was rigged. My other conclusion is, that converting what is a highly successful underwater weapon into an aerial delivery system, was never going to be a winner, especially if it is being considered as a dual purpose weapon. In my opinion the weapon we tested should have been designed for aerial use and should therefore be lighter in weight and have a longer range, It would obviously require different fusing and a means of identifying its selected target. With all the problems, the only purpose of the test we undertook with all the expense and personnel involved, had to be a diversion, a red herring for the enemy to swallow and follow up."

He sat back surprised at the conclusion he had reached.

The Admiral leant back in his chair, saying nothing, looking at John, then at Chloe. He considered for a moment rocking slightly in his chair. Then he leant forward placing his elbows on the desk. "Whatever made you come to that conclusion. I trust it is not reached elsewhere. As you say, the whole business was a sham, a ploy to distract the enemy while we continue to build up to the place and time that we will invade Europe once more. In the meantime, we have to keep the enemy under pressure. Whether they believe what they have undoubtedly seen or not, the fact is they cannot gamble and just discount it. Such a weapon would be a battle winner, on land, at sea, and in the air. We are developing weapons systems to make the difference, but it all takes time. Many of the tasks we provide are time wasters, set to lead them in the wrong direction." He sat back with a sigh. "Many of the tasks we give out for this reason are costly in lives as well as resources."

Chloe interjected, "But surely some of these tests are significant?"

"All of them are. It's just that some mean more than others." He snapped.

He paused, and in a softer voice said, "It still costs lives and resources, neither of which we can afford. Our problem is that there seems no way around it."

John said thoughtfully, "So far, we here seem to have managed to gain advantage from each exercise. Even in the latest scam it cost the enemy a U-boat. Thus the odds stay on our side, apart from the residual effect of scaring the pants off them with the suggestion that we are ahead of them with our research into weapon systems. As you say, believe it or not, they cannot just ignore what we are doing. It could cost them the war!"

"Well, we will close the book on the last exercise. The next month is going to involve the use of the ML rather more than we anticipated. It will mean that your officers will be sharing command, as the *Mavis* has commitments elsewhere, and the *Audax* has been requisitioned for an operation in Norway."

Chapter fifteen

Norway

The North Sea presented a sullen face. The grey waters under a lowering sky offered little to encourage waiting around, and the destroyer was actually taking the shortest, fastest route possible on her way to rendezvous for the raid planned.

In Skrova in Lofoten, the bay was full of ships. John could see the small craft carrying the Marines who had been involved with taking over the island, to enable the rendezvous to be carried, secured for the assembly. As he watched the MTB's and MGB's were streaming out into Vestfjord on their way to Bogenfjord then to Narvik. the heavy cruiser *Memphis,* a modified Southampton class cruiser, with 12 x 6 inch guns, was there to divert attention from the mini-submarines which were to make an attempt on *Tirpitz.* The pictures of the *Tirpitz,* the *Admiral Scheer* and the *Admiral Hipper,* all at anchor in Bogenfjord opposite the small town of Bogen itself, made a tempting target for the raiders. There were destroyers and MTB's among other craft in the vicinity, but it was the big ship that was the prize.

Privately, John thought that this was an attempt to reassure the Norwegian people that they were not forgotten. The threat of the *Tirpitz* was not really creditable, judging by the lengths the German navy had gone to in protecting it. The sinking of the *Bismark* in 1941 had demonstrated the way the capital ships of Germany were regarded by their Government. The

Army/Air force based administration had been happy to load their naval activities toward the submarine war, at the cost of their surface fleet. The few excursions made by the German Navy had resulted in losses, which had convinced the high command that the huge crews demanded by capital ships were a waste of manpower, better used elsewhere.

Thus, while the *Tirpitz* could be regarded as a potential threat to the Russian convoys, the presence of the battleship and the two heavy cruisers in northern Norway was arguably to keep them from harm, rather than to inflict it.

***

As the second wave of ships left the anchorage, John studied the chart of the fjord and the location of the pick-up at Narvik. While the other craft raided the big ships, there were people to be collected from Narvik. All the other activity was incidental as far as John was concerned. The reason for *HMS Audax* being present had nothing to do with the other activity in the fjord region, though it was a welcome diversion for their own enterprise.

The Major in command of the Marine Commando unit crammed into the destroyer was standing with John on the bridge assessing the odds quietly. The Major did in fact hold that rank. On board a naval ship a Captain in the Marine Corps became a major. There was room for only one captain on a naval ship. Major Michael Johnson MM RM considered the fact that information from sources in Norway suggested that there were possibly as many as two hundred German troops in and about the town. His 80 men would have plenty to keep them occupied, whilst the snatch party took out the German scientists and their Norwegian counterparts. The intelligence stated that a group of replacement experts were coming into the airfield tonight, for a conference tomorrow. He smiled grimly. Tonight would last nearly twenty hours at this time of year. It was what had made this raid possible. It also meant that the Germans would be on their toes for that very reason. At least, as far as the major was concerned; in their position he would.

The destroyer was hammering along at full speed close to forty-five knots, her huge bow wave impacting the starboard side of the fjord in a line of white water which would have given their presence away in different circumstances. The two reasons why they took the chance were that the occupation forces had cleared the banks of the fjord to prevent sabotage, and the night was black and long at this time of the year. Even the most enthusiastic watcher would be inclined to stay indoors.

The hint of daylight was lightening the intense darkness of the night as they approached the port at Narvik. The ship glided, with engines reduced to slow speed. As the ship came alongside the open side of the quay, the Marines leapt ashore, their suppressed, semi-automatic carbines ready. They disappeared almost as soon as they hit the quay. All had tasks to perform and by the time the major left the ship his men were involved. The silent arrival of the destroyer had taken the dock police by surprise. All had been rounded up and passed to the Navy, in the form of a group of armed sailors under command of Ross Sherman.

Within minutes a group of Norwegian people were on the quay. The local resistance had several people to be taken away during this raid, including survivors from earlier raids by naval forces kept hidden for an occasion such as this raid. The fishing boat transport service to

Shetland had too many demands on it to cope with the numbers of passengers involved.

As it was, it had been prearranged for the twenty-five people to join the ship. All were aware of the possibility of not making it out of the fjord, especially with the big ships at Bogen.

The last person to board from the quay was Amy Martin.

"Hello, John!" She said brightly, and collapsed in his arms.

Realising that she was wounded, John called for the doctor and had Amy taken to his cabin. He followed her, and only there realised that his hand was covered with blood.

Doctor Porter, the ships Medical Officer, was swift to locate the wound. He realised that he would need to operate swiftly, to prevent complications.

"Take her to the sickbay, and clear the others out."

The sickbay had several minor injured people waiting. But, as Porter had already realised, there would be a need for space for serious patients anyway. It was needed now for this patient. He detailed a sickbay attendant to deal with the minor injuries in the wardroom. The cleared sickbay was prepared for serious injuries and within minutes Amy was on the table under a sheet with her wound being swabbed with antiseptic, while Dr Porter washed and prepared. The stab wound was in her side had penetrated her lung. The blade, having entered below her left breast, had luckily missed her heart.

Within half an hour, the wound was cleaned, a drain inserted, and dressed. She was then taken back to the captain's cabin, to make way for other casualties, the Captain's steward detailed to keep an eye on her.

***

Major Mike Johnson crouched in the shadow of the barrack building. His men were scattered around the site, covering the other wooden barrack buildings. Using a whistle, the Major blew two sharp blasts. This signalled the attack to begin. Promptly six grenades smashed through the windows of each of the barracks. A flamethrower hissed and shot fire at the doorways of two of the barracks, before the operator ran to give the other three doors the benefit of the horrific weapon.

With all six buildings healthily ablaze ,the cries and screams from within the buildings were followed by bullets sprayed through the walls in the vain hope of dispersing their attackers. The stream of men who braved the burning doorways succumbed to volleys of 9mm bullets cutting them down as they burst forth.

Taking the risk, the major called the Sergeant Major over. "Keep your squad here to cover the supply building. Mine it to blow before we leave, though it might be worth a rummage to find anything else of possible use to maintain control while we are here. I will take my platoon to fetch the boffins. Lieutenant Mackay is on his way with his men to blow up the research building. We'll reassemble at the quay in two hours."

The Sergeant Major smiled grimly. He took a flamethrower from the supply building. He had noticed some portable anti-tank weapons, similar to the new Bazookas the Yanks had brought to the war effort.

The sound of guns could now be heard from Bogen fjord. The town of Narvik was awaking after the attack on the barracks. The Marine Commander was not under any illusion that the raid so far might have reduced the number of troops ranged against them to any great extent. The sound of vehicles from up the valley meant that probably reinforcements were on their way, to find out what was happening in town.

From the quay it was possible to see the road up the valley. As soon as the convoy of vehicles appeared, the portside Bofors was depressed to take the lead vehicle out and block the road for the vehicles following. The staccato sound of the first clip of five shells missed with three. But the remaining two did damage. One hit the roadway ahead of the first truck and ricocheted into the radiator, smashing the block, and causing the vehicle to stop abruptly. The last shell passed through the driver, low down, and carried on through the seat and into the rear compartment, shattering the legs of six of the twelve men, sitting with weapons ready in the rear compartment. The survivors bailed out through the rear doors, leaving their wounded companions to their fate. The following burst of Bofors fire shattered the truck, killing most of the wounded, and punching the wreck back into the middle of the single track road. A flicker of flame from the engine compartment caused by the sparking electrics, among the fumes of the spilt petrol. The truck became a mass if flame, the screams of the surviving wounded swiftly dying as they succumbed to the fierce heat of the burning vehicle.

The commander of the column assembled the rest of his men. Already, he had them by-passing the burning vehicle and making their way down to the town.

The Bofors gun had raised its sights and was hammering the remaining vehicles only half seen through the trees lining the road. The armoured car following the convoy operated its 30mm gun from the cover of the trees, in an attempt to silence the Bofors. The attempt failed, as one of the Bofors shells impacted the ammunition boxes strapped to the back end and the subsequent explosion disrupted the rotating turret mechanism and jammed it, trapping the crew within, and causing fire to break out in the exploding ammunition.

Lieutenant Mackay heard the racket and looked at his commander crouched next to him, awaiting the arrival of the German troops.

Mike Johnson said tersely, "Armoured car, taken from the Norwegians. Fine against ground troops without anti-tank weapons, but useless against a Browning .5, and only just effective against .303." He considered for a moment. "Had a decent gun though, 30mm." He turned back to the area in front of Mackay. "Blow the research building when the German troops get close enough to use it for protection." He then turned and left the lieutenant to his duties and returned to his waiting platoon, to complete his assignment and gather the scientists to deliver to the ship.

On board *Audax,* John was discussing a matter with the Norwegian leader of the underground."What do you need us to do?" He asked.

"I believe the men who were raiding the heavy water plant are held in the Bjerkvik administration building. They were taken and handed over to the Gestapo. I understand they probably will never reach Oslo alive, though the central government has ordered that they be brought there.

One of the MGB's came alongside the destroyer, to pass over wounded men for the doctor's attention.

John held up his hand to stop the flow of information from the Norwegian. "A moment, my friend, I must see to this."

He went down to the deck where the MGB lay alongside. He was escorted aboard by the Cox'n, Jack Lane. The Lieutenant RNR, in command, looked a little worn but otherwise was alert. "What can I do for you, sir?"

"There are some people being held at Bjerkvik, at the head of the fjord. If I give you some of my people, I would like you to go and fetch them. How are you fixed for ammo and fuel?"

"Just topped up on my way here, sir. The wounded I brought were from the attack ships. I'll need to get a move on for a trip like that."

"I will rendezvous with you at Ballangen. We will make the run home from there, in company. As long as we don't run into the Tirpitz or the cruisers we should be alright. We can refuel at Skrova; they will be holding there for the next three days for the benefit of stragglers."

John returned to the bridge of the destroyer and beckoned Ross Sherman, back from his shore party duties. In conjunction with the Norwegian leader, he explained the situation. With one of the partisans as guide, Ross took his landing party aboard the MGB, which cast off immediately and roared off up the fjord to Bjerkvik.

The sound of rapid fire from the road up the valley indicated that the Marines were involved with the local garrison. The firing slackened off and the building, nominated as the research centre, went up in flame as the explosives planted were set off.

The first of the Marines returned under the Sergeant Major. His men took over the perimeter from the destroyer's men. The party under Lieutenant Mackay returned carrying two wounded men. He had them delivered to the doctor, and reported that they had caused rather more casualties than they had taken.

The Major returned with a cart with the bodies of three of his men killed in the fire-fight with the German garrison troops. The injured from his party were all walking wounded. They took themselves down to the sick bay, while the Sergeant Major and the Lieutenant reported to their commanding officer.

John explained the arrangements for the rendezvous with the MGB, and Major Johnson suggested that he organise his men in an all round defensive formation, to secure the ship while they waited.

The Norwegians said that the rendezvous was well chosen as far as they were aware. There were no German troops in the vicinity. They settled down to wait. The remnants of the German garrison were left in no doubt that the raid was by British Marines and the Royal Navy. Though the garrison did probe the defence line, it was a tentative effort, judged by the major to be made to impress the commanders that the troops had been overwhelmed by superior force, but had continued to fight back until the enemy force retreated. With no further casualties the ship left quietly, sailing at slow speed down the fjord to the rendezvous point at Ballangen, where they awaited the return of the MGB.

***

Bjerkvik was not well lit, nor was it more than a small collection of buildings scattered along the shores of the fjord. With the guide leading the way, Ross Sherman and his mixed party of bandits crept ashore. They were taken to a building beside the quay, and a truck was pushed out, which they boarded. Ten minutes up the road the truck stopped. The party de-bussed. Through the trees ahead they crested a rise, bringing into sight a well-lit building with two armed guards visible. Still over a quarter mile distant, the ground between them was snow-covered and broken up with clumps of straggly trees and scrub offering cover for most of the way. The final stretch, the area around the building, was open ground.

Selecting two of the Marines from the MGB, Ross drew his finger across his throat and pointed at the two guards. Both men nodded, handed over their sten guns to their companions and slid off into the darkness.

It was only when both guards disappeared that the party realised the two men had done their job.

Ross stood and moved forwards toward the building, which apparently had been a school. The guide confirmed this impression when Ross questioned him. The man was able to describe the interior layout of the place.

"There is a main hall with three classrooms leading off. One will be used by the security team, probably the one next to the front door." He indicated to the left of the entry doors. As the men closed up to the walls of the building, Ross stood where he could look through the glass panels in the doors to short corridor inside, with the first door half open to the left as the guide indicated.

"Bo'sun," he whispered. He indicated the half-open door. The bo'sun nodded and pointed to three of the men to go with him. They opened the door quietly and slipped through, closing the door quickly after them. The Bo'sun pushed the next door wide. He stepped through and faced the four seated men, all around a table with cards and money. The man facing the door looked up and froze. Four sten-guns were all pointed at the men. They were carried by men who looked serious, and not at all bothered about the idea of opening fire. A draught of cold air wafted through the door as the other members of the raiding party entered the building.

In the guard room, the Bo'sun indicated for the guns to be collected. The fourth man went behind the four card players, and collected their MP40 machine pistols, and the belt guns of the four soldiers. All wore the edelweiss of Alpine troops, who specialised in mountain warfare.

In the main part of the hall were three people: a woman and two men. All were busy when the raiders entered. As the three were being secured, the other two rooms were opened.

In the far room, an operating table was placed. On it a body lay. Another man was preparing some instruments on a silver tray. As the men entered he spoke without looking up. "This man will not survive another treatment. we will need to fetch anoth....." He realised the men in the room were not those he expected.

The man was searched and his hands bound. The medic they had brought with them took a look at the man on the table. He then went to work.

The other room revealed a bunch of people, some injured, some still unhurt. All were pleased to see the uniforms of the Navy. The story they told was of their task to destroy the heavy water plant in the mountains behind them. They had got so far but had been betrayed in the end by one of their own.

Between the guide and the leader of the captives, Ross established that the heavy water plant was operating two hours away in the shadow of the mountains.

"Tell me. What security do they have there? I understand you were captured, but that was because you were betrayed."

"True. We were taken by a team of Alpine troops, like the men here. There are no more than 20 of the men there. I believe they depend on the isolation as much as anything. We would have taken them completely by surprise had we not been betrayed."

Ross considered the problem, "Would you be willing to try again with my support?"

The leader grinned, his teeth bared. "Yes! Our friend stayed behind when we were taken away."

"What about explosives?" The Bo'sun asked.

"They are all here. They were brought back with us. So they will be within the building."

"Then let us find them, check them out with anything else useful, and get on the road."

Ross spoke to the medic. "What about our friend? Can he travel?"

"I would say so. In the circumstances, do we have an option?" The medic was angry but positive. "The man has been abused and wounded deliberately, but his survival depends on rest rather than anything else. We can send him down in their wagon, with the prisoners. The injured underground members can escort them to the boat. They can wait there for us, and the boat SBA will look after the injured there."

"Good! Bo'sun. Explosives?"

"All here sir, including the box of detonators."

Ross turned to the guide, Petr, and the local leader, Anders Nilsson. If you agree we will take a look at the heavy water plant before we return to the ship. It would be a shame to be so near without trying to do something about it. Though what anyone would do with heavy water I do not know. In fact, I can only conclude that somebody does, otherwise we would not be here now.

With the enthusiastic agreement of Nilsson and Petr, Ross placed the injured and the prisoners in the truck the naval party had used, and sent them off, with the message that they would be following within four hours.

As the party departed for the heavy water plant, Ross speculated that the party were likely to take more time, rather than less. Unless they were lucky, that is. He shrugged with a wry grin and looked around at his party of eighteen men, all armed to the teeth, mainly with the German weapons taken from the school house.

The bo'sun commented, "Right bunch of pirates, if you ask me. I'm glad they are on our side, though they wouldn't look good at Whale Island, that's for sure."

Ross nodded. "Just the sort of men you need for a job like this."

It came as a surprise as the truck slowed down. They had arrived at a place where they would have to start walking.

***

The truck loaded with the prisoners and the wounded drew up on the quay alongside the MGB. Jack Lane, the skipper, appeared. "Get the wounded on board and anyone who cannot be left in Norway. We have a building where we can dump the prisoners to keep an eye on them." He turned to his Radio operator. "Message to Captain Macklin. Advise him Lieutenant Sherman will be delayed. I suggest I deliver wounded down to Narvik and return for Sherman and his party. Got that?"

"Yes, Sir. I'll get on the blower now."

"Will it work at this range?"

"Should do, Sir. I'll try anyway."

"If you get through give me a shout. I'll speak to the Captain myself."

"Yes, Sir!" The radio man went to the bridge to check and see if the TBS was in range.

"I will be here for the next hour. If you can make it in that time, fine. If not, it means Ballangen. That could be a risky proposition due to the time factor, as we have no way of knowing, apart from the sound of gunfire, how the diversion is working out. I do not look forward to crossing swords with a heavy cruiser, let alone a battleship. I will be at the rendezvous. Take your time getting down here, good luck. Out."

John Macklin sounded relaxed as he closed the conversation, but he was getting worried. The sound of the guns from the attack on the *Tirpitz* was getting less and less. That indicated that the attack was running out of steam, and the diversion would not be in place much longer.

Jack Lane considered John's suggestions. He realised that the Commander made sense.

He put the mike down and turned to the Cox'n. "Cast off. Let's get the show on the road.

The MGB roared off down the fjord for the delivery of the wounded to Narvik. He decided the sooner he was back alongside at Bjerkvik, and available, the better he would feel.

***

At the heavy water plant, Ross Sherman and the two Norwegians, Petr and Nilsson, split the men up into their arranged units. While Petr and his men kept an eye on the barracks, which was the only other building in the area, the others entered the plant.

They were aware that the guard unit consisted of three squads of men in shifts, the duty shift in the plant, the other two shifts on rest or training.

Petr sent his men to specific places around the barrack building, lacing explosives around the doorway in front and the other door in the side of the building. The wood construction would burn well, once it caught fire. Given the heavy glass of the windows with double panes, they were not what Petr considered easy escape routes.

So far there was no sign of any guards or alarm from within the building, despite the muffled noises emanating from the plant. Gunfire, and bomb blasts, audible from outside but with the insulation of the double glazing, could obviously not be heard from within the building.

With the flamethrower taken from the German's armoury in the village, the party got to work waking up the barrack occupants. The Norwegians had no qualms about killing Germans. Norway's occupation, from the very beginning, had been unnecessarily brutal. The ruthless destruction of lives carried out by the enemy troops had earned reprisals. Neither side had showed any sign of mercy.

This particular skirmish was started by the most horrifying weapon in Germany's armoury.

The flamethrower pointed at the front door. Its stream of fire ignited the explosives, but they did not blow-up in a spectacular explosion. The doorway disappeared in a sheet of flame which immediately started to engulf the front wall of the building. Petr was not surprised when the alarm started to sound, and the people within the building began to move about. The explosion of the front door trap started proceedings. The side door erupted when an attempt was made to sally from the building. The effect of the explosion set timber on the side of the building on fire.

From the plant, the sound of explosions could be heard and the first of the casualties came through the front door. Two men appeared carrying a third between them. They made straight for the truck where the medic waited. The two men then joined Petr and his men facing the barracks. The two new men took the offensive, throwing grenades through the now open, front and side doors. "Just to discourage the occupants a little," was the way they put it.

With the building well on fire, the sounds from inside were becoming frantic, and the, first of the windows was shattered by gunfire from within. The man who hurled himself through the window, was riddled with bullets before he crossed the frame.

As the explosions from within the plant became more dramatic, the demolition party emerged: two of their people with bandaged arms, all looking battered but all smiling. The one man not smiling was Norwegian. He looked scared. Nilsson led him from the plant with a halter round his neck. He was the informer apparently. Ross did not ask, nor could he blame the partisans for their ruthless attitude.

The heavy water plant had been systematically destroyed. In addition, because the troops set to protect the establishment had had so little to do, they had become careless and discipline had suffered. The attempt by the partisans to destroy the plant three days earlier should have put the troops on their guard. In fact, because of the recent attempt, they had presumed that there was no likelihood of a repeat performance in the immediate future. After all, even if there was another attempt, the partisans were a bunch of amateurs, not really a worthy opponent for the skilled Alpine troops defending the plant. There should have been three shifts of guards, one in the barracks, one in the plant and one exercising on the hill. The fact was that the unit supposed to be exercising took longer and longer to get ready, which had resulted in their eventual leaving that part of the cycle out. Thus, with two units in the barracks, twice as many were trapped inside. Because those in the plant were dispersed throughout the building they were picked off piecemeal. Thus the comparatively small numbers involved in the raid had had a very good chance of success, a factor that they exploited to the full.

The barracks had been left in a parlous state. The soldiers trapped within were wiped out with a rain of grenades. When the raiding party departed, several of the unidentified partisans remained behind to keep up the grenade assaults, giving the others time to escape.

Thus, when the party returned to Bjerkvik, they were able to catch the MGB which was, as promised, still waiting.

It was a tense time racing down the fjord to Narvik, though they were not surprised that the *Audax* had departed already for Ballangen.

***

The two British ships met as *HMS Audax* was approaching Ballangen. So, rather than stopping, both ships carried on for the open sea. The short period of daylight was rapidly decaying into night once more, as the *Audax* cautiously passed the entrance to the Bogen Fjord. The radar showed the positions of the ships still anchored there. It was possible to make out the wreck of one of the vessels, which John thought was probably one of the destroyers that had taken part in the attack. It was possible to identify the *Tirpitz.* Their seeker torpedo was locked onto the bearing, to either explode on contact or after six hours. With a silent cheer, John launched and left the torpedo to do its job, while sending the *Audax* racing after the MGB. The subsequent explosion echoed from the surrounding cliffs, so while they did not anticipate the sinking of the German Battleship, as the CPO remarked "We hopefully gave her a sore belly."

The destroyer caught up with the rest of the raiders at Skrova. The cruiser, showing some signs of damage from her excursion, left within an hour of *Audax* arriving. The small convoy of ships, including the surviving destroyers, quietly left the anchorage. They had the bulk of the long night to cover their departure.

The MGB refuelled and took extra on board to ensure she had sufficient to get all the way home. As the remainder of the raiding force signalled their readiness, the anchorage was vacated, leaving the quiet waters to the sea gulls once more.

Chapter sixteen

Counterspies

On instructions of the Admiral, Lieutenant Alec Randall PhD RNR assumed command of the modified ML, part of the special unit commanded by Lt Cdr. John Macklin RN. In the absence of John, who was currently in Norway, Alec Randall was in command of the unit.

Seated in the Admiral's office with Second Officer Chloe Masters WRNS, they were being briefed on an operation.

"This is going to be tricky!" The Admiral looked and sounded serious. "I would have left this until John Macklin returned, and I would be happier if Doctor Martin were here to undertake the second part of the operation. However, since there is a blackout on their movements and John is in Norway, we are left with the problem we need to solve." He turned to Chloe, "You may recall the operation, the first led by John in the ML. We had the problem of leaked information causing us to lose agents?"

Chloe nodded. "We never really solved that. I believe it ended with a 'bad luck' verdict, as the losses stopped Though John was convinced that there was a mole somewhere, and probably among the returning agents."

"Exactly!" The Admiral continued. "Well, it seems that 'bad luck', as we called it, has returned to haunt us. We were lucky enough to intercept a message between the mole and the enemy HQ in Paris. The contact in Paris is a part of the Gestapo counter-intelligence section. They are using former police detectives as part of their enquiry team, an action that the normal Gestapo hierarchy disdain. It seems that in Paris the senior Gestapo officer appointed has realised that, by employing experts to investigate, it saves time and resources, wasted by politically elected officers, who are inept, and more likely to invent answers than find them.

"Our problem is that, though our agents are gaining experience, it does take time, and the first three months are vital for an agent to survive. We are losing people too fast, certainly to the skills of street-wise detectives, but also to our friend, the mole." He relaxed back in his chair. He was looking a little tired, the cares of the continuous pressure of his command telling on him.

Chloe realised that the Admiral would normally have retired three years ago, his reason for staying on obvious—he was needed. But it worried Chloe that the health of the Admiral was beginning to suffer. She corrected the thought, had already suffered, through late hours and unremitting stress that were part of the job.

The Admiral stirred from his chair and stretched, then pulled down a screen on the wall with a map of Northern France and the Channel, showing beaches and quays and listed detail of facilities and, where known, enemy bases. "Here!" He pointed at the small town and port of Fecamp. "There is a fisherman who is part of the fishing fleet for the area, which are herded by two armed launches forty foot long, armed with Vierling 38 quad, flak mounted guns.

"The port is used by E boats on an 'on and off' basis. So you will approach and enter with the Nazi insignia, go alongside and collect the agents. There are German-speaking seamen to carry on your boat. They will handle any communication with German authorities. Chloe will have two Frenchmen with her, to help if needed. The pick-up will be set for three days time. I will expect the ML to be carrying normal armament plus at least one seeker, just in case." The Admiral sat back and sighed. He thrust a package of notes toward Alec and said, "Chloe knows the rest. Get together and sort yourselves out. Any extra staff, or equipment, let me know."

The pair left the Admiral's office silently, both absorbing the brief they had been given, and both concerned for the Admiral's health. By common consent, they boarded *Mavis* and sat down in the wardroom with the package of orders between them. They sat silent for a few moments. Then Chloe spoke, "I am not happy about the Admiral's health."

Alec nodded in agreement, "I know what you mean and I agree with you. The Admiral looks ill."

Chloe shrugged. "Well, there is nothing we can do about it, so the best we can do is get on with things and do what were are asked."

With that, they put aside their concern for the Admiral and got down to the planning.

***

In Calais, Klaus Richter studied Peter Schramm, his boss, as he waited for his orders. When, eventually, Schramm looked up he gazed sternly at his assistant. "Why am I still awaiting a report of the loss of a platoon of Waffen SS?"

"Because by the time I was permitted to go and examine the scene half of the German army had walked over the ground and destroyed all trace of the story of the events that caused the aforesaid loss. And that, boss,, was down to you. You have at your disposal a fully trained forensic investigator, yet you send a bunch of hooligans to investigate a serious crime. That is why there is no report. I presumed no report was better than a report that makes you look like a fool."

Klaus realised that he had gone too far. "Sorry, boss. I did not imply that you are a fool. Just that some office-bound idiot could very easily express such an opinion, based on the fact that the area was destroyed by the people sent to the scene."

Mollified, Schramm said, "I am well acquainted with the expression that 'blame, like shit, slides downhill.' I accept that I should have used your services first. Now I have something else for you to do. I want you to round up all the agents the opposition have in this area."

"Opposition? The Abwehr?"

"No, you idiot, the British. I presume we are aware of at least ten people in that category. With their help we should be able to find most of the rest. I have information that there will be a pick-up for most of them shortly. I would like to get hold of them before that happens.

"You can get the list from Gerda, my secretary." He returned to the papers in front of him, indicating the interview was over.

Klaus walked out of the office closing the door behind him.

The secretary, Gerda, was a new addition to the HQ staff. She was in civilian clothes, crisp white blouse buttoned, the hint of cleavage. Slim waist, blouse tucked into straight black skirt, black silk stockings, and court shoes. A jacket on a coat-hanger was hanging from the hat-stand, also black and tailored, a match for the black skirt. The blond hair was firmly retained in a style which clung to her head, neatly cropped showing the nape of her neck.

Klaus walked over to the desk and perched his bottom on the edge. "You have something for me."

The icy blue eyes looked up at him, "Klaus Richter?"

"That's me."

"I.D.?"

Klaus looked at her, astonished. "I am deputy chief of this department and you ask me for ID? Who are you, woman?"

"I am the Director's secretary and I need to know that you are who you say you are."

Klaus shook his head and grinned, "My ID."

She looked, nodded, reached into her drawer, and passed over an envelope.

"Thank you," Klaus said clearly.

"It's nothing." She replied equally clearly, and returned to her work.

Klaus went into his own office and sat down, ripping open the envelope as he did so. He swore as he tore the corner of the note inside.

Luckily, the tear did not affect the contents. He perused the list. There were 22 names on it, several known to him already. Three at least were names offered by jealous enemies hoping to exact revenge or punish an enemy. He guessed there would be others on the list for the same reason, and also to make up the numbers to prove that the investigators had been diligent.

Klaus always felt sorry for the latter. Unfortunately, the interrogators were not renowned for their forbearance with people who had nothing to admit. It was usually accepted that there was always something to be divulged, and people had been known to die as a result of their knowing nothing. He tucked the list into his inside pocket and left the office. On the ground floor he made his way to the office occupied by Mary Curtain.

He knocked and entered. Mary sat behind her desk typing notes. When she looked up and saw him, she smiled momentarily.

Making progress, he thought to himself. "Just called in to ask if you would care to visit the theatre on Friday. It would require evening dress. I am expected to bring a guest, and it would require that we dine beforehand. I would have been accompanied by my wife when she was alive, but, as I mentioned, she was an early victim of this bloody war."

Mary looked at him, half inclined to send him off once more with a refusal. Almost to her surprise, she found herself asking, "What is the play?"

Klaus was mentally already leaving after her refusal, when he realised what she was saying. "Oh. It is 'Liebestraum', described as a romance based on the music by Franz Liszt."

"Collect me from my apartment at when?"

He thought hurriedly. "You are in Rue Richelieu?"

"As I am sure you are aware," she said.

He flushed. Of course he had found out as much about her as he could. "I will collect you at six if that is possible."

"That will be fine. Long dress, you mentioned?"

"I believe so," he said. "Until then." He ducked out and went down the steps of the building his feet hardly touching the ground.

Klaus was quite surprised at himself in the circumstances. As he drove to the first address on the list, accompanied by the squad of Feldgendarmarie (military police) wearing the silver gorget of their occupation around their necks.

The first address was in the area of the Bleriot Plage, an area that had been growing in popularity until the commencement of the war. It was now partially deserted as many of the places had only been used as holiday accommodation.

Klaus had to concentrate to get through that day. The frustration of interviewing people who were patently not agents was demotivating. He discovered three people who would have taken part in the mass exodus of agents from the area, though there was no mention of the suggestion in any of the initial interrogations. However Klaus was having suspicions of some big event occurring he as yet knew nothing of.

***

The Mercedes drew up outside the house on the Rue Richelieu. Klaus, resplendent in black tie evening dress, carried the flower corsage to the door of the apartment on the first floor of the building.

When he knocked the door opened promptly, surprising him. Mary Curtain was standing there, looking beautiful in a deep orange dress which just cleared the floor.

"Please come in for a moment," she said, accepting the corsage. "How lovely. Though you shouldn't have bothered."

With a shy smile Klaus said, "If I had not bothered, my mother would had been most upset that I had forgotten my lessons so quickly."

Inside, the apartment was tidy and comfortable. "This is a nice place," he said, as much for something to say, as anything. He realised that he meant it. It was nice and had a comfortable feel about it.

"Why, thank you, kind sir." Mary said. "Please, sit I will only be a moment." She went through a door off the lounge, and returned within three minutes carrying her coat.

Helping her with the coat, Klaus could not help feeling that this was the first day of the rest of their lives.

Chapter seventeen

Chloe Secret agent

Alec Randall stood on the bridge of the ML chatting quietly to Chloe Masters, who was standing in for Amy Martin. Once more they were carrying a contingent of Marine Commandos to clear the ground for the pick-up.

"You may not land with the Marines this time," Alec said. "I have strict orders that you will be escorted at all times and whatever happens you must not be allowed to fall into the hands of the enemy. Are we clear on that point?"

Chloe nodded resignedly. "Orders from Commander Macklin, I presume."

"You presume wrong. Orders from the Admiral!"

Chloe shrugged. Whoever the order came from, she was in no position to ignore it.

The appearance of Toby Cummings on the bridge reminded Chloe to strap on her pistol belt, and check the MP40 sub machine gun she had been issued. Over time they had collected plenty of the weapons, and on the whole, these were more reliable than the Sten guns they were normally armed with. They were favoured by the agents. Her pistol was actually an automatic, a German Walther, using 9mm ammunition as was used also in the MP40.

A signal from the beach indicated all clear, so Chloe and Toby landed and made their way to the roadway running alongside the canalised river to the open sea.

The rendezvous point was 200 yards down the road, at a disused grain silo. The squad of Marines fanned out and disappeared in that direction. Chloe and Toby walked the ditch beside the road following the marine unit.

Chloe was leading when shielded headlights appeared, coming from inland. The sound of vehicle engines could be heard. She dropped down in the ditch and waited. Two vehicles drove up to the small building selected for the rendezvous, and ten armed soldiers dismounted from the small truck, The officer, still seated in the Kugelwagen which had preceded the truck to this spot, called the Sergeant over and gave him orders.

There had been no reaction from the small building. As Chloe watched, the men moved in, their guns poised ready. They all filed in through the door. There was a shout from within. Hearing it, the officer started to haul himself from the small open staff car. In seconds he was hurled back into the car, his spine smashed across the half open steel door. The driver who had risen to his feet was equally unfortunate. The small steel framed window in the wall beside the front door, exploded outwards. Spinning, it took the entire front of the driver's throat out on its flight across the open area ending up in the woods on the other side of the road.

Chloe was sickened at the sight, but managed to keep things together enough to swear under her breath. The fact, that the building had been mined, meant that the alternative rendezvous would be used. She rose to her feet and ran forward to the ruin of the building, meeting the corporal in charge of the Marine squad.

"Both truck and kugelwagen are secure and usable, Miss. I will lead with the truck to the second rendezvous, if I may." The report was polite and succinct, so she pulled letter two from her pocket and opened it.

"We need to follow the Rue de Pilotes to the Sente Bellet. It's the corner cottage. Go!"

She followed the man to the vehicles, the bodies had been removed. And someone had covered the seats with a blanket. Chloe took the wheel of the kugelwagen. Toby did not have a licence to drive, and, more importantly, had never driven in his life.

Chloe started the vehicle. "Remind me when we get back. You will learn to drive. No arguments."

"Thank you, Ma'am. I would be delighted to learn. I just have not had time, what with one thing and another, I have never been able to fit it in."

Nodding, Chloe drove after the small truck, leaving plenty of distance between the vehicles. "Eyes open, Toby. This may be an ambush." As they came in sight of the junction, she stopped the vehicle and did a three point turn. "Just in case."

They then left the vehicle and drifted along roadside, down to the cottage on the corner of the road, the rendezvous point.

The sound of voices within could be heard from the street.

The Marine on watch at the door looked at Chloe anxiously.

She nodded to him and went in. The corporal was standing with his three other men facing an excited Frenchman who was talking at a fast rate in a loud voice. The others in the room were all crowded in the corner behind him.

Chloe went in. As she stepped in view, the noisy man turned his attention to her.

She held her finger to her lips, the universal sign to be quiet. It had no effect. So, drawing her Walther

9mm, she cocked it and shoved it under the man's nose. "Shut up!" She said in French.

The end of the barrel of the gun was pushing his upper lip off his front teeth. He stopped talking.

"Right, Corporal. What started him off?"

"I do not know, Ma'am. I knocked and came in. He was having a go at the others. As soon as I appeared he started on me."

Chloe selected one of the other men in the room. "Who are you? What was that all about?"

The man shrugged. "My name is Pierre Rodin. Albert was trying to tell us that we should stay on station here, that the Germans did not know who we were, and, that if we disappeared, they would identify us, and take things out on our families."

"What do you think?" Chloe asked. She had recognised the name Pierre Rodin from her earlier list.

"I was visited by an investigator from the Gestapo at Calais. I believe he was a police officer from Germany, not one of the normal thugs the Gestapo usually sends. He did not indicate that I was a suspect. But during the week after he spoke with me, he had also spoken to Henri, and Calvet there. When the message came to assemble, Albert immediately started to say he thought the recall message was bogus. It was the Germans trying to bring us out of our hiding places. "

"Are you all here?"

"All those of us who are left and that we have been able to contact!"

Chloe called, "Everyone outside, and into the truck!'"

Albert hung back. "It is a trap. You will all be taken to prison."

Chloe stuck the gun out once more. "Move, or I will shoot you." For a moment she thought he would call her bluff. Then, with a shrug, he moved after the others into the truck. Following the Kugelwagen this time the truck kept up as Chloe speeded back to the waiting ML. At the quay there were several dead troops, mainly Wermacht Police. The Marine lieutenant, signalled them to stop and debussed the agents onto the ML promptly.

To Chloe he said, "There are six of my men holding the rest of the Krauts off. They are in there," he pointed down a side road leading toward the high ground of the offshore island, where an odd building stood. "I sent a party to take over the building as an observation post. It seems there is more there than a telescope."

"What did you have in mind?" Chloe asked.

"I will now have enough men to take the building and find out. I have a suspicion that it is an electronic surveillance site. See the aerials further up the hill?"

Chloe was able to make out the aerials he was talking about. "She looked at her watch. How long?" She said tersely.

"Half an hour!" The instant answer was a reassurance.

"Go! You have your half hour. Do you need more bodies?"

"No. We'll manage." He was gone, taking the corporal and his men with him.

Chloe boarded the ML and checked that all the agents were there, including Albert. Out of the twenty expected there were only eleven. Albert was on the list.

She called Albert into the cabin she had been allocated. Once he was seated, she asked the question. "What was all the fuss about?"

Albert Contran was a small businessman from the village of Valmont. He sold and repaired furniture and was well regarded in the region for his good quality work.

" I received a message from one of my contacts that the Germans were running a scam operation to collect all the agents in the area. They have already managed to lift eight of our people. When that message came through, they said the collection would be by people we did not know. I suspected a trap. My apologies for my doubts. Survival in this place is a deadly business."

Chloe understood. "My major worry was the noise you were making in the middle of an occupied town. It can be the cause of disclosure to the enemy, if only by the idle comment of an innocent bystander."

Albert was contrite, and Chloe had the sense to realise that there was no point in pressing him. "The matter is closed as far as I am concerned. Now, tell me about this information you received on the scam by the Gestapo. Who actually gave you the information? Is he here in the rescued group?"

"No, he did not make it. I was told by one of his agents that the policeman, Richter, came and took him off to Calais for interrogation."

"Richter? Who is this man? Not a regular member of the Gestapo, I presume?"

"Oh, no. He is much more dangerous. He is a Berlin detective. A real police officer who was successful before the war, having caught four murderers, and had all four convicted."

Chloe leaned back in her chair. That was not good news. Thus far, eluding the Gestapo had been a hit or miss arrangement, win some lose some. This sounded as if the ground rules had been changed. If that was the case, they would have to do some rethinking over the way things were run. Certainly, they could not afford the losses they were taking at present.

She sighed and shrugged, this was a problem they would need to sort out in Portsmouth. From here there was little to be done.

She sent Albert back to join the others, then went herself to the bridge to see how the remainder of the operation was progressing.

Through her glasses Chloe studied the small building on the offshore mound. The door was open with people going in and out carrying things. As she watched, the lights within the building went out. She made out the shadow of a person leaving and slamming the door, before disappearing against the background of the hill.

The roof of the building actually lifted and collapsed back. There was a splash of light inside, which swiftly went out. A line of men appeared on the quay carrying boxes and equipment.

Lieutenant Roberts RM appeared carrying a heap of files. He followed his men onto the ML. As he boarded he called, "I suggest we move off, skipper. They got messages off before we cut them off."

Alec gave the orders. "Cast off forward. Let the current take her. Cast off aft. Engines half ahead."

The ML cruised downstream to the sea. As soon as the boat rose to the first waves, he ordered the throttles open. The ML soared off out to sea with a flurry of white water.

Down in the wardroom, Lieutenant Roberts was seated with Chloe, going through the papers he had brought with him from the lookout building.

Chloe said, "Do you know what we are looking at?"

Roberts replied, "I haven't a clue. All I know is they were upset when I came and took their toys away."

"Well, for no other reason, pissing them off will do for a start!" Chloe said. Collecting the papers together, she stuffed them back into their file container, and dumped the file back into the box with all the other gear collected from the lookout building.

The loudspeaker bleeped, calling Chloe to the bridge.

Out in the night, Chloe pulled the neck of the duffle tight and joined Alec. "What's happening, Skipper?"

"We have company!" He pointed off to starboard, up-channel. Chloe made out two white darts in the water headed in their direction.

"Do you think they have spotted us?"

"It's a pretty good guess."

"What do we do?"

"Split the difference. Fly between them flat out. They won't expect the speed we are going, so we have a chance of getting away with a little noisy murder. Once through the gap, we should be well away homeward."

Chloe stood watching the approaching E boats.

Alec said, "You might be better off below. The Admiral will never forgive me if something happens to you."

"I prefer to take my chances up her," Chloe said. "The Admiral thinks I should be wrapped in cotton wool. I think it's because I remind him of his daughter"

"I didn't know he had a daughter?" Alec said.

"She was killed in the London blitz," Chloe said quietly. "Bombs don't discriminate. She was a nurse in St Thomas's Hospital. She and several others died in the same raid."

Alec nodded in agreement. Well, for my sake, get down behind the armour when we pass."

"Okay, Skipper, I will. But it's just for you, mind." As Chloe settled down behind the armour screen around the bridge, she heard the clatter of feet, as several of the Marines stationed themselves around the upper deck. Two of them set up Bren guns on the roof of the cabin next to Chloe. One stood with grenades in his hand waiting for the chance to pitch them onto the enemy boat.

It was all over in a mad rush. The clatter of the Oerlikons on both sides of the ML, the stammer of the Bren's, and double gasp as the two grenades were thrown by the big man standing beside Chloe. The crack of them exploding could only just be heard amongst the cacophony of noise at the time.

The ML made it back to Portsmouth with no further alarms. The Admiral was there to meet them. There was a contingent from SOE to load the agents into a bus and take them off to London.

Chloe supervised the offloading of the documents and equipment from the lookout house, ensuring that the Admiral was aware that Lieutenant Roberts who had been responsible for their collection.

As they walked up to the office, Chloe asked if there was any news of the *Audax* and the raid in Narvik fjord.

"So far, so good! The initial part of the raid has gone off well, but, at the moment, no news of casualties or of successes, apart from the news of damage to the *Tirpitz.* Sadly, we must sit and wait. Meanwhile, the boffins are excited about the goodies you brought back with you."

They entered the office and Chloe realised that she was tired. She stripped off her duffel coat and gun belt, returning the Walther and her MP40 to the arms cupboard in the corner of the office.

The Admiral took a good look at her and immediately called for the car to take her to her quarters, where she collapsed on her bed, exhausted.

***

The return of *HMS Audax* was greeted with relief by the staff at Portsmouth, not the least because of the safe return of John Macklin as far as Chloe was concerned, but also the return of Amy Martin, though she was injured and required surgery.

Neither John nor Chloe were ever able to discover what her part in the operation had been, or, in fact, if she had been part of the operation. The fact that she was there at the time was a surprise. On the journey home there had been no real time to do more than inquire if she was responding to treatment. As far as he knew she had spent most of the time asleep, under sedation. When they arrived she had been taken off directly to London for specialists care.

Over the next three months they saw nothing of her and Chloe now promoted to First Officer, carried out any duties with the agents that were required.

Chapter eighteen

The Med

The development team on *Mavis* had been busy working on refinements to the seeker torpedo and the depth bomb. The development of the proximity fuse was more difficult than they had anticipated.

The duties of the *Audax* were more varied than before, though the latest developments of the seeker torpedo were still very much part of the destroyers duties.

The activities of the Commando unit were becoming more diverse and the use of the ML for small landings continued.

Sub Lieutenant Martin Offord had not been home for several weeks, and since home was near Oxford, it was not that easy to get to for a weekend pass. His home in the village of Drayton Parslow was not served by any trains. The bus only came twice a day, stopping at the Three Horseshoes in the early morning and once again at six in the evening.

He found it difficult to be alone with Maddy. She lived just down the road from his mother's house, so they were always under someone's eye whenever they were together at home. Advised by Jim Fordyce he considered the idea of asking Maddy to meet in Thame or High Wycombe perhaps. They could stay in a hotel, in separate rooms of course, and it would give them a chance to get to know each other properly, without anyone looking over their shoulder.

He had written to Maddy to suggest that. They could have more time together if they met somewhere between Portsmouth and Drayton Parslow.

She had replied that there was this nice hotel she had once stayed at with her aunt in Reading. She had booked two rooms there for the Friday and Saturday night, if that was all right.

Martin had managed to get the train to Reading and, to his delight, because he found it hard to believe that Maddy meant what she had written, she was waiting on the platform for him to arrive. She kissed him when he got off the train and took his arm to show him where to go when they left the railway station. He checked into the hotel and they went out to explore the town. Both were shy and unsure in the circumstances, but it gave them time to get to know each other once more.

"So you are an officer now?" She mentioned the fact that men in uniform were saluting Martin as they walked down the street. Martin had mentioned it in a letter when he had been promoted, but Maddy had not really grasped what he had meant. He explained all about it and told her what it meant at sea, that he was left in charge of the ship during his watch.

Not surprisingly, Maddy was impressed.

That night he delivered her to the door of her room, and as he kissed her goodnight, they were passed by other guests. One whispered to them, "If that's your room, why not kiss him in there, out of the way of this gawking lot."

Maddy looked startled. It had not occurred to her.

She turned and opened her door and dragged Martin into her room. The curtains were open and it was not completely dark.

She slipped her coat off and put her arms round his neck, pulling his head down to kiss properly, just like she had seen in the movies. He responded, wrapping his arms around her, holding her close, as in the quiet and the privacy of the dark room, they began to get to know each other properly.

***

In Portsmouth the war was speeding up. There was a sense of urgency about the preparations for action. The tide of Axis expansion had slowed to the point where the Allies were beginning to regain land once lost.

Suddenly, the urgency for the development of new weapons was being overtaken by the need for greater production of existing ones.

The *Mavis* was transferred to parts unknown. Alec Randall found that his berth was now 2nd in command of *HMS Audax.* And she, plus the ML, had been transferred, initially to Gibraltar, for operations under the Flag of Admiral Cunningham.

The office of Rear Admiral Howard (Special Services) along with Chloe were also transferred to Gibraltar though his position was officially unaltered, the zone of operation no longer included development of new weaponry.

In *HMS Audax,* Ross Sherman had been promoted and given command of a Corvette operating in the North Atlantic.

Lieutenant Jim Fordyce RN was now skipper of the ML. His promotion came through with his posting. The command was appropriate as he had, on several occasions, been in temporary command in the past several months.

The Special Operations section stationed in Gibraltar was enhanced by the addition of two further ML's, both commanded by Sub Lieutenants RNVR. Though both boats were new they were equipped with the standard Packard petrol engines. They did carry up to date radar and sonar equipment, and were suitable for conversion to alternative configurations if required.

For John Macklin the move removed some of the extra stress of the post at Portsmouth. The need for Chloe to go to France on a regular basis with the agents was his main cause of anxiety, which he had not anticipated.

The base in Gibraltar was also a revelation. Carved out of the native rock, the offices were windowed, but the staff immediately labelled themselves the trogladytes. The address was embellished by a crossed stone axe emblem drawn as a doodle by the Admiral himself.

The situation in the Mediterranean at the time meant that air cover was still based on a carrier being part of any convoy sailing for Malta and Alexandria. Escorts were in short supply. So the appearance of *HMS Audax* in Gibraltar was regarded as a useful addition to the next convoy for Malta.

The order, under the circumstances, to take part in convoy escort duties as part of Force H, was not surprising.

John discussed matters with Alec who was unused to convoy operations. "When we attend the convoy briefing, take especial note of the two forms of attack we may face. The main will be aircraft, bombers and torpedo bombers. Also the submarine threat, though not as critical as the Atlantic, they still pose a threat in the Med.

"Since the Italian navy got clobbered by Admiral Cunningham and Commodore Vian, there had been virtually no sign of them leaving port. It does not mean they won't appear, but the odds are against them coming out."

"I'm told the convoys can be pretty lethal as far as escorts are concerned?" Alec commented.

"That is because the air element loses a lot of aircraft to the escorts. We use a block barrage when things get rough, putting up a shield of fire over the convoy. Each gun aims at a particular part of the sky and shoots it. The result is that there are no gaps for the planes to get through. It pushes the bombers up too high to get accuracy and gives time for the ships to take evasive action."

Alec had a lot to think about when he sat awaiting briefing that afternoon. He shrugged. What the hell! Had he gone with the other boffins on the *Mavis* he would have been bored to tears.

"Gentlemen, Admiral Somerville!"

He leapt to his feet with all the others in the briefing room.

The Admiral had little to say. Just a reminder that the best they could expect is what they always got, a surprise.

***

Surprisingly, the weather was dull and showers of rain swept over the collection of ships making their way west through the moderate sea. Torpedo gunner's mate (Torps), Albert White, known as Chalky to his friends, commented to the after Oerlikon gunner, Peter Finch, "It's always the same. 'Come to the sunny Med', they say. 'Enjoy the balmy breezes as you relax in the warm Mediterranean waters.' Fancy a swim, Pete?"

Looking over the side at the sullen grey waters alongside, Pete commented, "Not this week, Chalky. Re-apply in a month's time, I'll consider your suggestion then."

"Pipe down, you two. And keep your eyes open. This is not a bloody picnic excursion." The voice of the Chief Petty Officer interrupted the conversation, bringing their focus back onto the matter at hand.

On the bridge, Alec Randall was walking back and forth, keeping his body active, anticipating the end of his watch in just ten minutes.

The Savoia Marchetti S79 torpedo bombers appeared three minutes later, being detected by the radar in the AA cruiser, part of the convoy escort. All escorts went to action stations, the klaxons and bell warnings being heard from the closest ships as they reacted to the information. Leading Seaman Peter Finch RN kicked his loader awake, said loader Burke being one of those people who could sleep on a rope. Once awake, Burke joined his gunner in searching the sky for the air attack.

The dry voice of Torps suggested they lowered their eye to the horizon. "Bloody torpedo bombers coming. They'll not be up there. They'll be down 'ere skimming the water. You'll see."

Sure enough that's where they were, dropping height from the first warning. They were accompanied by dive bombers as well, now showing themselves through the clouds. The AA guns were already in action as the convoy commodore ordered the alterations of course, dictated by the first of the falling bombs from the high level bombers, forming the third element of the air raid.

Martin Offord looked at the sky apprehensively. He was bothered by air raids, mainly because there was little he could do about them. He was not a coward. He just disliked not having control for whatever reason. The bombs dropping did not seem to have any particular target, mainly falling into the sea, though the odd flash and roar indicated that some unfortunate within the convoy had been hit.

The sight of the torpedo bombers approaching from the flank was rather more of an immediate threat, as the ship was in between the bombers and their supposed targets. As he saw the main 4.7inch guns swivelling to port toward the approaching threat, he suddenly remembered to get the ear plugs from his shirt pocket. He pushed them into place just in time. The broadside crashed out, the noise loud despite the earplugs. To his surprise the shells were fired into the sea, sending a wall of water into the air in front of the torpedo bombers. Martin saw some rise above the wall of water though most went straight through, emerging streaming water, one had an engine coughing and lost height crashing into the water, its torpedo still attached. The others started releasing the weapons, either levelling-off and steadying onto a course toward the passing ships, or plunging too deeply and not reappearing to track as they were designed.

John called the light gunners to target those they could see. The Oerlikons immediately opened fire, luckily catching two, causing them to sink. The machine gunners were doing their best, but still several of the torpedoes got through passing into the convoy, missing the *Audax* by very little in one case. The aircraft took a beating, three of the first wave plunging into the sea. A fourth lost one of its engines, and jerked to one side into the next aircraft to his starboard, causing both to crash into the sea in a tangle of wreckage.

The raid lasted just over twenty minutes. It cost the convoy two ships. Others also suffered damage, sufficient to cause the convoy to slow down. The remainder of the day was tense, as the slower ships repaired their damage.

By evening they were back up to the fourteen knots speed expected of them. But, with several days still to go, nobody could afford to let up on their vigilance.

For two days there was nothing but rough weather, but on the third day the sun shone, the sea turned blue, and the aircraft came back.

It was just one at first. He was chased off by one of the Seafires, one of the first of the converted Spitfires used as a carrier aircraft. With the calmer weather there was no problem flying off the aircraft from the carrier at the centre of the convoy. When the first raid approached the Seafires were into them before they could reach the convoy itself. The air seemed to be full of whirling, spitting aircraft, and soon the smoke trails of falling planes were tracing paths across the sky. When Seafires were forced to return to refuel and rearm the escorts got the chance to do their bit. It was during that period that *Audax* suffered her first damage. A 250 lb bomb hit the after 4.7 gun turret causing it to jam in place,, luckily pointing fore and aft. Meanwhile the anti-aircraft guns claimed another two of the Italian aircraft. The gun crew had suffered shock but no actual injuries, apart from ear problems caused by the noise of the bomb impact.

When they reached Malta there was considerable celebration. The convoy had lost only four of its fifteen ships, a record result up to that time.

In the historic world that was Malta, the crew of the *Audax* had time for a brief excursion around the beleaguered stronghold. John had been stationed there during his service as a midshipman he found it heartbreaking to see the damage the enemy had caused the beautiful city of Valletta. At the same time he was heartened by the defiant attitude of the people he met.

At Naval HQ the escort ships from the convoy were reassigned, either to return to Gibraltar, onward to Alexandria or to remain in the harbour for further assignment. For *HMS Audax* it was a modified wait and see. The after turret needed to be cleared to rotate once more. From there on, they would have to wait and see.

Alec Randall was fascinated. Having never visited the island before, the sheer antiquity of many of the buildings dating back to the time of the Crusades and beyond, the whole island breathed history. He walked around and out of Valletta. Got a lift in a friendly RAF truck to Mdina, where religion mixed with pottery and glassware, and winemaking was still a way of life.

As he wandered the streets of the old walled city, time seemed irrelevant, until he realised that he was really quite hungry, noticing that it was way past three o'clock. He had not eaten since seven in the morning. He turned sharply, recalling a restaurant he had passed a short way back. He encountered a body. Perhaps 'crashed into' would be a better description. However described, Alec found himself lying down on the recumbent figure of the person who had been right behind him on the pavement. That it was a she popped into his mind, and that she was apparently stunned by the impact of his body and the hard surface of the ground beneath her.

He rolled off her and knelt to lift her head off the ground to check for any injury. He found none. He felt her looking at him and turned to look at her.

She was studying him gravely, her face calm. "Do I pass?" She said quietly.

Alec leaned back. "I am sorry," he said, and stood helping the woman to her feet in turn.

She stood with her dark hair reaching his eye level, her brown eyes calm studying the man in front of her. She was well-dressed, sensibly with walking shoes rather than heels. Tweed skirt and white cotton blouse. He guessed twenties rather than older, and attractive.

"Are you hurt?" He said anxiously.

"Pride perhaps, otherwise not really." Her voice was cultured, her English natural and without particular accent.

"Please," he said "I am so sorry. I realised I was hungry and remembered the restaurant just there and turned without thinking. Would you allow me to take you there and get coffee or something stronger to revive you, or at least to allow me to make amends?"

The lady collected her fallen handbag and a carrier bag of provisions. As she straightened up she said, "That would be most acceptable." She turned and walked back to the restaurant alongside him.

Inside the waiter greeted the lady as if she was well known there. They were seated before she explained. "I live in this street and I know the people around here. More importantly they know me."

"I am Lieutenant Alec Randall, Royal Navy. I have just arrived with the latest convoy."

"My name is Julia Wallace. I am the local Archaeologist."

"How do you do? May I call you Julia?"

"You may, but only if I am permitted to call you Alec."

"Agreed. What will you have?"

"You said you had not yet eaten, so I will just have a glass of wine while you order something to eat. The lamb here is very good."

Chapter nineteen

Special Ops

The bridge of the destroyer was quiet. Alec Randall had little to do for the rest of his watch, and the time hung heavy on his hands. His mind kept going back to the encounter on Malta, analysing the conversation, trying to work out if he had been a complete fool or just a hopeful idiot. It was quite evident that, as a scientist of no mean skill, and a naval officer, he was regarded as pretty well endowed with grey matter. Yet, while he was with Julia, he had felt very much, the differences between them. Having said that there was the matter of the attraction between them that he did not, could not deny. As he leant against the bridge rail he could see her in his mind's eye, the lovely face with the hint of a smile, and her eyes gazing into his as she made some idle comment about the wine, or the weather. His sigh was audible and heard by John Macklin as he came on to the bridge.

"Wow! That does sound as if there was something going on in Valletta. Why have I not been told of this?"

Alec turned at the sound of John's voice. "Basically, Sir, it's none of your business, though I suppose it is all over the ship anyway?"

"More or less," John confirmed. "So tell all and relieve your straining conscience."

With a resigned shrug, Alec unburdened his soul.

When he had finished, John looked at him with an amused smile on his face. "So why the long face? Are you giving up on the lady?"

Alec shook his head. "Oh no. That is the last thing I considered. It is just that I have not been in this position before." Seeing John's look at that point, he gestured impatiently. "I have been with a woman before and I am aware of how bodies work together, but this is something else. I have not felt like this before over any woman, and I am having trouble coming to terms with it."

John nodded thoughtfully. "It happens to us all at some time in our lives, and we all have our own way of coping with it. Some say the best way is to just go with the flow, and see where it takes you. Others fight it, often spend the rest of their lives regretting the fact that they let slip the one person in their lives who might have made them happy.

"I personally feel that the 'go-with-the-flow people' are the wisest. But that is just my opinion. I, myself, nearly got it wrong. I believe I corrected my mistake in time." He shrugged. "It's really all we can do. If you think another will be coming along shortly, like a number 7 bus perhaps, remember, they are often followed by three at once. Confusing, I believe!"

John walked away to speak with the Engineer, who had just appeared on deck.

Alec resumed his perusal of the waters of the harbour. It seemed that he would just see what his date tomorrow produced. The thought of the exploration of the cellars of Mdina was intriguing even to a scientist, and the company doing the guiding added interest of course.

For Owen Jones, now senior midshipman, Malta was exciting. His boyhood reading had included the Crusades. Tales of the Knights Templar and Hospitaller had been a feature of the boy's stories of his youth.

Exploring the narrow streets of the old town and finding odd graffiti dating back centuries, was a thrill he had never anticipated. In the museum there was armour preserved from the time of the occupation of the island, and religious relics hidden away at the time, but brought out once more in the more enlightened times of the 20th century.

Around the harbour the clatter of metal on metal and the noise of winches and grinders were a permanent reminder that the war was close by. The regular air raids were less effective now with the enhanced defences, with the addition of the carrier aircraft stationed ashore while the carrier was in Malta available to help in the defence of the island while they were there.

Having linked up with junior members of the crew from other warships in harbour, Owen found the other side of life in Valletta, notably the area known as the Gut. That place in ports all over the world where sailors gather to drink and carouse, and generally let their hair down.

It was there that Owen discovered that activities, that would have shocked the people of the Chapel in his home village, were in fact normal and enjoyable elsewhere in the world. He discovered that there could be possible repercussions for the abandoned behaviour, newly introduced. In Owens's case, the ship's doctor had been able to prevent the consequent infection from ruining his life. On the advice of the Doctor, Owen decided to seek gratification elsewhere in future.

The sojourn of the crew of *HMS Audax* in Malta was longer than expected but shorter than some of the crew at least wished.

She sailed early evening for Gibraltar and was in position to rendezvous with a returning ML damaged in transit from the Italian coast. The transfer of people from the damaged boat to the destroyer was accomplished swiftly and efficiently. The crew of the ML undertook to stay with their boat and head for their base in Bone, the recently-recaptured port on the north African coast. The wounded from the ML were taken on board *Audax,* where the doctor was able to treat them on the voyage back to Gibraltar.

For John the chance to get together with Chloe was appreciated. The erratic nature of the events he had been involved with since war began had been stressful to say the least. Time spent with Chloe had allowed him to relax however briefly, and the Gibraltar visit gave them three days to explore and enjoy each other's company without pressure. They spent most of the time scrambling about the Rock, exploring the many caves and avoiding the notorious Rock apes, of which there were an extraordinary large number.

At the Spanish border John was surprised at the active antagonism displayed by the Border Guards. In all the years of occupation since the Rock had been taken, this attitude had been maintained, creating the stubborn refusal of the British to allow the Spanish to take over control, whenever attempts had been made to this end. On the last occasion the arrogance of the Grandee, sent to negotiate the treaty, earned a rejection before a word was spoken. Apart from his manner, it appeared that the Marques had been drinking prior to his visit to the flagship of the Governor of Gibraltar.

The Governor did not make a habit of receiving diplomatic missions on board ship. On this occasion, since the Spanish government persisted in claiming the British condominium as Spanish, the Governor decided to prevent the Ambassador from officially setting foot on Gibraltian soil while no diplomatic agreement existed.

The Grandee was sailed over from the port of Algeciras and piped on board the flagship, where the meeting took place. When it was over he was sailed back.

The episode did little for inter-country relations because it upset the Spanish, though it gave the presiding Governor considerable satisfaction.

His three days break was soon over. John returned to *Audax* to find that most of the remedial work had been completed.

Called to the office of Admiral Howard, he was informed that arrangements were still under way for Special Operations. In the meantime, his ship would take part in convoy protection until required elsewhere.

Happy to be busy rather than sitting at anchor, this suited John, and especially Alec Randall as he would have the opportunity to maintain contact with Julia Wallace, in Valletta.

She had begged off the idea of writing, as she was only too aware of the number of women in Valletta who discovered that they were not only pregnant, but the promised husbands were suddenly not to be found or available.

When the arrival of *HMS Audax* became known she was apprehensive but not hopeful. However, when she saw Alec, who appeared with flowers in one hand, and chocolates in the other, she was happy to see him and her doubts were set aside.

As for Alec, the smile on Julia's face was enough to confirm what he guessed already. Julia was the woman he had been seeking, knowingly or otherwise. He knew he wished to marry her, after only meeting her twice.

They went out to the Phoenicia Hotel to dine. Over dinner Alec told Julia exactly how he felt about her. He also told her that he demanded nothing of her but her company, until she had herself made up her mind about him. He did, however, warn her that on each occasion when they met he would ask the question.

"The question?" Julia asked interestedly. "What question?"

"Will you marry me?" Alec answered.

She flushed. "But you hardly know me?"

"Perhaps that applies now, but how about tomorrow, or the next day, perhaps on my next visit. What then?"

She looked away. It was difficult to keep her head in order when he was looking at her like that. "I.....I'm not sure...."

He took her hand in both of his. "Where will we go tomorrow?"

She shook her head, lost for a moment at the change of subject. "Oh, I thought perhaps Gozo."

"Good. I'll ask you again on Gozo. Now forget it. Let us dance and enjoy the evening together."

The next trip to the Island was a vicious battle from beginning to end, there were German troops being evacuated from North Africa. The cover for their ships was seriously interfering with the convoy to Malta. Out of fourteen ships, seven survived.

It was one month later, after two more convoys had run the gauntlet, though as Alec commented, the actual pressure was lessening as the days went by, that Julia said "Yes."

Earlier, having posed the question, Alec had continued to speak as the answer to the question floated in the air uncomprehended. This got through to Alec, and he spun round to look at Julia, still unsure that he had heard her correctly.

"You said, yes?" he stuttered.

"I did? Yes. I believe I did?" Julia said, almost unbelievingly.

"You will marry me?" Alec insisted.

"I usually mean what I say," Julia said, still nervous that she had come to such a momentous decision in such a short time, still apprehensive, though she was feeling more and more certain that it was the right decision for her to make.

Alec swept her into his arms and hugged her, kissing her, lifting her off her feet and swinging round and round in the middle of the room. Then he placed her carefully on her feet and looked into her eyes.

"The jewellers!" Looking at his watch, it was 6.30pm. "They will be closed," he said disappointedly.

"This is Malta. The shops close at 10.00 pm, sometimes later." Julia said quietly.

In the shop beneath a huge stone building, Alec realised in fact that it was a cellar. The lights were on, reflecting and splintering from the selection of diamond, emerald and sapphire rings. Julia was examining a ring with three rose-cut diamonds in a platinum mount.

The jeweller, a small man with a bald crown surrounded by greying black frizzy hair, explained that he could enlarge the ring if necessary.

Alec took it and slipped it on Julia's left hand ring finger. It fitted as if it had been made for her. She looked at him and nodded. He turned to the jeweller, smiled and said, "We will take it."

The jeweller went to remove the ring to place it in its box.

Alec stopped him. "Now it is in its place." He smiled at Julia as he saw her smile back at him, pleased that he had spoken and not allowed the removal of their engagement ring.

Alec spoke to John when he returned to the ship for the Gibraltar run.

John looked at Alec, surprised. He had known about Julia, but had not realised the seriousness of the relationship between them.

"Congratulations!" He said. "Does this mean a long engagement or are we thinking of a special licence marriage?" He smiled as he spoke, thinking of his relationship with Chloe.

"No long delay. I was hoping for the next time we are in Valletta," Alec said a little uncertainly. "I rather hoped you would be my best man."

"With pleasure, Alec. But how about one of the others? What about the bride? Her family are dead, I understand. Is there someone to escort her down the aisle?"

Alec stopped in mid-stride. "Oh, hell! I did not think of that," he spoke dejectedly.

John grinned. "Right. Phone her. The line is still linked. We don't sail for three hours. If there is no-one to give her away, then I will. One of the others can be best man. How does that sound?"

"Sounds great to me." Alec said.

"How about the Chaplain? Have you spoken to him yet?"

As Alec shook his head, John said, "Do it now! Call him and he will come on board before we sail if he is free. First though, make sure all is ok with Julia."

The Chaplain, Lieutenant Commander Peter Blake DD, decided that he had business in Gibraltar and used the opportunity to thumb a lift from *HMS Audax*. It gave him time to discuss matters and make arrangements at leisure. This suited both Alec and the Chaplain.

The convoys continued and John was beginning to believe that there was no real demand for the services of the destroyer for the Special operations they had been promised.

Alec was back on board, after the week off they had arranged at the time of his wedding. John was called to a conference on the Rock, where he was advised of the operation being planned for a series of landings along the Italian coastline.

Since the Allies' next objective was going to be Sicily, the landings on the mainland were a diversion to mislead the enemy. The locations were in Northern Italy. Two in Liguria, one near Albenga, the other near Genoa. The remainder of the landings were between Genoa and Livorno. The idea was to provide maximum distraction with minimum effort. All the troops involved would be in standard Marine battledress, with no commando insignia. There would be no excuse to brand them spies and summarily execute them. All were charged to cause as much mayhem as they could, just to confirm that they were serious. The rendezvous chosen meant that it would take time to get there, so the pick-up schedule required three pick-up dates. This would allow the three teams to pack-up and move out in time to make rendezvous on schedule.

"Of course, as you all here know, advanced planning, however complex, will only take you as far as the first steps of the plan. From then on it's in the lap of the gods and your own sharp wits." Major Archie Cameron MC RM of the nominated commando unit sat back and contemplated the others around the table. "Comments anyone?" His soft Scottish accent belied the steely warrior worshipped by his men.

It took a few minutes. Then the first of many questions flew from the audience to the platform.

"Supply will be impossible except in certain circumstances. There is no overlooked forgotten dinghy or Liferaft, nor are there likely to be allies in the area. So, if help is needed, unless the *Audax* or the ML is offshore, there will be none to be had. Your best bet will be keeping a low profile and only coming out to commit mayhem."

The group split up into its parties and went to gather their gear.

As the coast of Italy loomed to starboard in the darkness of the oncoming night, the destroyer made for the first of the drop points for the raiders.

The first three parties were dropped without incident. Dawn was beginning to show at the fourth drop, and, though the drop was successful, the ship was spotted and reported. When the spotter aircraft appeared, the Italian insignia and flag was very much in evidence. Officers dressed in Italian Naval uniform waved and saluted the seaplane which came to check them out. The fact that, on this occasion, they seemed to have got away with it, John put down to the Italian air force. Had it been a German aircraft, he thought there would have been a completely different result. As it was, they made their way to the coast of Corsica, where they sheltered in one of the many wrinkles of the coast line, assisted by the use of, netting coloured to blend with the rocks around them.

The night was slow to return. In the good weather darkness took longer to settle over the area, and it was late in the evening before *Audax* could sail discreetly and drop off the other two raider groups.

Having seen Major Cameron and the last group dropped, the ship turned, and heading round the southern coast of Sardinia, made its way back to Gibraltar without further incident.

The experience gained, when setting down the raiders, convinced John Macklin that future contact should be made using the ML. The fact that it could pass for an Italian MAS or even one of confiscated French Naval ML's, meant that it had better chance of evading interception than the destroyer. It also had the speed and endurance to accomplish a round trip, plus a better chance of concealment in the cove on Corsica.

Contact with the partisans on Corsica had enabled the Allies to set up regular radio communication with them. The use of the cove would also allow frequent delivery of arms and ammunition, and create the possibility of reciprocal assistance between the Allies and the partisans.

John made the suggestion that he should take the ML on the next circuit, in view of the fact that, having briefed the groups in the first case, he should be best able to judge the plans made on the spot for the diversionary raids.

The final date for the invasion had not been divulged though John was aware that it should be during the first two weeks of July.

1943 had not been a year for the best weather in the Mediterranean. The wind and rain were at once an advantage and a disadvantage. It tended to make the sentries less efficient, but it also made the ground more difficult to cover.

***

Archie Cameron was twenty-nine years old. He was a professional Marine. His service followed tradition in his family, passing from public school direct to the Royal Navy, where he had graduated and been gazetted as a second Lieutenant in the Royal Marines. His family had had a tradition of service with the Royal Marines since the

18th century, with Ensign Donald Cameron serving on *HMS Temerere* at the battle of Trafalgar.

Here in the close vicinity of Livorno, a city he knew from his travels as a youth, he had the fate of eight men in his hands directly. In the commando training a unit of multiples of two was paramount. Trained to operate in pairs, and all trained to think and act in whatever conditions they found themselves landed in, his group were at the same time the most lethal gathering available and with the most potential for disruption he could imagine. Using them to best effect was what he was here for. The other unit within the area was at Las Spezia. It would be possible to contact Sgt Pete Hardy, in charge of the second unit, if cooperation would be worth arranging. A dead drop had been arranged in advance by the agent who had checked the area out in the first place.

Meanwhile, the first option was to check out the airfield in the area. Cameron despatched three teams to survey the airfield and the possible points of access. The group had been able to occupy an abandoned barn, once more found by the local agent in the area.

The team settled in, with fields of fire marked off, and sleeping arrangements quickly set up. The agent within the area was an Italian national whose hatred of the Fascist Government was evident to Archie the moment the subject arose.

Paula Manfredi was the widow of the lecturer in archaeology at the University of Padua. The agent Giuseppe Mancini, operating in the area had made the mistake of being married to Paula. She was a woman to turn the head of any red-blooded man. The local Fascist Party leader decided that the removal of the husband would make the wife available. His plan succeeded, or so he thought. Mancini died within two days of his arrest. He apparently had a weak heart and could not survive the vigorous interrogation he was subjected to in the hands of the OVRA, the Italian secret police.

Paula was persuaded to go to the house of the local Party leader, whom she rightly presumed had enabled the arrest and subsequent demise of her husband. There she had been offered food and fine wine, in the company of her host.

She flattered the man despite her disgust at his groping hands approaches, and waited until he sent the servants off before she borrowed one of the steak knives from the dinner table and stabbed him, six times from throat to crotch. The throat stab was to stop him screaming. He died knowing he was dying, and she made sure he knew just why.

She left the house through the window. She left her host on the floor in a pool of his own blood, the steak knife rammed into the floor pinning his private parts to the carpet.

Her assumption of the position formerly occupied by her husband, was unchallenged by the partisans.

With the return of John Macklin, the raiders re-assembled for the final briefing for the first attack on the airfield. The fact that there were German aircraft present as well as Italian made the target particularly attractive.

The prepared bombs were fitted with standard ten minute fuses, all _packed in bags for each of the raiders, who were otherwise armed with their selected weapons of choice._The only stipulation regarding weapons was that ammunition should match all weapons, so that reloads could be passed from one to the other. Thus their selected weapons were all 9mm in this case. In addition, ten-second fuses were carried in a separate box, to be used in extreme conditions. The outer fence of the airfield was not electrified. It was impractical in the circumstances and tests had indicated that continuous maintenance of such a length of fencing would be difficult to manage. The security was maintained by regular patrols.

The raiders simply entered by individual cuts in the fence, spread over a known area, each person leaving some marker to indicate where his or her entry cut was situated. Though it was not the safest way to get in and out, with multiple cut places the chances were pretty good that all could get out through at least one of them.

Within the airfield the raiders moved silently over the grass covering the area either side of the concrete runway. There were aircraft dispersal areas for the swift turnaround of the fighters when air or sea forces were in conflict. At present they were filled with aircraft sheeted against the possibility of the rain that the cool moist air seemed to presage.

The raiders ignored them for the moment, as they intended to take out the buildings and accommodation to start with. Hopefully, they would deal with the aircraft on the way back.

The buildings, of what had been a pre-war airfield, included a control tower and several reception and administration buildings. For the military the control tower was the focus of the occupation. It was an obvious target and the raiders had decided that, come what may, the Axis occupation troops would be denied its use. The supporting buildings that were used as accommodation and administration would also be taken down.

With their black overalls covering their uniforms and the balaclava helmets,— there was little to give the raiders away in the darkness of the cloudy night.

Splitting into pairs they each went to their preselected target and placed the charges, using the ten-minute fuses.

The sentries at the tower were despatched swiftly and efficiently.

Six minutes after dispersing, the pairs rejoined before attending to the aircraft, replacing the ten-minute fuses with the one-minute versions.

Three other sentries were despatched silently, then the party of raiders were at the wire, slipping through as the first explosion went off. They quickly disappeared, accompanied by a series of explosions. The aircraft blew first, then the more sombre explosions of the barracks, and finally the control tower. The tower stood higher than any of the other buildings and, considering it contained the hub, the movement control centre for the area, it had been a very important place. Now it was a heap of rubble. All the buildings had collapsed.

There was a roar of vehicles and clatter of troops deploying, as the main body of the airfield defence ground into action.

A warning, based on a tip-off from a trusted source, had caused the barracks building to be vacated, the defence troops had been temporarily accommodated in the main hanger.

Fortuitously for them, they had not been targeted, as their move had not been announced and the transfer accomplished after dark.

The raiders were back in hiding before the airfield troops managed to deploy. Too late to be of use in the defence, they were employed in the rescue and recovery of anything left intact on the airfield.

There were four other episodes in northern Italy coinciding with the raid at Livorno. All were attacks on airfields. The result was that aircraft from inland airfields had to be provided for the patrols normally carried out by the raided fields from Livorno north.

The following day the airfield to the west of Genoa suddenly erupted with delayed action explosions. Aircraft in the act of taking off exploded, as did the armoury and the arsenal where bombs were stored. The security arrangements were completely disrupted as there was no warning given and the defence troops were caught off guard at their duty posts and in their barracks.

The most significant result of the raids was the only casualty of the six raiding parties, Corporal 'Chalky' White. In the raid on the Spezia airfield, the corporal had slipped from the roof of number one hanger, he had not survived the fall to the concrete below. The unfortunate commando had been left behind and, though he carried nothing personal except his ID, his uniform alone was enough to create serious worry on the part of the General in command of that area of Italy.

Elsewhere information found with the of the body of a Major on the coast of Spain had already indicated any invasion would be via Greece. Here they had evidence of British troops raiding the northern Italian coast. Immediately, the other raids were taken into account as it now appeared there could be a link between them.

Chapter Twenty

Eliminate or snatch

The Gestapo Headquarters in Milan are not as elaborate as those in Calais, thought Klaus Richter. He looked moodily around the drab office ruled by a pasty-faced, bespectacled toad who insisted in being addressed as Reichskriminaldirector. Like most of the other Gestapo officers Klaus encountered, Herman Stoltz was a creep and a failure in civilian life. With the arrival of the Nazi party had come the opportunity to advance rapidly through the ranks, provided only that you had no conscience and were prepared to sell your mother to a pimp, as Klaus picturesquely put it.

He, currently, was in Milan to assist in the battle with the emerging partisan force in Italy. So far, it seemed the total contribution made by the local Gestapo had been the arrest and detailed examination of the majority of the good-looking women foolish enough to be found in the city centre after breakfast time, 9.00-10.00 am, when the office opened.

Klaus, having arrived during the evening, had encountered a bored night-duty Kriminalassistent (Sergeant) and promptly made his way to the best hotel in town and crashed out until morning. He had reported at 09.00 and discovered that the place did not awaken until 10.00 am at the earliest. His encounter with the Officer-in-charge was not a happy one. He guessed the CO was completely inept at any form of police work, with the possible exception of the ability to detect if a suspect was a virgin or not. Male prisoners were the exception here apparently.

He had been dismissed from the presence of the CO with the instruction to keep out of the way of his men. His posting, to assist in the work of the Milan office, had not been requested, and was not required.

Klaus had only made it as far as the outer office when the telephone rang, and the operator had called the Reichskriminaldirector (Colonel) to accept a call from Herr Himmler.

Klaus decided to relax and await the outcome of the call.

It ended and Reichskriminaldirector Stoltz came out of his office almost running. He was calling his assistant, "Find that bloody policeman from Calais who came here this........" He saw Klaus sitting beside the reception desk, apparently concentrating on the local newspaper.

Klaus folded the paper. "Did you want the bloody policeman from Calais for some reason?" He asked politely.

The Gestapo chief looked as if he would like to strangle the Kriminalrat (Major) who sat looking innocently at him.

"My office! Now!" Herr Stoltz was not happy.

Klaus moved into the office and closed the door. Stoltz went behind his desk and sat. He did not offer Klaus a chair.

Klaus pulled up a chair and sat down.

Stoltz said, "You will commence working with my investigation branch and report to Kriminalrat Hauser." He bent his head and ignored Klaus, apparently awaiting his exit from the office.

Klaus got to his feet leaned across the desk took Stoltz's chin and lifted it so that Stoltz looked directly into Klaus's eyes. Klaus spoke in an icy tone, freezing the Colonel in his chair. "You will give me no orders. Nor will you interfere in any way with any enquiry I am involved with. If you attempt to push me about, you will discover what it is like to be in the basement when you are not in charge. I am under the direct orders of the Reichsfuhrer himself. I am also aware that he has ordered you to give me any assistance I require. You and your position here depends on my goodwill, and you have made a bad start. Understand?"

He released the man's chin, the two white marks where his fingers had held the man clear on Stoltz's face.

Pale-faced, Stoltz nodded.

Klaus stalked out of the office and left the Gestapo Headquarters.

Making his way to the Carabinieri office, he strolled in and introduced himself to the desk officer and asked to speak with the Commandant.

Tenente Colonnello Manfredi Fabrittzi had been in the Carabinieri since leaving University. He had always intended to follow the career his grandfather had chosen, despite the fact that his father was a successful banker. The banking profession was not of interest to Manfredi who yearned for a life of adventure. In the police force he had seen his way of achieving it.

The arrival of the Tedesco (Germans) had been a shock and a disappointment to Manfredi. The attitude of the Gestapo and the Wermacht Police units had been contemptuous to their Italian counterparts from the very beginning. The methods used by the German elements were both distasteful and barbaric in his eyes.

As the Gestapo officer entered his office Manfredi rose to his feet to greet him, a surprising politeness that Klaus appreciated.

"Tenente Colonnello Fabrittzi at your service." The announcement, accompanied by a polite nod of the head was immediately answered by Klaus, "Kriminalrat Klaus Richter, on attachment to the Gestapo."

Klaus sat in the chair indicated by Manfredi. "Coffee?" his host suggested.

"Please." Klaus settled in the chair, studying the Lieutenant Colonel sitting on the other side of the desk. He found he liked the look of the man sitting opposite.

The coffee arrived and the formalities dealt with, Manfredi spoke. "Now, sir, I presume this visit is not just a polite announcement of your arrival in Milano."

Klaus grinned. "As you so rightly point out, I am not here for a social chat. To explain, I should point out that I have been seconded to the Gestapo from my position of Detective/Inspector in the Berlin Kriminalpolice. It appears that my colleagues in the Gestapo have little or no experience in criminal investigation or crime detection, hence my attachment. It also appears that my posting is not popular with my commander, who is of the opinion that his own cut and thrust methods are all that is required to maintain law and order."

"I'm afraid I do not have the pleasure of knowing the Gestapo commandant here in Milano. We have not yet met."

Klaus thought for a moment. "He has been here for six months and you have not yet met?" He spoke the words but did not disguise his surprise at that Italian's comment.

Manfredi smiled cynically. "I presume you are here about the series of raids by the Allies on the Italian coast here."

"That is perceptive of you, sir." Klaus was impressed. "Do you have any information about these raids?"

"Very little, I'm afraid. I had the first reports but was banned from going to the scene of any of the raids because they were all on German airfields. My local informants do tell me that they were made by British soldiers in uniform. Not partisans. What have you heard?"

"Nothing. My leader has no information of the subject because the Luftwaffe handle airfield security. The Gestapo are kept as far away from the Luftwaffe as possible."

Manfredi raised one eyebrow. "I am surprised. I was under the impression that the Gestapo was all-powerful in terms of security."

Klaus grinned. "My finding thus far is that the Gestapo would have difficulty in locating the left cheek of their arses, if the label was left off."

Manfredi looked at Klaus in astonishment, amazed at hearing such a comment from a German officer. He then burst into laughter, and reached into the bottom drawer of his desk for the bottle of Grappa that he kept there for emergencies and celebrations.

He lifted the bottle and his eyebrow at the same time. Klaus nodded and the two professionals settled down to a realistic discussion of the genuine situation regarding crime and espionage in the area.

The bottle was considerably depleted by the time the two men had gone over everything. In fact, there was not that much known in terms of political crime. The usual level of crime was still there, though the criminals were managing to keep a lower profile these days. The Gestapo had a cavalier approach to crime and punishment. Most criminal offences merited a death penalty, possibly a stay of execution, if there was a chance of gaining information on the movements of the partisan groups who were becoming bolder, as Mussolini lost his grip on the people of Italy.

When Klaus left the office the pair had a firm agreement to only share information between each other. As Klaus pointed out, after the months of occupation, there was no excuse for the lack of cooperation which had existed up to now.

It made little difference at the moment. Whatever information was available, local sources would be the only news of any worth from the look of things.

***

For John Macklin, the success of the raids initially seemed to have little effect on the movements of troops in the area. Everything that was achieved was being concealed to ensure that nobody got the wrath of the hierarchy down on them for failing to secure their own units. It seemed that all the raids had been put down to partisan activity, the attacks were going to have to be higher profile to have the effect required.

In the circumstances it made sense to consider a raid on the coastal batteries, though it would require at least two of the raiding units to do the job properly. The other units were tasked to locate more open targets and it was suggested the local Gestapo offices in Spezia, Livorno and Genoa be nominated.

Leading the first raid on the coastal guns was priority, as time was catching up with the raiders. John took command of the raid, nominally taking the responsibility, while allowing the experts to plan the actual assault.

The plan called for a silent approach to the site and the securing of the sentries. In the event, they managed to reach the bunker without being discovered. At that point it was necessary to blow open the steel doors, using shaped charges of plastic. What they had not anticipated was the result of the blast from the doors. The men within the main bunker were found sprawled all about the place. The guns had all been retracted with the shields in place to keep the rain and wind out. The result had been the compression of the air inside the bunker caused the collapse of the gun crews when the doors blew in. All showed the blood leaking from their ears, caused by the blast. The people were disarmed and secured and the guns were run out on their slides. Each barrel was stuffed with an explosive charge, then the guns were partially run back over more explosive charges. The entire explosive program was wired to one detonation circuit. The bunker was emptied of personnel and the magazine given its own specific explosive charge.

This did not go unremarked by the enemy, who had become became aware that something was wrong. The alarm had been sounded. However, it took time to get troops from the barracks to the gun-site, and that time had been sufficient to complete the wiring.

Thus the final act of the drama was that when the reinforcements arrived they were in time and in the position, to be part of the general explosion destroying the site and killing many of the troops sent to save it.

This time there could be no cover-up. The troops were despatched all over the area searching for the saboteurs, all of whom had departed for their next projects: the Gestapo offices in the coastal towns, which were all scheduled to be hit at the same time.

John still had the idea of the Gestapo office in Milan, but decided that it was a bit too far at the moment, worth looking at in future perhaps.

The uproar caused by the gun emplacement explosions was made more dramatic when the local Gestapo was targeted. The three offices were no great achievement as far as damage was concerned. But in terms of propaganda, the fact that they had hit the Gestapo seemed to be popular, even with the other German units in the area. The area was now alive with search parties. Retreating to the various pick-up points became a difficult and time-consuming process.

The scheduled night was luckily moonless and clouds obscured the stars. The ML arrived to take the raiders off. The group which included John Macklin managed with difficulty. During the escape and evasion after the coastal gun episode, two of the commandos had been hurt with bullet wounds. Neither had been actually fired-at. The wounds received by both men, were the result of ricochets, and more damaging because of this. Both men had to be carried out of the area.

Among the extraction of the other groups was the collection of the dead soldier, whose body had been recovered during the raid on the Genoa Gestapo office.

After spending the following day at the new site in Corsica, the ML made the long run back to Gibraltar and the security of the naval base.

Chapter twenty-one

The Commodore

Rear Admiral Howard had been suffering from ill heath for some time. Though the mild climate of Gibraltar agreed with him, his health now dictated his long overdue retirement. His replacement was sent out from Portsmouth in the form of Commodore Henry Carlisle DSO RNR.

The still-dark hair and flashing blue eyes were in a six foot frame that showed not an ounce of fat. With hat at a rakish angle, he strode into the office like a breath of fresh air. He was followed by a Commander, who appeared to have been carved from a slab of granite.

"Morning all! I am Henry Carlisle, come to give you all a good kick up the arse to get this show on the road. Commander Harris will introduce himself as we go along."

He looked at Chloe with approval. "Are you the secretary?" He asked.

"No, she is not!" John Macklin snapped. "The First Officer is an essential member of the planning team and was aide to the Admiral."

Completely unabashed, Carlisle smiled and said, "Oops, I beg your pardon; First Officer Chloe Masters, is it?" He reached out and took her hand. "You'll soon get used to me. Still not quite used to being back in uniform."

Chloe recovered her hand.

Carlisle carried on as if nothing was amiss. Swinging on John he said, "I presume you are the senior active naval officer, in command of the destroyer, the ML, and a ship called *Mavis* which is elsewhere at present."

"Commander John Macklin. RN," he announced.

"So you are the intrepid Macklin. I have heard many good things about you from my friend, Amy Martin."

John looked up sharply at the name.

"You know the lady quite well, I understand?" The Commodore said.

"We were at university together." He said quietly.

"I understand you have met her since?"

"She was one of a group we collected from Le Havre at the time of Dunkirk."

The Commodore decided to leave it at that, and then demanded to be introduced to the rest of the team present.

His disturbing influence seemed to invade into every action that the team discussed.

It appeared that he was a temporary appointee for the Special Services section having been axed from the navy in 1936, during a round of cuts in spending indulged by successive Governments at the time.

When war broke out he was recalled in the rank of Commander and served in Alexandria with the SAS, mainly operating small craft collecting and dropping off agents and partisans on the islands of the Aegean and Tyhrrhenian Sea.

He had earned a reputation as a dashing innovative officer and was rapidly advanced to the rank of Captain. Now it seemed he was on the track for higher things. the Special Operations unit in Gibraltar was the next step on the ladder.

John was back on the bridge of *HMS Audax,* as the convoy formed up for the dash to Malta. The routine was well established now and the escorts were all practiced at their tasks. The new members were swiftly placed in position.

There was the usual anti-aircraft cruiser, with the aircraft carrier placed centrally in the convoy. As usual *Audax* led the parade.\

Prior to sailing, Lieutenant Commander Robert Watt, RN, Chief Engineer on the destroyer, joined John on the bridge.

"What brings you to these exalted heights, Robert?" John smiled. It must be something special to lure the engineer to the bridge.

"Nothing to really put my finger on, but I'm a wee bit wary about the main engines."

John swung round to face Robert. "What's the problem?" He sounded sharper than he intended. "Sorry, Robert," he apologised. "Bit jumpy these days. So what is the problem?"

Robert shrugged. "That is the problem, boss. I am not sure what is wrong, I'm just thinking that there is something not quite right, and I cannot put my finger on it."

"What should I do about it?" John asked.

"That's the problem. I do not know. I suppose all I can ask is you try to avoid sudden changes of speed, and as few bangs and shivers as possible."

"Carry on as usual then." John smiled.

Robert's smile was a little strained. "I suppose so."

The incident bothered John more than he made out. Robert was a very good engineer. John trusted his instincts. If he felt that there was something wrong then there probably was.

There was little to be done at the moment and John just had to put the problem on the back burner, until something either happened or didn't happen.

The convoy went through a certain amount of interference. But now the invasion of Sicily was under way, the pressure was not so pronounced on the Malta run. There were still air raids and torpedo attacks, but the invasion fleet was suffering the brunt of the pressure from the Germans. The Italians were wavering and needed more pressure from their German partners to press home attacks in the face of the withering firepower of the convoy, plus the air cover provided by the carrier.

The return to Gibraltar was in the company of two other ships, the anti-aircraft cruiser and one of the other destroyers. The guns of the AA cruiser opened up as they passed to the south of the island of Sardinia.

She had detected a group of bomber aircraft wheeling high above.

The radar operator on *Audax* called out the identity of the aircraft. The klaxon sounded action stations throughout the destroyer.

John shrugged, 'No peace for the wicked' and stuffed earplugs in. The guns started to bark as they found targets.

It was still fifty miles from Gibraltar when the beat of the engines faded. *HMS Audax* lost way and drifted to a stop. The engine room voice pipe whistled and the engineer reported that they had suffered from an overheated shaft main-bearing. They would be unable to clear the problem for some hours, as rapid cooling could crack the bearing with serious consequences.

John reported to the cruiser Captain who commanded the small force. The answer was for the other destroyer *HMS Hector* to take *Audax* in tow, and deliver her to Gibraltar where she could be effectively repaired.

The feat of seamanship involved in the transfer of the tow from ship to ship was the stuff of life for the Bo'sun. The duty watch was lined up, ready to receive the line as *Hector* brought her stern close to the bow of *Audax.* The hand at the stern of the *Hector* whirled the knot at the bitter end of the small line around his head. As the stern of his ship rose on a wave he cast the line over to the bow of the *Audax,* where it was caught and taken to the waiting line of men. The light line was swiftly taken in, and the hawser attached to it was drawn up through the hawse and attached to the towing bitts in the bow of the crippled ship.

The *Hector* moved slowly forward to allowed the towline plenty of scope before actually taking up the strain and finally starting the long haul to Gibraltar.

On the bridge John heaved a sigh of relief. Though he kept it to himself, he had been worried about the possibilities of an enemy submarine being presented with a dream target of a stationary destroyer. They entered Gibraltar in the dark, and tugs took control at the earliest opportunity.

The Commodore was not pleased. It almost seemed that he blamed John for deliberately sabotaging the engine to cause him problems. Surprisingly, the dour Commander smiled at John as they left the Commodore's office together. "Don't take any notice of our leader's displeasure. His problem is that he is always trying to get things done in the face of the Navy. He looked at John's straight rings. As a regular you realise that that is brick wall science, and you need an immovable force to breach it. At the beginning when we were losing, he was able to get away with it. Now we are no longer losing, the routine is back to normal. With the honeymoon over, poor old

Henry is suffering from what we professionals are accustomed to. Administrative inertia.

John looked at his companion with surprise.

Noting it, Commander Phillip Harris smiled grimly. "I have always suffered from the opinion that my rather grim visage hid a rather grim person. In fact, I am known among my friends for a wicked sense of humour and an amiable disposition. On the other hand, there are those who never bother to get past the outer shell. For those people I maintain the mask they prefer. Poor Henry has never bothered to get to know me at all. He is quite happy to use me as a threat to those who can be threatened. Let's get a drink, and, for God's sake, call me Phil."

The pair went into the town and sat down with drinks in the hotel used by the officers of the garrison.

Phillip Harris had been at Dartmouth before John. Though John knew the name, they had never really met. He now discovered that his companion was the man he had himself described, dry, amusing and witty. John found himself talking about the way he had finished up in Special Operations. This led to Phil and his story. Both confessed to being happier when they were doing traditional naval tasks.

Later that evening, Chloe spoke with both of them. "Tell me, Philip, how does the Commodore get his information so much faster than even the Admiral?"

"You should understand that the Commodore was far more famous prior to his return to the Royal Navy. His exploits after joining an archaeological dig in Afghanistan are the stuff of 'Boy's Own Paper'. A hero with a large 'H'. He rescued the damsel in distress from a wicked Afghan lord, and then followed up with an epic Greek escapade about which there is some doubts. The penny papers had a field day. Then when the war started he was in Egypt and got involved with David Stirling in the SAS. The Navy recalled him. He did an island operation involving the Greeks. Now here he is a member of the armed forces. His impatience is directly linked with the fact that here, he is very much a small frog in a very big puddle. The nearer he gets to London, the bigger the puddle gets. My problem is trying to keep him within the bounds of reason. Two hundred years ago he would undoubtedly have been a privateer or even a pirate. He is having difficulty restraining his enthusiasm for operations which would involve unnecessary loss of life. So far I have been successful in restraining him. How long that situation lasts is anyone's guess.

"You cannot be serious?" Questioned Chloe, "Surely the man is aware of the basic rules for any operation from the Allies' point of view. Whatever the enemy may do, we do not descend to their level."

"There is a school of thought that says 'fight fire with fire'." Phil said mildly, and this man regards David Stirling as a rival?"

"If you are suggesting our leader is advocating such methods, then I think it may be already the time to do something about it." Chloe had definite opinions about such matters, as John was only too aware.

Phil, on the other hand, was not aware. So John jumped in before any more was said on the subject and asked Chloe if there was news of the next operation.

"The Commodore is being very secretive about his thoughts on the matter. As far as I am aware we will still be carrying out the Admiral's last order, which involved the return to Spezia to actually remove the Kriminaldirector-Oberst. Apparently, Stoltz is still blaming the Italian people for the raid on the office, and the release of the political prisoners. Which occurred at that time.

"In the circumstances, I suggest you carry on with the planning for the operation. The Commodore is currently pretty busy with other matters at present."

Chloe looked uncomfortable as she passed on the information, but did not explain the reason for the Commodore's current preoccupation.

Neither Phil nor John pushed the point. Both put their heads together and cooperated with planning a raid to create the maximum impact on the German forces in Italy. The invasion of Sicily was already in progress. Diversion was no longer the first priority. It was now regarded as an opportunity to bloody the nose of the Germans, at a time when they would not be expecting it. The removal of the local Gestapo chief would be an important demonstration to the Italian people that the master race were in fact, not the masters.

Once again the ML was deployed for the drop off, but the destroyer was also despatched to cover the operation. The intelligence, received from the French and Italian coast, was that the naval elements of German and Italian fleets were not expected to react quickly, with the exception of the E-boats. The Italian MAS boats attached to the German forces were dangerous, but those operated under Italian command did not constitute much of a threat.

HMS Audax would, in addition, use her guns to inflict damage within the dock area of Spezia, and intervene with any attacking U-boats.

The date was set as soon as Archie Cameron, commanding the Royal Marine Commando, confirmed he was ready to go. Archie would lead the assault, and much against his will, John delegated Alex to accompany the raiders, to liaise and identify the Gestapo chief, for capture or otherwise disposal.

The picture of Herman Stoltz was placed on the display.

"Dead or alive?" Queried Archie, adopting a gunfighter's stance, right hip thrust forward, hand poised above an imaginary six shooter.

John smiled, "Just remember this is not a game. Stoltz has been responsible for the death of hundreds, here in Italy and in both France and Germany. The man is a monster, whose basic ethos is self-preservation. Ruthless removal of people is only one of the methods he uses. Blackmail and extortion, torture for amusement, and, to entrap people he thinks can help his upward progress, everything and anything to keep his upward progress going, and to ensure his survival.

John put another picture on the board. "This is Kriminalinspector Klaus Richter. He is a professional police officer, detective from the Berlin police, attached to the Gestapo as a bloodhound, mainly because the Gestapo have proved themselves inept at any form of realistic investigation or detective work. Oddly, though we have no evidence of anything but straightforward detective work, he also is a target, should he be in a position to be taken. Otherwise? He shrugged, leaving it at that.

The two ships were underway before the Commodore was aware of it. The message announcing the departure of Operation 'Pizza' was in his 'In' tray, as yet, unread.

The message ordering the return of the group could not be acknowledged, and on the orders of the Officer in Command, ignored.

John smiled grimly as he read the message, despatched despite the official radio silence instruction supposedly in being. "He seems to be of the opinion that he is above such things," he commented to Archie Cameron.

"Ah, well, of course, rules are for the obedient to obey, the brilliant to interpret, and genius to ignore."

John nodded. "Ah. So now he will classify us as brilliant or genius?"

"Now he will classify us as disobedient serfs, who will be court martialled upon our return from what we hope will be a successful mission. In that event it will all go away, and he will either have spun matters to show that he was responsible for our success, or try to turn it to our detriment in some way. Whatever, we will now have to accept that we have made an implacable enemy, by having the audacity to steal his thunder with this operation, thunder planned for and rightfully his, gained no doubt, from stepping firmly on the necks of anyone in his way."

"Cynical, Archie?"

"John, I was in Alex when he was operating a Greek ketch-rigged fishing boat, landing and collecting agents from various places in the Islands and mainland of the Greek Aegean. He returned on one occasion from an expedition, shaken and tired out, having single-handed the boat for 600 miles. There were two of my men on that boat. Both had died. According to the Carlisle chronicles. the boat had been strafed by an ME 109 and the rest of the crew were killed. The only body he could produce was Marine Potter. Our medic looked him over and questioned the fact that though there were three body wounds from heavy calibre bullets, none was actually lethal. The lethal wound, he guessed, was 9mm. Because of the condition of the body it was not possible to be certain of the time of death. Though, once again, the medic guessed the 9mm was after the heavier calibre wounds."

John looked at Archie, "What are you saying, Archie?"

"Sadly, nothing I can prove. But I would be wary of having an armed Commodore behind me in a tight situation, especially if I stood between him and the exit." Archie smiled wryly, "Know who your friends are, eh!"

Neither mentioned the conversation again, but it gave John considerable food for thought.

Command is a lonely place. It's where you stand secure and guarded, giving orders for others to risk their lives and obey.

John paced the bridge of *HMS Audax* as the destroyers 4.7in guns rotated, sniffing at the targets in Spezia harbour.

The guns would not fire until the basic task had been performed and either, the captive/s were aboard, or dead. Only then would the guns speak.

Ashore, Archie and the first snatch group were crouched outside Gestapo HQ. The lights were on and there were people walking about looking busy. The security had been beefed up with Wermacht troops from the local garrison. Archie looked at his team, all in black with balaclava helmets on. He pulled his up, rolling it so that it now looked as if it was a wool hat. He whispered for the others to do as he had. In the alley where they were crouched there was room for them to stand and form ranks. "We will be marching in. Sling your weapons over the left shoulder. Be prepared in case someone notices. Last two take out the door guards. Ready?"

A low chorus responded. "Good. By the left," he said quietly. "Quick march!"

The party marched smartly and confidently across the square to the door of the Gestapo building.

Nobody took any notice, at the doorway the Major entered followed by his men. The last two peeled off and removed the door guards, and took position in their place.

Inside the Major snapped at the reception, "Oberst Stoltz."

The receptionist, a corporal pointed down the hall. "Room 4, sir."

Nobody hesitated, nobody queried, the squad of black-dressed men who marched down the corridor to room 4. Archie knocked at the door and immediately entered, followed by the first two-man file. The Sergeant halted the remainder of the men. Then, having noted the empty ante room, brought them in and, about to close the door, changed his mind. Nodding to the corporal and holding up two fingers, he watched two men take positions at the open doorway, each able to see in one direction along the corridor without exposing themselves.

In Stoltz's office, the man himself sat petrified in his seat, as Archie explained that he should do everything he was told, the option to that being shot, or knifed without further warning. Klaus found it difficult to stop himself from smiling. He knew he should be raising the alarm, but he was technically not there. The room he occupied was a small store room, which had been unused for years before he came. He had taken it over and made certain private adjustments, one of which was the installed camera in the office below, Stoltz's office. Using a wire recorder that was voice and noise operated, it started the camera and recorder when anyone entered, and switched off when they left.

Currently supposed to be in Livorno, Klaus had sent his deputy to the city in the southern section of Liguria and remained, anxious to get something on his boss so that, if he needed to, he could use it as a 'get out of jail' card, just in case. It seemed from his current observations that problems with this particular man were being resolved for him as he watched.

It did not occur to Klaus that he should interfere in any way with the situation. Stoltz was a waste of space in his opinion. His replacement may be better or worse. That was something to be dealt with at the time. Now was a good time to lose Stoltz.

As the office below emptied, Klaus sat back. After giving the raiders time to clear the building, he made his way through to the private back exit used for discreet visitors. Once in the car, he tore off down the road to Livorno. He would need the alibi for the enquiry.

Chapter twenty-two

Corsica

The raiders marched out of the HQ with Stoltz in their midst. Nobody said a word as they passed through the office. Stoltz, stone-faced, gave no indication that he was detained. He marched rigidly in the group through the rooms and out of the front door. The two men stationed there indicated a half-track vehicle that was now parked outside. The entire party boarded the truck and departed the scene, the noisy truck creating echoes from the old stone walls of the city.

The second group was nominally a snatch group, with the secondary target of creating mayhem, as they had on the last occasion they visited the city.

The vehicle park of the troops was an obvious suggestion and timed charges had been left to get the their attention.

Elsewhere, the barracks of the garrison were located. Once more charges were laid and the sentries silently disposed of.

The commander of the troops, Oberstlieutnant Helmut Reichs, was unhappy with his situation. Running the Feldgendarmarie was not the easiest of jobs, and had often led to unpleasant interviews with the Gestapo Oberst. He was sitting in a gloomy mood, expecting the worst, when the news came through that the Oberst had been removed from his office by Special Forces. Reichs was elated to hear this news, until he heard the first of the explosions in the barrack area of his own headquarters. Reichs was a professional soldier. His reaction was to collect his MP3 from the rack beside his desk, leap to his feet a call for his orderly to sound the general alert.

The whooping noise of the alert signal accompanied the first rattle of gunfire, as Reich's veterans opened fire on the raiders.

The bombs placed in the barracks accounted for seven of the occupants. Most of the men were on duty or in process of handing over, which meant that 33 of the force was active and available. All were time-serving professional soldiers. They reacted instinctively and were currently attempting to cut off the raiders from the sea.

Marine Lieutenant William Harding Fitzwilliam Arnold MC RM, Fitz to his friends, shrugged when he saw the reaction of the Feldgendarmarie. "It had to happen sometime." He told Sgt Pete Hardy.RM. "Get the third squad around to stop them cutting us off. We will hold here and, when you are in place, we'll stage our withdrawal, in steps."

Hardy saluted. "Back to the grind again," he muttered as he dashed off. The two parties of Commando retreated in steps, each covering the other. The German troops were keeping the pressure up. It only eased as the guns of the destroyer started their destruction of the foreshore dock equipment. The ML added its guns to the racket, their fire being directed by Fitz who arrived on board, the first of the raiders to arrive.

The other groups boarded, trailed by Archie Cameron who had four wounded and one dead with him. The Marines added their fire power to that of the ML. As they drew away the whole of the waterfront seemed to be afire, as the shells from the destroyer laid waste the stacked supplies and the railway trucks which carried the goods elsewhere in Northern Italy.

As the two ships left Spezia, John reckoned that the authorities at the port would be forced to remember this occasion.

***

The engines on the *Audax* started to overheat before the Island of Corsica loomed out of the darkness. An unscheduled visit to the cove on the island was necessary, as the engineer was worried that they would not make it to Gibraltar. As soon as they tied up in the cove on Corsica, the engineers were stripping down the filters on the seawater distillation units.

Camouflage covers had been attached and silent routine initiated by the time the engineer reached the bridge to report on the problem.

John looked at the Engineer wearily. "Well, Robert. How do we stand?"

Lieutenant Commander Robert Watt looked angry as he reported his findings on the subject of the engines. "Bastard saboteurs! The filters were stuffed with rubbish, meaning each one had to be stripped out and cleaned out. We do not have the material to replace the filter medium, so it will be start-stop all the way home, a sitting duck."

"Brief Alec on what we need from Gib. He can go off and come back tomorrow night with the correct gear."

Robert thought for a moment, then he smiled. "I'll make a list," he said and disappeared below once more, calling for his chief petty officer.

With the departure of the ML, armed with the spares list from the engineer, and the wounded, life on *HMS Audax* settled down. The Marines stepped ashore and dispersed, setting up watch places to ensure the security of the area. The local partisan leader came to visit and was entertained in the ward room, where information was exchanged and problems discussed.

Archie Cameron was intrigued to hear that there was a problem with the local garrison, created by the mayor of the local town. It seemed that the mayor expected the Germans to remain permanently to rule the people of the island. He had been using his relationship with the Commandant to dispose of enemies and business rivals.

Andre Cabral, the partisan, had no personal problem with the mayor, but he had been approached to do something about him. "I could of course kill him. But that would upset the Commandant. If, however, he was abducted or killed in a raid, all would be clear. I could not be held to blame."

Archie grinned. "You would like me to solve your problem?"

Andre Cabral nodded, seriously.

"Why would we raid Solenzara? There is nothing there."

"Oh, but you are wrong. There is something there that is most important. Just above the village there are, as you already know, the big guns." He paused. "They are only kept manned because of the production units in the magazines, a series of rooms below the gun platform itself."

John looked at Andre keenly. "Production units?"

"They make anti-personnel mines. They jump up and blow your knees off. At least, one of them does."

"Why haven't I heard of this place before?" John Macklin asked?"

A smile appeared on the face of the partisan, "Your sphere of operation is Italy. So you didn't need to know."

John realised immediately that this was the reason. However, since they had established the hideout in the inlet, a fact known to HQ at Gibraltar, it surely became a matter of interest to any ships using the newly-established secret island base.

***

There was an interesting note from Berlin signed by Martin Bormann. It dismissed any idea of maintaining a security cover, as it would draw attention to the location of the production unit. The Commandant of the region headquartered in the area was not impressed with the logic of the writer of the note. Having been involved in the administration of several areas in the past where so-called secret bases had been established, his experience was that such secrets were seldom kept longer than the first interested enquiry.

It did mean he had to maintain a security unit dedicated to the base. A waste of men and resources, which he did not dare skimp on.

***

Archie looked at the diagram that Andre produced.

"How many men has the Commandant got?"

"Probably some two hundred in all, but there are only about seventy here at the moment."

"Do they work overnight in the production area?"

"The local people only do the day shift. At night they check the day's output, with German staff. They pack and ship at night also. The day staff are locked in all day and so they cannot contact anyone, and they stay in a special barrack overnight. They are not local people, they have been brought in from off island." Andre paused. "I do have a contact inside, but I cannot speak with him without notice. The next contact will not be until Friday, two days time."

Archie smiled, "We'll do it tonight. If we do it right we will take out the guns as well."

The Marine officers and the Sergeant sat round the table in the wardroom and planned the takedown of the gun battery and the production facility. Fitz was detailed to take his platoon and pin down the garrison in their barracks. Sergeant Hardy would deal with the guns themselves. The Major would concentrate on the production unit, and set off the ultimate bomb—from the bomb factory—hopefully to take down the battery in addition to the production unit.

Crouched under the concrete base of the gun platform, Archie Cameron looked at his watch. Still three minutes to go. As he waited he ran through his mind the sequence of events leading up to this moment, like all the other moments he had waited just before the operation began. He knew that the slight queasiness would disappear as soon as the action started. He thought briefly of Margaret, his wife. Her last letter had not been a major event in his life. The plea for his understanding over her affair with her boss was hardly the most heartening event of their married life. He shrugged, looked at his watch again, two minutes. He often wondered why time slowed down on occasions like this. He eased his knee. The wound he had received at Dieppe had never really ceased to remind him to keep in cover when in the presence of snipers.

Then it was time. The doubts and worries disappeared. He was on his feet and the satchel charges had been thrown in through the gun-ports, along with grenades. Everyone ducked. With the crash of exploding charges the attack began.

His radio squawked. The report was that they were in the gun mount. The other aspects of the raid could now go into action.

"Rome, Foxtrot, Go!" Archie transmitted, then slinging the radio on its strap, over his shoulder, he hauled himself up onto the concrete platform and entered the gun chamber.

The explosives had not been kind to the occupants. There had been, he thought, only two by the looks of it. The doors to the ammo store were open and, recalling the sound of automatic gunfire, he was not surprised to see the scattered bodies of the men who had been playing cards at the time the raid began.

The corporal pointed to the door in the corner. "Production unit, upper floor."

Archie went straight through, ignoring the bodies and the stench of shit and blood, through the door and down to the room slightly below the ammo store. The dead soldier and his lady had died from the pressure of the explosives in the next door room. The door must have been slightly open. The couple had been caught in the middle of their lovemaking and, still joined, died in the act.

The room otherwise was a clutter of tables and jigs and metallic objects in process of assembly. "Touch nothing," Archie ordered. "There is no way of knowing how dangerous this stuff is. How about the next level?" As he spoke the doorway to the next level opened. As the steel panel moved, it hit some of the debris and there was a whirring noise. "Bomb!" Archie cried and hit the deck. The others in the room all hit the floor. The blast was not great, but, as Archie described it later to John, "With the top door open, it had somewhere to go."

The searing scratches on Archie's back were a testament to the efficiency of the explosives produced. Though the wounds were superficial, they were painful and could have been disabling and deadly, with the door closed and the explosion contained.

The men recovered, and Archie led the way through the lower door, now clear of the debris that had caused the blast. The room below was still in a neat layout. Stacks of pre-cut pieces of explosive were against the wall. Once again, the only live human presence was the corporal who had opened the door, thrown back by the slamming door. He was just a little dazed.

When they opened the lower door the sound of firing could be heard. The party tackling the defending troops had discovered that they were dug in and awaiting them, occupying the base section of the gun mounts.

Archie signalled the others to deploy through the double doors leading to the external passage. On his signal two men burst through the doors and rolled into the middle of the passage, each facing a different direction, both opened fire immediately, the answering fire was erratic and short lived.

"Clear!" the lead man called. Archie and the next wave went through into the corridor and spread out the length of the passage. When ready, they slammed open the room doors where the defending troops were in cover. It could have been a massacre. It was not, simply because Archie gave the Germans the chance to surrender. There were no senior German officers present. The Oberleutnant in command called his men to give up their weapons, and the resistance was over. The Marine detachment lost two men dead and six wounded, including their leader Major Archie Cameron.

The Oberleutnant and his Leutnant were discussing matters when information about the headquarters in the local town was mentioned. Archie realised that the sparse distribution of German troops on the island made it possible for the island to be recaptured without the Germans have much chance to do anything about it.

Having thought it over, he decided that, though he would not attempt the island takeover, there was nothing stopping him taking over the local town and putting the Germans on notice. If they tried to retaliate, or in fact stop the process, it would cost them dear. The vehicles of the garrison were standing where they had been left when the troops had debussed for the defence of the gun mounts.

Interrogating the Oberleutnant was not difficult. The arrogant young man was younger than his junior and, having been an aide-de-camp to a staff officer, was also less experienced in warfare than his junior, who had been promoted from the ranks. After service in North Africa under Rommel he would have been worth listening to. As things were, the Oberleutnant was happy to boast about the other troops in Solenzara, and the fate of the raiding party, when his Commandant would take the matter up personally.

While the iron was hot, Archie radioed to John that he would be visiting the town and expected to be back in time from breakfast. He explained that the Germans would not be expecting him and, he believed, that despite the risks, he thought the risk worth taking.

John turned to Alec. "I'm just popping out for a jaunt with our Marines. I'll be back for breakfast. He was collected by the kugelwagen once used by the Oberleutnant, and was present with the bandaged Major Archie Cameron MC RM, when the town of Solenzara capitulated without a shot being fired.

In the town Mayor's office, John turned to Archie. "Now we have it what do we do with it?"

To his surprise, Archie said, "We use it to recover the entire island."

On the table in front of him was a chart showing the disposition of all the German assets on the island.

"With only one thousand men on the island, and two hundred already accounted for, we really would have a good chance of clearing the island of German influence."

John Macklin looked at Archie sadly. Shaking his head, he said, "You and I both know that it will never happen. The powers-that-be have plans, and that does not include taking the island at this time. So it's now best forgotten. As it is, we can only hang on here for a certain time, until the Germans get together a force big enough to shift us out of here.

As they drove back to the concealed ship, Archie said, "It was a good idea, you know."

"I know it was." John replied, "And it would have wrapped up German troops needed elsewhere."

"It made sense." Archie said with feeling.

"Since when in war did sense come into it, or anything?"

"I see your point." Archie said bitterly. "So my men are expected to continue to die because some politician has had a fall-out with another."

"Exactly!"

"Well it stinks, the whole system stinks." He sank into a morose silence for the rest of the journey.

The ML returned that night and the German officers, taken prisoner, were loaded aboard for return to the Allied HQ at Gibraltar. The engineers went to work fitting the new filters, their priority to get the ship into a condition to defend itself as soon as possible. As the ML left the small base, there was now the risk that the engines may not start. It was with some trepidation that the crew of *HMS Audax* waited to hear and feel the presence of the engines now silent for three days.

Chapter twenty-three

Escape and evasion

In Spezia, Klaus returned to the Gestapo office to discover the absence of Stoltz. It meant in simple terms that Klaus was in charge. He immediately inspected all the facilities under the control of the Gestapo. The interrogation rooms downstairs sickened him, the mockery of the doctor's surgery, by appearance only, the trays of implements, none directed at healing, all used and directed at hurt. It was as he stood in the passage with cells on either side he made his mind up. He spoke to the three men on duty in the office at the entrance to the cell block.

There were seventeen prisoners, eight of them women, all were currently awaiting interrogation.

His mind was screaming wrong. This was wrong. He frightened himself, the feeling was so intense. Looking around, he wondered if he had spoken aloud. But there was no one there. He spoke with the officer responsible for the cells. "Are all the cells locked?"

"Of course, sir. As always."

"What about your staff? Are they in place down there?"

"Yes, sir. All located in their office at the end of the cell row."

"Very good. I am pleased to hear it." Klaus went into the office and located two cans of knockout gas.

Closing his office door he picked up the telephone and rang Mary Curtain in Calais. "Have you booked your holiday yet?" He asked.

"No, though I can leave at any time. I am in charge here."

"I have realised that the people I work with have made a mistake in bringing me here, so I have decided to leave."

"Where will you go? What will you do?"

"I thought a little travel, and perhaps make clocks?" He held on breathlessly hoping that she had understood his message.

She was very quick on the uptake. "I was considering going to my aunt in St Louis de Chaussee. I can be there by tomorrow evening. Will we meet perhaps?"

"Of course. I will do my best to be there when you arrive, though I may be a little late. Traffic, weather, you understand?"

"Always. A tout a l'heure."

There was a rear entrance to the interrogation section, a private rear entrance to allow for the quiet disposal of embarrassing bodies.

Klaus looked at the occupants of the cells, and selected a cell containing two mature-looking men, who were sitting quietly conversing in low tones.

He stopped and approached the cell. Motioning one of the men forward, he asked who they were. "The nearest looked puzzled, "We are members of the Church management here. For some reason we have been arrested and brought in for questioning."

"Wives? Families?" Klaus queried.

The first man said, "Not me. I am a widower and my son was killed in Tunisia. My friend here. His wife is in the cell over there with the other women." He indicated a cell further down the hallway. His other daughter is in America."

Klaus said quietly, "I am going to release you all. I will need to get a truck to the exit." He pointed down to the exit doors. "If I leave you the keys, can you collect everyone and control them quietly. I will bring the vehicle and we can all leave here. Those who think they can hide in the town may leave separately. The others I will take to the Swiss border. The Gestapo will not be kind to anyone they catch, including me. So once again, I caution quiet and orderly. Will you do it?"

The two men looked at each other, then turned and nodded to Klaus. "We will do it."

Klaus unlocked the cell and passed over the keys to the other cells. "Gentlemen, I will see you shortly at the rear door."

Back in his office he armed himself with an extra automatic. Taking the two knockout gas grenades from a box, he put them in his coat pocket, Carrying his own documents taken from Stoltz's files, he stuffed them into his briefcase, then removed several other passports from the safe with the mixed bag of money. He adjusted the combination, altering it. And after a last look to see if he had forgotten anything, he slammed the door and spun the combination. He removed the keys for the crew van from the keyboard and went to the garage to collect the vehicle, parking it behind the building. Entering by the side door, he made his way to the detention wing and popped his head through the door to the security office.

The three guards were playing cards.

He popped the cap on the first knockout gas grenade and rolled it into the room. He heard the three men crash to the floor. So he opened the door quickly. All three were sprawled on the floor. Popping the other canister into the room, he shut the door and kept holding his breath, until he was as far as the cell block and the cell occupied by the two men.

They came out when they saw him and followed him, unlocking the doors as they passed.

At the back door Klaus held up his hand and opened it carefully. Then he stepped out and opened the double doors of the van, waving the escapees in. He closed the doors, climbed into the cab and drove off north, heading for the Swiss border.

The rescue of those people from the clutches of the Gestapo, made Klaus feel like a real policeman again. Doing the job for which he had been trained once more.

***

The village of St Louis de Chaussee lies right on the Swiss French border. The city of Basel sat on the hill opposite. The slender arch of the bridge over the river Rhine was outlined against the sky.

Two days later, the distinguished Swiss businessman, Karl Wagner, crossed into St Louis to collect his wife, who had been visiting a clinic with medicines. Herr Wagner brought more medicines with him and, later that day, the couple crossed back into Switzerland, leaving the horrors of war behind, in occupied Europe.

Klaus had wondered if he would feel guilty at leaving his country. He found that he did not. Nor, it seemed, did Mary Curtain.

Chapter twenty-four

Sabotage

HMS Audax sailed into Gibraltar harbour, with her engines once more running smoothly, coming up to her mooring quietly, without a fuss. The launch carried Archie and John ashore to report to the Commodore.

Chloe greeted them warmly, happy to see that they were both well and without serious injury after the operations they had undertaken. Archie had first made a visit to the doctor, who expressed his approval of the treatment so far. He had the wound dressing changed.

She ushered them through to the Commodore's office and took a seat along with them.

The Commodore was busy at his desk. Having waved them to seats kept his attention on the documents he was working on.

John was not impressed, but waited patiently until the classic head rose and acknowledged their presence with a broad smile and, "Welcome back, gentlemen. A most successful exercise."

As John watched, Henry Carlisle raised the document in front of him and spoke, "I would have cancelled the last operation had I been aware that it was due. The job I have here is of much more importance. And it needed urgent action. As it is, we have lost irreplaceable time."

"The sabotage that delayed our return was the main cause of delay." John said politely.

"Yes, yes. I realise that aspect of the delay was not avoidable. But had you not disappeared when you did, it could have been discovered earlier." He shook his head in annoyance, "Anyway, water under the bridge now. This project is really important and it requires immediate action. What is the condition of the *Audax?* Will we be able to depend on it for the next two weeks?"

"You will, sir!" John's reply was sharper than he intended, but the Commodore was seriously annoying him.

"This task is to land the Marine commando in Italy. Because of the current stalemate of our forces at Salerno, their objective will be to raise enough noise to disrupt local communications and make difficulties for the expected German forces trying to prevent the handover of Italy to the Allies.

Turning to Archie, the Commodore added, "Your part in this operation is to secure the area, and make it possible to channel Special Forces into the countryside. Given the success of this incursion, we will be able to secure more advanced beachheads up the length of the country, and cut off any pockets of German military, isolating them from supplies and support.

"The First Officer can pass over the full briefing notes, based on moving out within three days. Both ships will be involved."

He rose to his feet, "This is an important part of the effort to cross Italy off the axis map.

"The landing at Salerno was, in effect, unopposed. Delays were due to the lack of inspired leadership, and bad intelligence at the time."

His tone implied that, had he been involved all would have gone off like clockwork.

The pair left the Commodore's office and joined Chloe in her office for the briefing documents. Neither of them had any time for the posturing of their leader. Any illusions they had entertained when he first appeared had been sadly dispelled.

"This is rubbish." Archie held the briefing notes in his hand. "There is no reason to suppose that we will be in a position to do anything to prevent the German army marching down Italy, without a regiment of our own troops to back us up."

"Ah!" John said reflectively. "But we are Special Forces. The normal rules do not apply."

"What on earth do you mean by that?" Archie asked quizzically.

"Bridges, railways, and roads." John said succinctly. "That's the way we can slow them down if we have the time, depending on which way they choose as their main route south. Once they are decided, it will take time to alter their line of march. We concentrate on mining the bridges and tunnels on the chosen routes. Actually blowing them only when they are committed. If we have time, we can possibly cause even more problems by getting into alternative routes. It will delay them regardless, even if it does not stop them. But what would you do if you were finding annoying opposition to your land forces in a country like Italy?"

Not waiting for the answer, John said, "Use sea. Convoys, and coasters, following both sides of the country. Delay, delay, delay!"

Archie looked at John, "Bodies?"

"Partisans." John said. "Starting with Corsicans. They have contacts on the mainland. We can ship them over. They can team with your lads for the initial booby traps. And remember, our crews are the biggest bunch of pirates in the Med. All can use small arms and we have plenty of explosive expertise between our boffins and the torpedo rates. We can target the harbours they need, and ambush any convoys they manage to run. But first things first! The land traps."

Chloe found maps of the mainland of Italy and laid them out on the planning table.

"Do we have any SOE assets in Italy?" Archie asked, "If so can we contact them and get help from their local contacts?"

John and Chloe exchanged looks. "The boss won't like it," Chloe said.

"Then we won't tell him until we have to. If we have to. Try the High Commission here and the Office of Naval Intelligence. They should know or can find out. But impress on them to keep it quiet."

John left it to Chloe to get on with that, while he and Archie bent over the maps, seeking suitable choke points. There were not many in the northern part of the country, so it was there they concentrated. They were driven by the urgency of the need to act before the German machine got up to speed.

***

They selected Montepescali as their first point of attack. The rail and road crossings followed the western coast of Italy. Then Chiusi and Perugia. Both were choke points on secondary routes south. All three had road and rail links through the mountainous country to the south.

There was still stalemate at Salerno. Elsewhere in the country, the unrest of the civilian population became more widespread. Elements of the Italian army rebelled against the injunctions, placed officially on action against their former allies. And the German reaction became more violent. Suppression of insurgency, so called, was ruthlessly carried out.

Archie and his men were sent in by air and sea. Selected points were prepared for destruction. Bridges and viaducts were the prime requirements, mountain passes and road complexes, especially those where by-passing was not possible. Any partisans encountered were recruited, where they willing, to make life difficult for anyone trying to by-pass or clear the obstructions created by the saboteurs.

Chloe's efforts with the High Commission spooks paid off with contacts. These were mainly of people willing to hide agents and pass information about troop movements and other activity by the occupying forces.

They also received enthusiastic support from the Air Force, who were roped in to drop supplies to the units on the ground. Explosives and weapons were dropped to the teams in country.

A major contribution came from the SAS based in Alexandria, whose attention was divided between the Greeks and the Italians. Their small craft activity on both sides of the Adriatic Sea had gathered contacts on the east coast of Italy. Now it made for a more complete picture of the problem John and Archie faced.

With the mainland side under way, they chose that time to approach the Commodore.

John undertook the task of briefing him, and also bringing him to take an active part in the operation. Chloe and John made their presentation, pointing out that Archie was in Italy and unable to attend at this time. Having gone into the planning so far in detail, John played his ace. "Sir, we have done as best we can with the land aspects of this task. We wondered if we could persuade you to command the sea operation. We need to mine harbours and intercept convoys, if this operation is to work to the lengths that you planned. You would need to rally extra support for the interdiction of any enemy convoys both from the Air Force and the Navy. You would obviously be in overall command of the operation, to ensure things occur in the correct order, to forestall any reaction by the Germans."

John could tell from the gleam in Carlisle's eye that he had hit the right buttons. Suddenly, the operation he had thrown at his team looked workable. In overall command, the glory would fall where it belonged. After all it was his idea.

"I will run this past the RAF and the Navy. I'm pretty sure we will get the co-operation that we need.

"I do agree that this is one job where the rank would count. Well done to you all! You have earned your salt on this one. I will see that the powers are made aware of how much this is down to the efforts of you three."

As they left the office John shrugged. To Chloe he said, "We best not hold our breath waiting to receive the credit for this."

Chloe grinned, "Unless it all goes wrong?"

For an operation of that size and style there was no way of predicting its success or failure, it was a matter of 'suck it and see'.

As John said afterwards, "It was like the curate's egg, good in parts."

***

The opening salvo was the rail line at Montepescali. The first of the major arms-carrying trains had been loaded with tanks and APC's when the culverts beneath the marshalling yard exploded spectacularly. There was no question of its effectiveness. Points, the signal box, and every line passing through the area, were blown far and wide. In addition, the trucks in the shunting area, loaded with coal and iron ore, were shattered, their contents projected through windows and even walls, creating an enormous area of devastation right through the centre of the yards.

Following the blast, A second explosion from the direction of the road junction created a machine gun hail of shattered asphalt, which wounded when it hit flesh. The troop convoy on its way south lost the first three trucks as a culvert, packed with explosives, shattered the lead truck. Incendiaries on the second truck ignited when it struck the wreck of the exploding leader. The third truck took the brunt of the double explosion, and troops packed in the rear were shredded by metal shrapnel from the exploded trucks.

The convoy commander was frustrated by the fact that, in neither case, was there a way round the obstructions created. Because of the pressure being put on him, he sought ways of bye-passing the blockage. There were some cargo ships in Livorno, so he arranged to backtrack to the port, while crews got to work to clear the obstructions to road and rail services.

The coastal ferry at Livorno was normally used on the service to Ajaccio on Corsica. He arranged for it to be loaded with as many trucks as possible, and despatched south to Civitavecchia, the next port down coast capable of handling the unloading of the ferry. The ship survived the passage out into the open sea, but then abruptly lost its propellers and all means of propulsion, the wind and the sea pushing it inexorably towards the coast and disaster.

Tugboats sent to rescue the ferry suffered a similar fate. Both lost the entire stern of their craft and sank at the narrows, where the two arms of the harbour construction reached out to the open sea.

The delaying methods used on the east side of the country were sadly not as effective as those on the west. One road explosion was only partially effective. As a result, apart from the immediate damage inflicted on the trucks, men, and equipment involved, the remainder of the column was able to get through. A rail embankment was mined to collapse spectacularly which delayed the rail traffic, but it was cleared within the week and the flow restarted.

The Commodore collected the plaudits for a job pretty well done in the circumstances. He actually managed to recommend both the senior officers involved for decorations. John received a bar to his DSC. Archie received a DSC. The Commodore received a bar to his DSO, so all were covered, with the exception of Chloe. The omission was remarked by both Archie and John and, somewhat reluctantly, by Henry Carlisle, who still seemed to have the idea that Chloe was some sort of secretary, and therefore not on the list for consideration for an award.

Chapter twenty-five

Portsmouth

The Mediterranean theatre became more and more the province of the major armed forces. The SAS from Alexandria continued its activity in Greece and the Greek islands, but in the Western Mediterranean, the Commando sections of Marines and Army took over more and more of the activities, up to now handled by the Commodore and his section.

It was with some relief that, after interview with the Admiral-in-Command in Gibraltar, the ML and *HMS Audax* were relocated to Portsmouth once more. The Commodore was also transferred there, but in an altered capacity, working directly with the agents and a section of small craft which were still employed to smuggle people in and out of the still-occupied coast line.

Chloe was in charge of the Communications section in Portsmouth.

HMS Audax underwent further maintenance and was back escorting coastal convoys, commanding a flotilla of four frigates and two corvettes, while the ML, still nominally attached to John's command, was utilised for commando raids along the French coastline. The year faded into 1944, and, though the corner had been turned, the battle was still a determined grimly-fought affair. The flotilla commanded by John was now exercising with other ships and landing craft, prior to the invasion of Europe.

Amy Martin appeared in Portsmouth once more. John and Chloe were now unofficially engaged. An open secret among the staff in the Dockyard, they were both invited to a function in the wardroom of the Headquarters, to celebrate the engagement of Amy to Rear Admiral Henry Carlisle DSO and bar RNR.

John and Chloe managed to get together. As they snuggled down in each other's arms, they talked of the sort of things that couples discuss in the circumstances. They had received the invitation. John mentioned it to Chloe, "I see the Commodore made it then. What does he do now?"

Chloe smiled. "He is currently running the North Sea coastal services, sending coal to Newcastle etc. Generally keeping the seas open for law-abiding ships to pass without let or hindrance. I believe that would be a correct interpretation of his duties."

"Not a happy man then?"

Chloe nodded. "Influence only goes so far, I'm afraid. I met Vice Admiral Howard when he visited the yard, while you were involved with that business of the E boats at Slapton Sands. I asked about the Commodore. He mentioned that Carlisle had been promoted to keep him out of direct action scenarios. It seemed he was too casual with other people's lives. The echoes of his early days in the Med seemed to have caught up with him and his present posting will be his last active post."

"They didn't tell you then?" John said.

"What?" Chloe asked.

John looked at her, and then slowly told her the real story of Slapton Sands. "Not everyone knows the true story. There had been in effect a massacre. Troop-filled ships were moving to Lyme Bay. They were unescorted through an admin, balls-up. E-boats attacked them without opposition and had a field day. We lost troops and ships, which were unable to defend themselves." He paused, white faced at the memory.

"We arrived too late to really do more than help to clear up. The entire action actually took place off Portland Bill. The story of Slapton was propaganda. They were caught with their pants down. The escort for the LST's had been damaged and pulled out, and no one had requested replacements. *Audax* could have been there had we been told. There was also a flotilla of MTB's in Portland harbour which could have taken over the escort. As it was no one acted, and the E-boats had a field day. We arrived on the scene and saw the tail end of the departing enemy boats, and then were neck deep in finding survivors and removing the evidence. No one was prepared to admit officially to being the cause of the disaster. With large numbers of US and British troops gathered, they did not want it known that the attack had been so close to home. So moving the scenario to Slapton Sands was dreamed up, and we shifted all the evidence to that location, Needless to say, we were all sworn to secrecy."

He stopped pale-faced. The effect of the blunder with the resulting carnage had really upset John.

Chloe held him close, as he relived the scenes of the sinking ships and the bodies floating on the surface of the sea.

After a while John stirred and kissed her. "So what was it you were saying?"

John looked at Chloe brow raised.

With a sigh, Chloe said, "I was told this under strict instruction to keep it to myself. There is an operation scheduled, that you may be involved in."

John smiled wryly. "I told you mine so I guess you can tell me yours. Your secret will be safe with me.

Archie has just returned from Italy. He was wounded again apparently. He said that one of his contacts in the war office told him that he would be just in time to join me in some madcap scheme that Carlisle had dreamed up. From what you say, his friend has it wrong. I confess it's a relief."

Chloe looked concerned. "Did he say what it was? The scheme. I mean."

It was John's turn to look serious. "He said something about Rotterdam."

Chloe looked worried. "If that is true, it's bad news. The job is critical and was set to be run by the specialist Captain who set it up. If Carlisle has managed to get his oar in, you could be in serious danger."

"But, if Carlisle has been sidelined, there should be no problem surely?"

"The trouble is he is still in a position where his influence can gain him support, and many still think of him as a modern version of Sir Frances Drake. I'll put my feelers out when I get back in the office. You will know as soon as I do."

She turned and looked at him anxiously. There was the odd grey hair beginning to show, and he was looking tired, she thought.

***

Lt Col Archie Cameron DSC MC RM sat facing John Macklin in the day cabin on *HMS Audax*, his beret on the chair beside him and both men were looking at the brief on the table between them.

Archie looked up at John. "We will be pushing our luck to get away with this."

John smiled. "Why am I not surprised? When I look at this program, I see the fine hand of a man who believes that divine light shines from his backside. The actual rail terminal covers a huge area of ground, and will undoubtedly need an enormous amount of explosive to stop its operation."

Archie shook his finger at John. "The order calls for signal lights to direct air bombing only."

"But it also calls for prepared measures to be taken, in the event that the bombing is ineffective."

"Having examined the worst case scenario, let's look at the basic task and see if there is a better way to deal with the problem. The train is coming to the junction on Thursday in three weeks time.

"It will stay overnight before proceeding to Koln via Dusseldorf. The train will be empty on arrival, but it will have a full complement of staff and passengers when it departs in the early hours of Friday morning.

"It will include superior Pullman carriages, with sleeping accommodation, dining facilities and a lounge, sufficient for eight people and their partners. It is expected that the passengers will include Albert Speer Herman Goering and Martin Bormann. Others will be present but, on the basis of the three alone, the exercise is worth it. It will undoubtedly be well guarded. So where does it come from in the first place?"

Archie smiled. "Where else? From Dusseldorf. The main attraction is a meeting in Rotterdam of the three main actors, all will either be there or passing through at the time.

"Martin Bormann is the instigator of the meeting which, I believe, is rumoured to be held because there seems to be a move to sort out Herr Hitler's replacement, in the event he becomes an embarrassment or gets killed in the interim."

John looked at Archie open-mouthed.

Archie watched the questions coming up and burst out laughing. Got you!" He said, laughing at John's stricken look. "Fact is we have no idea. It says so here," he pointed to the last page of the briefing document.

"How do we sabotage the train when it will be under security control from Dusseldorf onwards."

"What we do is substitute the carriages."

"You have to be kidding. How do we substitute carriages?" Archie sounded bemused but interested.

John continued, "The train is being brought through to Rotterdam. It is being checked over there and refurbished. We have a copy of the main lounge car already. The others are undergoing alterations as we speak. Luck was on our side. The closed bodyworks in the yards at Rotterdam were reopened to inspect the train, though half of the works are still closed because of bomb damage. The substitute carriages will be on a line next to the real train, screened from view by a false wall."

"What do we do about blowing things up?" Archie asked.

"Basically, we use this." John rolled a piece of pipe over the desk to Archie.

When he picked it up, he realised that it was lighter than it should have been. He looked up in surprise.

"It's not metal, It's just made to look like it. We have replaced several of the under-floor pipes with this stuff. It's all explosive. At the right moment it will be set off, hopefully destroying the entire train."

John sat back, his dissertation complete.

"Where does Admiral Carlisle come into this?"

"Originally, sitting offshore in *HMS Audax,* unless he becomes involved, in which case, I suggest he will be in town with us."

Archie looked stunned. "We cannot have an Admiral in Rotterdam with us."

"We may not have the choice. Just pray that the rumours are wrong. Or that the powers decide that the Admiral stays and supervises from here. While I agree his presence anywhere where we are involved is not welcome, at least then we will be able to get on with things, without him there looming in the background micromanaging everything."

The air of foreboding was not dispelled, as the orders came through assigning Rear-Admiral Carlisle to the operation. Unfortunately, his part was not detailed specifically, which placed John and Archie in no man's land, until the clarification was received. The Admiral would be responsible for the outline planning, leaving the conduct of the operation to Commander Macklin DSC RN and Lt Col Cameron DSC MC RM.

It was with a certain amount of trepidation that the two officers presented themselves at the Admiralty, to discuss their part in the operation with the Admiral.

Neither was re-assured by the manner of the Admiral when they entered his presence. The breezy, smiling face deceived neither man, as John mentioned afterwards. "It is déjà vu. That man had not changed in any way, apart from adding two inches to his waistline. He is still the 'boy's own hero' in his own mind. I do not trust him to stay out of our faces. There is a blaze of glory in his future, and we are showing him the way to get there."

"Surely, he cannot interfere with our part. He is under direct orders of Vice Admiral Harrison." Archie, despite his words did not look too sure.

"Admiral Harrison has other things on his mind. This must be a small part of a big picture. Someone else will be persuaded to give Carlisle full hands-on control of the operation. He still has friends in high places." John shrugged. "We can only hope it does not happen."

He did not sound too hopeful when he said it.

The two friends made their way to the Strand where they met Chloe at the Savoy for lunch.

She did her best to cheer them up, but it was difficult. It seemed that she also agreed with John, that Carlisle would be involved fully with the upcoming operation, and that would place her two favourite men in jeopardy."

***

The team was all lined up in the wardroom of the ML. Chloe sat at the table with a pile of packages beside her. All the packages had codes on them. Each had a designated purpose. Beside the list of team member's names was the list of codes. As the men stepped up they gave their name. A code package was checked off against it for the package passed over.

The ML set off across the channel. The men had all been briefed. Offshore from the Dutch coast, they took their places in the rubber dinghies as they came alongside, in turn.

While the transfer was under way a second power boat appeared, an MTB. It gave the recognition signal and came alongside the offside of the ML. John had already been landed and was organising the raiders, despatching them to their locations and making sure that their combined headsets (ear phone and mike) were working before they set out.

Archie was still in the ML, waiting for the final few men to be passed through to the dinghies. His heart sank as the voice of Carlisle could be heard snapping, at some dilatory seaman who did not move fast enough.

Carlisle appeared, dressed in a roll neck sweater with epaulettes ablaze with his rank, and wearing a black beret, with an RN badge. The gunbelt and holster housed a Browning .45 automatic, with a loop hooked over the hammer, to prevent it being jolted out of the open holster. Archie stood open mouthed at the sight.

"Don't you salute senior officers in the Royal Marines?" The caustic comment jerked him to his feet.

Archie saluted hurriedly. "With respect, sir. I did not expect to see an Admiral in an enemy harbour, on a secret operation at 20.00hrs. I can only presume that some important matter had caused the cancellation of the operation, or that the invasion of Europe is about to begin here in Rotterdam harbour. Since I see no sign of an invading army, I presume it is a cancellation. I will inform the Commander."

"Stop right there, Colonel, there is no cancellation. I am merely here to support your operation, not to cancel it."

The MTB that had brought the Admiral had already cast off, and was making it's way quietly out past the breakwater.

"With all due respect, Admiral, you presence here is an embarrassment. Far from being helpful you have created a security risk that we could well do without." He turned to Alex. "Please escort the Admiral below. If there is any attempt made to come ashore or interfere in any other way, lock him in the brig."

Alex looked a bit worried.

Archie looked at him, "We have 24 men including the man WHO planned this entire operation, ashore in enemy territory. The last thing we need is a maverick lumbering about and upsetting the entire operation, putting everyone at risk. As officer in charge here, I have given my orders and I expected them to be obeyed. Understood!"

Alex snapped to attention, saluted. "Yes, Sir." Turning to the Admiral, he said, "If you will just take a seat, sir. We will despatch the remaining members of the team. Then we will be able to brief you on what is happening, and hopefully, what we expect to happen thereafter."

Alex indicated a seat at the inboard end of the cabin and turned to see Archie into the dinghy.

Furiously, Henry Carlisle made to step forward. He was stopped by the right arm of CPO Peters. "Now, sir. If you will just take the seat the officer has indicated, we will soon get things sorted out."

Carlisle started to raise his voice. "Stand down, P.O.! I'll have that hook, and you....." The voice died away, as Rear Admiral Henry Carlisle DSO RNR collapsed silently into the waiting arms of CPO Peters.

"Doc! Bring your bag, now!" The urgent voice of the CPO made it clear it was urgent.

The SBA arrived with his bag, took one look at the Admiral and dropped to his knees beside him. Turning him on to his side, he drew out smelling salts and waved them under Carlisle's nose.

The Admiral awoke with a jerk, shying away from small bottle. "Put that damn thing away," he said. "What is going on....?" He realised where he was and obviously remembered what had been happening.

He sat up looking at the CPO. "I collapsed?"

Peters nodded. "Yes, Sir. Just as you were getting into your stride."

The SBA spoke, "Can I do anything, sir?"

"I'm afraid not. They tell me that there is no cure. I'm not supposed to get upset." The messman brought a cup of tea, and a glass of rum which Carlisle took gratefully.

"What is the problem?" Peters asked.

"Brain tumour!" He sat back. "It's inoperable. I decided I would rather go during action, than tamely in bed. I should have realised that I could be putting others in danger. But I could only think of the horror of dying by inches." He took his head in his hands.

"What does your fiancée think?" Alex asked.

"She doesn't know," Carlisle said. "She will not be interested in me now."

Alex looked doubtful, then to the CPO he said, Keep him here."

Peters nodded. "He'll be fine, sir."

***

The team assembled at the rendezvous and were given their last minute instructions. John and Archie stood and watched them disappear in their multiple directions before heading for the section of the yard where the switch was being set up.

The landing party, with the exception of John and Archie, were all supplied with explosives designed to reduce the yards to rubble. Once they had been placed, the team would re-assemble to perform their other assigned role, that of acting as back-up in the event the explosives in the substitute carriages failed to go off.

The soldiers surrounding the Pullman carriages were being relieved. The critical time for the operation had arrived. A winch at the far end of the carriage group started to slowly pull the cleared carriages away. The soldiers had been assembled in the warehouse beside the line, ready to march off, while the relieving troops, Feldgendarmarie, were noisily climbing from their transport. The two guards, keeping an eye on things for the entire critical period, were distracted by the two replacements, who were in fact Dutch partisans from Arnhem, relieved them to join their departing unit.

Properly dressed in Wermacht uniforms, the bi-lingual men had passed as Germans on several occasions in the past.

The cleared carriages disappeared into the darkness, the substitute carriages were towed into place unnoticed. These carriages came to rest as the relief guards streamed out of the warehouse

Watching, John and Archie gave a collective sigh of relief. Phase one complete.

The team gathered at their assembly point, alongside the substituted carriages, now switched to an alternate line. The group gathered in silence. When all were accounted for. John stood by while Archie led them off to attack the yard control offices.

***

Henry Carlisle, Rear Admiral, was confused. The problem with his brain tumour had created gaps in his memory. Occasionally it created painful spears of fire which almost paralysed him. At the moment, he was aware that the Chief Petty Officer was looking after him, and now he must stay here in the bunk. There was something troubling him however. There was a detail about the current operation which could cause things to go dramatically wrong. He lay trying to remember what it was. The answer came in a single instant and then was gone. The important thing was he remembered what it was.

He sat up, surprised to find how easy it was once more. Swinging his legs off the berth, he stood swaying slightly, but upright.

Donning his cap, he opened the cabin door and walked through to the wardroom. Alex and a Marine Lieutenant, Ken Ord. were drinking coffee. Carlisle could smell the sharp scent of the brew. As he entered he spoke. Only the words came out wrong, He knew what he wished to say, but both Alex and Marine looked at him blankly, unable to understand what he was saying.

"Oh no!" Alex said. "That bloody tumour has caused a stroke or something like it. We'll need to get him back to bed."

Carlisle heard and understood her but, realising he could not understand him, he turned and strode through to the hatch on to the side deck. There was a dinghy alongside with a seaman at the helm. Henry jumped into the boat and waved to the shore. Unhesitatingly, the seaman started up, slipped the mooring rope, and made for the shore. The quiet electric motor, unheard, in among the overall clutter from the surrounding sea.

On the shore the figure of the Admiral disappeared in the direction of the marshalling yards. The Marine Lieutenant Ken Ord and Alex landed in time to catch a glimpse of the figure disappearing in the direction of the yard. They dashed off in pursuit.

In the spot-lit area around the train, there were several people waiting, both men and women boarding the train.

The Train Conductor met the people at the door of the Pullman car. He invited some in others not, though there seemed plenty of seats available.

To Carlisle's clouded mind it was trivial. He opened his mouth to say, 'Warn the Commander that this is a trap'. What came out was gibberish. Desperate to find his men and give warning, he ran into the lighted area beside the coaches.

The sight of a British Admiral appearing in the spot light in an enemy city stunned the troops for a moment. Henry pulled out his Browning.45 and cocked it, then fired three shots into the sky. As Alex and Ken Ord stood in the shadows watching, a blaze of fire from concealed positions around the area, caught the Admiral, jerking his body back and forth as he fell to the ground.

Several of the figures boarding the train fell also, as they were caught in the crossfire.

Watching, Ken lifted his Sten gun, only to feel Alex grip it and force it down. His whisper, clear to him at least. "Don't you dare. That has warned the Commander and the Colonel. It's up to them now."

After a sad look at the crumpled figure of the Admiral, they returned to the dinghy and back to the waiting ML.

John, able to see the carnage as the Admiral was shot, realised that they had nearly fallen into a trap. The attack on the yard offices had been planned by John and Archie without reference to anyone else, so John was forced to wait at the rendezvous, until Archie and his men returned.

John filled Archie in, and indicated the area still floodlit, the bodies still where they had fallen. "We can do nothing about this, I'm afraid. The ambush is still in place." As he spoke, men began to appear, in all some thirty SS troops. They wandered through the scatter of bodies turning them over with their booted feet. Showing a callous disregard for the dead, they removed the wounded.

As they watched, an engine and tender chuffed busily down the line and attached itself to the string of carriages. The soldiers ran and boarded the train as it began to move off. They left the dead lying where they were. John looked at Archie. He lifted the detonator. Archie shrugged and a smile crossed his face. As the train disappeared into the darkness beyond the floodlit area, John turned the key on the detonator and Archie pressed the button. The train had made 200 yards, when the button connected and the train dissolved into a million pieces.

John and Archie and their party were sheltered, but they were still affected by the suction created by the explosion. Both being prepared, recovered first. John looked out into the area still lit by the wildly swinging arc light.

"Fetch the Admiral." John called. Four of the men ran out, picked up the body of the dead man and hurried it into the shadows once more.

The party made their way back to the shore and set up defence positions, while the dinghies shuttled back and forth, taking the people back to the ML. As the ML left the shore the explosive charges planted by the raiders started to create their own part of the mayhem of the evening.

In the small sick bay, the body of the Admiral lay. Ken, John and Archie stood looking at the body.

"He saved us from the ambush." John said quietly.

"How did he know?" Archie asked.

Ken produced a signal. "This was in his pocket."

The message was a decoded warning from a Dutch mole in the local SS HQ.

"Why did he not say in the first place?" John wondered.

Ken once more came up with the answer they could all accept. "He knew about his condition, He did not want to die like a cabbage. He intended to die in battle somehow. I think he would have passed the message on when he was ashore with you."

"It will go down as 'killed in action' while saving the lives of the rest of the party."

And that was the way it was reported.

***

The section carried on under the temporary command of Captain Harry Winchester DSO RNR, a retread from the 1938 cutback of the navy. His career had covered service in China and India, where his experience of dealing with subversive groups in both nations had given him the right attitude to the infiltration of agents and raiders.

John and Archie found an instant rapport with Harry. The three entered into the planning and disposition of their resources based on the needs of the many departments involved.

The regular traffic to and from the continent was undertaken by the ML. With the additional services of Chloe where a bilingual person was needed, there was no need to expand the team.

With the invasion of Europe well under way, there was a decreasing length of coastline to infiltrate, and less reason for the retention of HMS Audax for the use of the Special Operations section.

The Captain called John into the office. He arrived to find Archie was already seated, awaiting the Captain's arrival. Archie was as mystified as John over the sudden call. But the pair had to wait another half hour until their patience was rewarded. Captain Winchester arrived with Chloe in tow, and a bundle of files under his arms.

Harry Winchester got straight down to business.

"I have a train for you, running from Alborg down Denmark to Hamburg in Germany. The train will be carrying heavy water from Norway."

"What is heavy water?" Archie asked.

"I'll explain later. First find a place and a way to stop the train, so that we can steal the shipment.

"The train is carrying ball bearings and gold. I expect the Germans to think the raid is for the gold and ball bearings, the water theft being collateral, because it was there."

Archie said, "Surely they won't fall for that? Why would anyone want to steal water?"

John corrected him. “Heavy water. Imported from Norway?” he looked keenly at Captain Winchester. “We are talking about an atom bomb?”

Startled, Harry Winchester’s eyes narrowed. “What do you know about atom bombs?”

John grinned, “Not a lot, but I do know heavy water can be used in a suggested process to split atoms. I cannot think of any other reason for Germany to import it, or in fact for us to steal it.”

The Captain relaxed, “Ideally, we take over the train and divert it to a coastal station where we can transfer the goods to our own craft.

“Esbjerg would be ideal. It is a ferry port and thus set up to deal with heavy freight. All we need to do is make sure we get it there.”

“And of course make sure that the port conditions are secure to load and transport the goods safely back to England,” John added.

“All with the help of a company of commandoes, I presume,” Archie added. “Diverting the train is the first item on the agenda. That is best achieved by chopping off the alternative lines. Sabotage, I presume. We will also have to make sure that the enemy do not suspect that the damage is linked to our exercise.”

The planning for the series of sabotage attacks commenced immediately. A provisional group of targets was selected to include the rail junctions needed, for their routes to stress the random of the partisan activity.

Having made their choices, each of the group, Captain Winchester, Chloe, Archie, and John adopted a quarter of the sites to examine in detail. It was important to choose targets where the collateral damage would be minimised. Despite the importance of the core target being successfully achieved, nobody wanted to bring retribution down on the local civilian population.

Captain Winchester took the list of suggestions. Having studied them, he selected the first three. "The links between Randers and Aarhus, Esbjerg and Kolding Struer and Herning, and Skjern and Herning. All are possible easy routes to the east coast. I believe we have to concentrate on keeping that train from the east coast ports."

"I agree. I also see the point of scattering our sabotage. It makes it more like an attack on the railways, rather than forcing trains to use a specific route." John thought for a moment, then added, "I think we should do (Esbjerg and Kolding) first, and work north. That way we should cover our purpose until the last minute."

Archie said, "How are we situated with the local partisans."

Chloe answered, "Better off than anywhere else in Europe. The Scandinavian countries all have dedicated partisan networks. Elsewhere, the setup is much more casual. In France, for instance, despite the groups that we encourage, in each of them there are two so-called, who profess but do nothing. When they act it is to steal, often from their own side. Now we are in Europe, there are suddenly more members of the Maquis than ever before. All, I believe, to cover either previously committed crimes, collaboration, or cowardice. Whatever the reason, the example set by the Danish partisans so far has been committed to freedom from the occupation. Simply, they can be depended on."

"Thank you, Chloe," The Captain added, "That needed to be said, and it has to be kept in mind with our dealings with the rest of Europe." He paused. "I will leave you with your planning, and recommend you get together with Chloe over the use of partisans in the operation.

All three presented workable plans for the attacks within the twenty-four hours. The operation would call for the destroyer to participate, since the protection of booty from the train was more important than anyone was really admitting. Before the expedition was committed it had been cleared with a back-up situation arranged.

Given the limited time available, the team were pleased to get things set up so fast. The main problem, as far as John was concerned, was that he could not get over the feeling that he had forgotten something.

All three went through each other's plans' to cover for errors and omissions. Only one or two minor things came up.

When the final departure was set, all had done all they could to make sure they had covered everything.

***

The voyage across was not taxing. There was time to reach the target area in darkness. They had detoured north before returning southward, arriving at their destination as dusk faded into night.

The partisans had arranged to meet the landing parties. Soon, the only group still around was that scheduled for the removal of the most northerly of the rail attacks.

John stood on the beach, watching the tail lights of the group going to Aarhus disappear down the road east. With a sigh he turned his attention to his own group.

The small convoy consisted of two vehicles. Dressed in the uniform of as SS officer, John travelled in the first, alongside his CPO also dressed in SS uniform. The driver was a genuine German, actually a Jew, and a full time member of the Jewish Battalion in Britain. When German-clad soldiers were required to pass as the genuine article, the battalion could provide, and did so.

The explosives were packed in both vehicles. In the bigger one were six soldiers including a sergeant, all in Waffen SS uniform, plus four civilians, partisans, apparently prisoners. The small convoy started out to the south to cut the line between Esbjerg and Kolding.

The flat countryside was vaguely visible in the starlight and, though the moon would appear later, it was liable to be dimmed by the hazy layer of cirrus cloud that was creeping across the sky and blocking out the stars as it progressed.

The guide muttered that they were approaching the roadblock, a problem for which they had prepared. The small vehicle pulled up at the barrier. The guard on duty stepped over to the car, rifle on its strap over his shoulder, his cigarette placed on a tin lid on the small table set next to the chair he had been using.

The driver, wearing the rank of Sergeant, took one look and snapped at the man as he climbed out of the vehicle.

The unfortunate guard suddenly snapped to attention, fumbling with his rifle getting from the slung position into his hands. Not surprisingly, he almost dropped it in his panic.

The noise of the snapped orders from the Sergeant brought the guard commander out of the small building that had, over the occupation period, become a permanent roadblock.

Leutnant Horst Staffen was a frustrated firebrand, forced to wear glasses because of an astigmatism. His chances of field promotion were nil. His only real outlet was to bully his men and any junior rank who passed through his barrier.

Peering at the kubelwagen, he made out the Untersturmfuhrer (Junior Lieutenant) sitting in the rear of the vehicle, and snapped, "What is going on here?"

John, dressed as Sturmbannfuhrer (Major) stepped out of the vehicle and turned to look at Leutnant Staffen.

It has been said there are people who can, with a look, reduce a grown man to tears. While Staffen's vision was impaired, and it was at night, the lights on the barrier were not exactly blinding. He was not actually made to cry. It was a close run thing. His body spasmed into a rigid state of attention. The salute was equally correct, only released when the casual wave, given by John in acknowledgement, indicated his acceptance.

Without a word, John waved at the barrier casually, and reboarded the kubelwagen followed by the driver.

Staffen shouted to the guard, "Open the barrier."

Fumbling with his rifle and almost tripping over his feet, the guard managed to raise the barrier and wave the two vehicles through.

After a further short conversation with the hapless guard, Staffen returned to the building and noted two vehicles passed through. Realising, that he had not got the number of either vehicle, he carefully erased the entry. The lack of ID for the two vehicles might have reflected upon his efficiency. After all, he reassured himself, both vehicles were German Army, with German personnel aboard.

CPO Peters smiled to himself as the kubelwagen continued down the road. He enjoyed his job, and especially working with his present boss. Too many of the regular naval officers were peacetime ornaments. Whatever else Lieutenant Commander Macklin was, he was no ornament. He would do for Chief Petty Officer Peters, that was for sure.

Out of sight of the roadblock, the driver allowed the truck to overtake, then settled in behind it. The partisans in the truck guided it to the agreed location of their target and the men de-bussed. The cutting chosen was a quarter mile long. The men immediately set to with spades and picks, digging holes in the near vertical banks. Two of the soldiers disappeared, one to the right, the other left, to watch the approaches to the railway. John strolled down the track with the leader of the partisans. "Shall we lift alternate rails before we blow the cutting?"

Nils Jordon smiled looking at his companion with respect. "Are you always as devious as this?" He asked.

John shrugged. "Needs must!" I have to confess I enjoy tripping the enemy up wherever I can."

"Then let us do it, by all means," Jordon agreed. "We will be cutting it fine for time. Getting back to the ship, and out of sight of the Germans, will be difficult if we are as late as I suspect we will be."

John looked at Nils. "Were you not aware that the ship is long gone. All the sabotage groups are here for the duration of the exercise. When all the tracks are blown, my men and I will leave. Just for a while, of course. We'll all be back for the celebrations when the Germans get kicked out of Denmark."

"The sooner the better." Nils added.

The work took as long, maybe longer than anticipated. They managed to remove two rails, which were dropped into the nearby river.

The men tidied themselves up beside the river and reboarded the truck. Once more the convoy set out, back the way they came. At the barrier there was no delay, the bar was lifted as soon as the convoy came into sight. As they passed the hut beside the road, one of the partisans dropped off a special parcel which rolled under the floor of the hut. It was standing on low concrete blocks to provide a level floor on the uneven ground. Timed to go off when the main charges were set to explode, the charge solved any problems of Leutnant Staffen and his small command at the roadblock.

The unscheduled train that set out from Aarhus to Vejle contributed to a series of railway disasters which all hit the system in Denmark at that time. The careful check up by the occupation troops of the other railway lines produced unexploded charges on several other lines, a situation that would have crippled communication between north and south, as well as east to west. The administration for the rail services heaved a sigh of relief that there was still a useable route from north to south, and even from east to west, albeit a tortuous one.

John, Chloe, and Archie looked at the chart with the blown areas of track illustrated. "Now, all we need is the train itself." Archie looked at John. "Any change? Do we know?"

Chloe answered, "No change, apart from the addition of the cruiser *HMS Wilmington,* which will be on hand when we take over the loading dock at Esbjerg. Her eight inch guns should make a difference.

The succeeding days, while the target date approached, were for John Macklin rather fraught. The number of things which could go wrong seemed to multiply whenever he lay down to sleep.

Going over in his head, he was still astonished at the fact that the only casualties from the sabotage raids had been three men with hernia's, acquired carrying lengths of rail away from the track, before exploding the charges.

All the teams were scattered around the area, concealed in barns and private houses throughout Jutland. Taking command of the train would not be a simple matter. Once taken, getting it to Esbjerg and offloading it was even more difficult, though the addition of the cruiser to the enterprise would improve their chances.

There were suggestions that air cover may be in the area at the time of the breakout from Esbjerg. No promises, but it would be useful. Everything seemed to depend on delaying the train takeover until it reached the immediate area of the ferry port. The less warning that was given the better. The partisans had volunteered to raid as many of the airfields as they could. The main bulk of available aircraft was involved against the invasion forces still fighting their way across France. However, nobody had any illusions that the Germans would not be very hard to handle when their precious cargo of difficultly acquired heavy water was involved.

The area selected for the takeover of the train was the area of Gjesing, as the train prepared to change lines to the cross-country line avoiding the direct route to the dock. It was pointed out that it was possible that the train would go into the docks, to relocate the engine to the front of the train, using the turntable. If that happened the team was ready to follow it in and take over at that time.

Three days to go, no change in the situation, though there had been an increase in activity among the counter-partisan troops. That task was currently undertaken by inefficient SS rather than the Feldgend-armarie, which could well be the reason that, apart from the extensive increase in mobile stop and search teams, the actual capture success rate remained at the same low level as before.

The partisans were hoping that the raid and capture of the special train would take the pressure off the local people, as the operation would be obviously a commando raid based overseas.

The list of targets that had been hit did not seem to have inclined the occupation troops to do other than increase security on their established bases. The partisan attacks on airfields had made it clear that the airfields were vulnerable. The numbers of damaged aircraft were important, as each one meant less pressure on the escaping raiding party. That, of course, depended on the raid being successful.

For John, finally back on board *HMS Audax,* the next few days were critical. He would much rather be ashore with Archie and his men in the circumstances. The next part of the raid was down to the Marine commandos. They were tasked with taking the train and making sure it reached the ferry port. The destroyer had to make sure that the port area was under British control long enough for the cargo to be transferred safely.

With the selection of the ferry port as the locus for shipping the goods out of Denmark, a fast ferry, which had been used on the service between Esbjerg and Harwich, was added to the raiding party. This had the effect of providing a skipper who knew the harbour and a custom-fitted ship for the efficient transfer of the cargo.

The plan to distribute the cargo between the destroyer and the ML had always seemed impractical, due to the sheer bulk and weights involved. The use of the ferry port had demanded that the vessels made a swift escape, which meant a fast ship for the cargo, preferably purpose built.

John Macklin sat in his cabin, as the report of the arrival of the *Orca* was announced. She was the latest of the ferries, completed just prior to the war; 28 knots and 8000 tons, the *Orca,* had been painted grey. Her lean shape had been altered with the addition of Bofors and pom-pom guns. Crewed by RNR, the ship had been a valuable addition to the harbour defence of Harwich.

Her skipper. Lt Commander Michael East RNR was experienced, having been the assigned captain of the *Orca* when she was taken into the ferry service in June 1938.

The TBS squawked. Michael East established contact with John Macklin, reporting the arrival of his ship and the fact that she was ready in all aspects for the task at hand.

For the two succeeding days, the two ships kept company and maintained their distance, ready for the final dash into the port.

Ken Ord and his platoon of marines were on board *Audax* ready for the initial dash ashore, to seize the quay and hold it under the guns of the destroyer until the train came alongside. The critical time would be the early hours of the morning, as they approached the harbour. Archie should by then be in control and in touch with the ships.

Archie had had problems. After all a plan could only be expected to survive the first move. From then on it was in the lap of the Gods, and down to the quick thinking of the raiders.

So far, the train had made up time and was approaching earlier than anticipated. There were extra troops on the train, and it was carrying 24 prisoners, to do the hard work for the arrangements of ramps and hoists, for the trans-shipping of the goods to the interisland steamer scheduled to take the cargo over to Kiel, in Northern Germany.

Archie had stationed his men at the junction on the outskirts of Esbjerg. With his two platoons spread both sides of the track, they began swinging aboard, as the train slowed to pass through the yards at the junction.

The troops on the train were relaxed, having passed without alarm through peaceful countryside for the last several hours.

The boarders were on the other hand, poised and alert for any threat, swiftly secured the men they encountered. They then moved up the train taking over the carriages one by one.

It was mainly a silent operation, the surprise complete. The sight of khaki-clad soldiers seemed to mesmerise the men they encountered. The SS men had, up to now, only encountered the uniforms on prisoner of war. The men, they had under guard in the second carriage, were in fact wearing similar uniforms. It had led to the impression that the prisoners had somehow escaped. The seconds, thus gained, gave the raiders the advantage, added to the effect of the blackened faces and the steady submachine guns in their hands.

The first real resistance came in the Pullman carriage where, it seemed, the officers had foregathered to eat dinner. An ill-judged grab for a gun, was answered by a burst of three bullets from two guns. The unhappy officer was not able to appreciate the joke, as he died from his wounds later that afternoon.

The train was going to the railway quay to rotate the engine and place it at the other end.

The prisoners were discovered and released. All were armed with the seized weapons of the enemy troops.

A Marine climbed over the tender to ensure the driver was aware that they would continue to the dock quay without stopping. This was the only other shot needed. The SS sergeant stationed with the driver tried a snapshot, and missed. He did not get another chance.

Thus the train was reported entering the dock side yards. The signal came to John that Archie was in control. There was no real reaction to the arrival of the two ships. John thought that the fact that both ships were flying the German ensign at the time had something to do with it.

Then the swift arrest of the officials and guards on the quay meant that the word did not immediately get out. The first sign of activity was the appearance of a half-track full of troops, led by a kubelwagen, at the end of the quay. The officer in the lead vehicle found himself looking down the barrel of a 5.0 inch gun.

The casual approach by Lieutenant Ken Dole RM would have seemed to some to be taking things too far. In fact, his manner reassured the German officer, who submitted to force majeure and surrendered his vehicles and men.

The train arrived. The trucks were halted opposite the *Orca,* and the unloading commenced.

The first shells from a concealed tank arrived, and struck the engine, creating a spectacular cloud of soot and steam, along with three boiled bodies. The half track, now manned by Marines, the 20mm cannon mounted in the rear manned and ready to fire, went off with a crash of gears into the streets of the town to locate the source of the tank gunfire.

The cool clipped accents of Ken Dole were soon heard, giving the location of the tank, and, at the same time, requesting fire to be directed at the bus station, currently in use as a tank park. The guns of *HMS Wilmington* dropped a salvo of three shells into the bus station, smashing seven of the close parked tanks. These were followed by a second salvo which brought down the building at the entrance to the area, reducing it to rubble and burying a tank on its way through. The three remaining tanks within the bus station were trapped. The crews bailed out hurriedly before the next salvo arrived. The tank that had opened proceedings was settled in between two buildings and had a supporting platoon of men with it. Ken signalled his sergeant to bring the bazooka, a handy weapon poached from the US army, specifically designed for anti-tank warfare. They worked their way into a position where they could get a clear shot at the Panther tank.

With the bazooka loaded and ready, Ken raised his captured MP40 sub machine gun and sprayed the entire magazine at the supporting German troops. He lifted a second weapon and repeated the action, emptying another magazine. As he finished, the sergeant lined up the bazooka and fired, dropping immediately to the ground.

The round impacted the turret of the tank, jamming it in place, having struck the joint where the turret rotates. The mounted machine gun fired in the general direction of the two marines, causing them to keep their heads down.

The clatter of the 20mm cannon from the half track, traced a line of destruction from the rear of the tank. The troops, surrounding the Panther, were caught exposed and several were injured before they could relocate. The support gave the two pinned down with the bazooka another chance at the tank. They reloaded and this time made sure that the tank could not move, the round taking the nearside track and front wheel. The lid opened and the crew tumbled out, accompanied by smoke and a flick of flame which rapidly became an inferno.

More troops were appearing, so Ken ordered his men to drop back to the quay. They all piled into the half-track and rumbled back to the protection of the destroyer.

Archie deployed his men. Their prisoners were all locked into one of the warehouses to release men from guarding them. The POW's brought on the train to unload the cargo were all now armed and helping with the unloading.

The garrison in the port was deployed to retake the quay, but their weapons were no match for the secondary armaments on the destroyer. The cruiser was targeting sites proposed by the partisans, the airfield being a priority.

The 8inch guns were firing explosive shells to create the maximum damage possible. The three big hangers were all in flames, and the runways had been peppered with shell holes, to the extent that no aircraft had been able to get off the ground.

The shell that hit the bomb store reduced the effectiveness of the base to zero, killing or injuring most of the people trying to save what they could.

The unloading of the train had to be done entirely by hand. The loading of the ship was a much easier task. The ferry side ramp was dropped, forming a gangway on to the main vehicle deck of the ferry. Using the lorries already on the quay, it was possible to load them from the train and drive them onto the ferry fully loaded. The entire operation took two hours. By the time they had extracted everything they wanted and the ships were ready to move, daylight was gone.

The two ships cast off, made their way out into the North Sea, and set course for the cruiser already seven miles offshore. They made contact and commenced their high speed dash for their lives.

The night gave them cover and would last for about ten hours. At maximum speed they could make about 250 nautical miles, still well within range of German aircraft. When dawn broke the sound of aero-engines put everyone on edge, until they realised that it was a squadron of Beaufighters, who took up position over the three ships.

Heinkel 111's appeared, accompanied by Messerschmitt 110's, and the air became filled with whirling, shooting aircraft. The ships began zigzagging and the Heinkels dropped low to attack the ships. All the guns on all three ships tracked round to the attacking bombers, and a storm of flack peppered the sky in front of them. The aircraft maintained their course though two dropped out trailing smoke and crashed into the sea. A third exploded, damaging the aircraft on both sides, causing both other aircraft to veer out of the formation. The other five aircraft flew steadily on passing through the ack-ack bursts. John could see the opening bomb doors on the leading aircraft. The formation was now weaving to line up with the changing course of the three ships.

The German fighters were losing the battle and a Beaufighter appeared behind the lead bomber. A burst of cannon fire sent the bomber into the sea, following the bombs tumbling from the open bomb doors. The bombs missed the ships. But the falling aircraft took the full impact of the bomb load dropped by his wingman, as his aircraft dropped its port wing and slipped below it's neighbour. The explosion from at least one of the bombs testified to the early activation of the bomb fuse. The unfortunate aircraft and crew disintegrated in the blast. The other bombs joining in added to the effect. The aircraft whose bombs were involved, also disintegrated as did the following aircraft.

The two surviving Heinkels jettisoned their bombs and turned for home, chased by another Beaufighter.

The two bombers, damaged by the exploding bomber, now returned to the attack, this time from the beam. Both were smoking from engine fires, so were unlikely to make it back to their base. Neither scored a hit. One scored a near miss, actually scraping the paintwork down the portside of *HMS Audax*. The engine room voice pipe whistled. John picked up the call.

"Bridge?"

"Engine room here, sir. We have stress damage just forward of the engine room bulkhead. I suggest we do something about it, before we break something. That will mean slowing down, Sir."

"I see." John looked around. The two smoking Heinkels were both skimming the water. While he watched they splashed down fairly level. To John it looked as though the survivors would have time to get out. The British fighters were forming up, the lead aircraft flashing a signal, which said that other aircraft were on their way to provide cover for the rest of the way home, ETA ten minutes. The cruiser answered with a swift 'thank you', and the aircraft departed.

John discussed the problem with the engine room, then informed the other ships that he would need to reduce speed. He instructed that the *Orca* and the *Wilmington* both continue to Harwich, leaving *HMS Audax* to make her way back at reduced speed.

A Catalina arrived on schedule shortly, followed by a trio of Mosquito fighter/bombers with extra fuel tanks, to take up the role of air cover.

With her speed cut to fifteen knots the destroyer was soon left behind, though the Catalina remained in sight for some time. John stood down the crew from action stations, but kept them in place, sending food around to be eaten at their post.

Leaving Alec on the bridge, John made his way down to the engine room to examine the damage in the compartment forward.

There was what John described as a pleat in the metal of the hull. When he touched the metal he could feel it flexing under his hand. He looked at Kit MacNish, the chief engineer, the question unspoken? Kit shook his head. "It should get us home, but....."

"What does that mean? 'but'"

The engineer looked at John seriously, "But we may lose her anyway."

John could not believe it. "Surely, this can be repaired?"

MacNish shook his head. "We cannot see the frames below this. The geometry of the lower hull has been distorted. The work required will be a dockyard job at least. That is, if the damage does not worsen by the time we get home."

"Is there anything I can do?" John asked. "Slow down more? Go astern?"

MacNish grinned and shook his head. "Skipper, if I think of something, I'll be in touch. Otherwise the odd prayer might help."

The sea was getting up as the wind rose. Alec commented on the forecast for gale force winds by the following day. "With luck, we'll be in harbour by then."

John thought about the damage and hoped he was right. The Catalina had returned to keep an eye on them, and *Mavis* came out to stand by *Audax* as she prepared to enter harbour.

After seven hours they were in sight of their destination. The sea was rough, the waves breaking up to ten feet. No problem at all for a healthy ship to be troubled by. *HMS Audax* was clearly not healthy. As she passed through the harbour entrance the crack, clearly heard across the harbour, was not a good sign.

On the bridge the engine room voice pipe tweeted. "Bridge," Alec said.

"Kit here, Alec. let the skipper know. The lower portside frame had snapped. We are taking water, though the bulkhead is holding. We'll need to shore it, until we get into dry dock."

John received the news calmly. He had a feeling that the luck that had followed the ship all this time had just run out.

Two harbour tugs came to take the ship in tow. The main engines were shut down. The generators were all working keeping the pumps going, but it required the additional pumps from the two tugs to keep the levels down.

The tugs dragged the destroyer to the dry dock. Her bow was down. The tops of two of her screws were projecting out of the water. The lines were passed to the handlers on the dock walls, and the ship was winched into place.

Three men had been caught by the final break. As the water drained out of the torn bow, the three bodies were recovered.

Captain Winchester was delighted with the result of the raid. His comment on the proposed loss of the services of *HMS Audax*, was, "Thank goodness it did not happen three years ago."

With the work load carried by the Harwich dockyard facility, it was decided that the Audax be given a temporary repair and so that she could be sent to Newcastle for a rebuilt bow section.

John was posted to the Portsmouth Office, still in charge of the *Mavis* and the ML. The Captain was posted to Whitehall, and the department was scaled down at this point in the war. The allies, According to John. 'Were now approaching a point where the armies of the east and west would meet and the quarrels would start.'

With the reduction in staff and the transfer of experimental duties from *Mavis* to the government labs, the actual workload for the department had reduced to a level where there was a chance for John and Chloe to think about their own private lives. They had plans to marry, arranged for the end of Chloe's service agreement.

Under the terms of her service she was not allowed to marry while serving in the WRNS.

The ML was called upon to perform other duties on loan to SOE and OSS. It was of interest to John that neither organisation showed any sign of wrapping up, despite the increasing certainty of the end of the war in Europe. Within, some ventured, six months.

John's thoughts strayed to the *Audax*, still waiting in the dock at Harwich. Alec was in command, at least until she had been repaired. John could not resist a sigh, as he recalled the feeling of being on the bridge in the sunshine of the South Atlantic.

Alec was given the task of sailing *HMS Audax* north, after her bows had been patched and a concrete plug inserted.

John and Chloe met Admiral Harrison and Captain Winchester on the quay at Harwich to see her off. Having dined well, they were all enjoying coffee in the wardroom there when the steward brought a message to the Admiral.

"I have just been told that *HMS Audax* has suffered a disaster in heavy seas. Her repair had been compromised. The plug had become detached and broken through taking the bow forward of the engine, away. The remainder of the ship was still afloat, but leaking badly from holes in the bulkhead. Support was on its way, though the other ships in the convoy had gone ahead, leaving a corvette standing-by. The ship was still under power, but making no progress.

Off Lowestoft, the stricken ship was being tossed about in the rough sea. From the bridge, Alec ordered the crew to prepare to abandon ship. The bulkhead had shown signs of collapsing.

Kit MacNish shut down the main engines and came on deck. His staff was on deck already. The life boats and rafts were poised for launching.

Alec was still on the bridge, keeping in touch with the corvette on the TBS.

Kit climbed up and joined Alec on the bridge.

"She will not last much longer." Alec commented.

Kit looked at him. "It's as if she decided she would go on her own terms," he decided.

"I think you may be right. The sad part is, after all the hassle and fuss throughout the war, she had to go out with a whimper."

The corvette came alongside and started taking off the remaining crew. The whole action was quiet and orderly. Finally, with just Kit and Alec still aboard, Kit heard the sound he had been dreading. The bulkhead gave way with a crack.

Kit stepped over to the corvette and yelled at Alec.

Alec jumped over the gap and the corvette clawed away from the sinking destroyer.

When they were well clear, the rescued crew stood and watched the dying throes of their former home. There was still a depth charge in the rack, despite the orders to set them at safe and ditch them. As the remains of *HMS Audax* sank below the surface, the depth charge went off, destroying the stern and allowing air to explode from the compartments where it had been trapped. The ship levelled off to an even keel, and sank, with dignity, to rest upright on the sea bed of the North Sea.

CPO Peters summed it up for the benefit of the members of the crew standing around him. "That's what I call a dignified demise. She decided that it was time to go, and went, not with her arse in the air like a trollop, but like the lady she was."

Chloe had tears in her eyes. She held John's arm tight when she heard about the passing of the ship that had been so much a part of their life for the duration of their war.

~*~*~*~*~

Meet our Author
David O'Neil

Frequently compared favourably to noted author, W.E.B. Griffin, O'Neil is an avid student of military history, especially during the time of sea battles and political uprisings. A native of the United Kingdom, artist and photographer David O'Neil started writing seriously with a series of Highland guide books. His boyhood ambitions were to fly an airplane, and sail a boat. As a boy he and his family were bombed out of their home in London. He learned to fly with the Royal Air Force during his National Service. He started sailing boats while serving in the Colonial Police, in Nyasaland (Malawi). He spent 8 years there, before returning to UK. Since then he lived in southern England where he became a management consultant, for over twenty years. He returned to live in Scotland in 1980, and became a tour guide in1986. He started writing in 2006, the first guide book being published in 2007. A further two have been published since He started writing fiction in 2007 and has now written five full length novels. A student of history and formerly military, O'Neil has been compared favorably with the UK's Ian Fleming and is frequently referred to as the "W.E.B. Griffin of the United Kingdom" due in a large part to his insightful recounting of exciting military exploits and his unique ability to develop credible characters.

Also by David O'Neil

Action/Adventure/Thriller series
Counterstroke # 1

Exciting, Isn't It?

O'Neil's initial entry into the world of action adventure romance thriller is filled with mystery and suspense, thrills and chills as *Counterstroke* finds it seeds of Genesis, and springs full blown onto the scene with action, adventure and romance galore.

John Murray, ex-Police, ex-MI6, ex management consultant, 49 and widowed, is ready to make a new start. Having sold off everything, he sets out on a lazy journey by barge through the waterways of France to collect his yacht at a yard in Grasse. En route he will decide what to do with the rest of his life

He picks up a female hitch-hiker Gabrielle, a frustrated author running from Paris after a confrontation with a lascivious would-be publisher Mathieu. She had unknowingly picked up some of Mathieu's secret documents with her manuscript. Although not looking for action, adventure or romance, still a connection is made.

An encounter with Pierre, an unpleasant former acquaintance from Paris who is chasing Gabrielle, is followed by a series of events that make John call on all his old skills of survival to keep them both alive over the next few days. Mystery and suspense shroud the secret documents that disclose the real background of the so called publisher who is in fact a high level international crook.

To survive, the pair become convinced they must take the fight to the enemy but they have no illusions; their chances of survival are slim. But with the help of some of John's old contacts, things start to become... exciting.

Counterstroke # 2....

Market Forces

Market Forces, Volume Two of the Counterstroke action adventure romance thriller series by David O'Neil introduces Katherine (Katt) Percival, tasked with the assassination of Mark Parnell in a hurried, last-minute attempt to stop his interference with the success of the Organization in Europe. As a skilled terminator for the CIA, Katt is accustomed to proper briefing. On this occasion she disobeys her orders, convinced it's a mistake. She joins forces with Mark to foil an attempt on his life.

Parnell works for John Murray, who created Secure Inc that caused the collapse of an International US criminal organisation's operation in Europe, forcing the disbanding of the US Company COMCO. Set up as a cover for money-laundering and other operations designed to control from within the political and financial administration, they had already been partially successful. Especially within the administrative sectors of the EU.

Katt goes on the run, she has been targeted and her Director sidelined by rogue interests in the CIA. She finds proof of conspiracy. She passes it on to Secure Inc who can use it to attack the Organization. She joins forces with Mark Parnell and Secure Inc. Mark and Katt and their colleagues risk their lives as they set out to foil the Organization once again.

Counterstroke # 3....

When Needs Must...

The latest action adventure thriller in the Counterstroke series opens with a new character Major Teddy Robertson–Steel fighting for survival in Africa. Mark Parnell and Katt Percival now working together for Secure Inc. are joined by Captain Libby 'Carter' Barr, now in plain clothes, well mostly, and her new partner James Wallace. They are tasked with locating and thwarting the efforts of three separate menaces from the European scene that threaten the separation of the United Kingdom from the political clutches of Brussels, by using terrorism to create wealth by a group of billionaires, and the continuing presence of the Mob, bankrolled from USA. An action adventure thriller filled with romance, mystery and suspense. With the appearance of a much needed new team, Dan and Reba, and the welcome return of Peter Maddox, Dublo Bond and Tiny Lewis, there is action and adventure throughout. Change will happen, it just takes the right people, at the right time, in the right place.

Young adult action/adventure/ romance thriller series
Donny Weston & Abby Marshall # 1

Fatal Meeting

A captivating new series of young adult action, romance, adventure and mystery.

For two young teens, Donny and Abby, who have just found each other, sailing the 40 ft ketch across the English Channel to Cherbourg is supposed to be a light-hearted adventure.

The third member of the crew turns out to be a smuggler, and he attempts to kill them both before they reach France. The romance adventure. now filled with action, mystery and suspense, suddenly becomes deadly serious when the man's employers try to recover smuggled items from the boat. The action gets more and more hectic as the motive becomes personal

Donny and Abby are plunged into a series of events that force them to protect themselves. Donny's parents become involved so with the help of a friend of the family, Jonathon Glynn, they take the offensive against the gang who are trying to kill them.

The action adventure thriller ranges from the Mediterranean to Paris and the final scene is played out in the shadow of the Eiffel Tower in the city of romance and lights; Paris France..

Donny Weston & Abby Marshall # 2

Lethal Complications

Eighteen year olds Donny and Abby take a year out from their studies to clear up problems that had escalated over the past three years. They succeed in closing the book on the past during the first months of the year, now they are looking forward to nine months relaxation, romance and fun, when old friend of the family, mystery man Jonathon Glynn, drops in to visit as they moor at Boulogne, bringing action and adventure into their lives once again.

Jonathon was followed and an attempt to kill them happens immediately after his visit. They leave their boat and pick up the RV they have left in France, hoping to avoid further conflict. They are attacked in the Camargue, but fast and accurate shooting keeps them alive. They find themselves mixed up in a treacherous scheme by a rogue Chinese gang to defame a Chinese moderate, in an attempt to stall the Democratic process in China.

The two young lovers, becoming addicted to action and adventure, link up with Isobel, a person of mystery who has acquired a reputation without earning it. Between them they manage to keep the Chinese target and his girlfriend out of the rogue Chinese group's hands.

Tired of reacting to attack, and now looking for action and adventure, they set up an ambush of their own, effectively checkmating the rogue Chinese plans. The leader of the rogues, having lost face and position in the Chinese hierarchy, plans a personal coup using former Spetsnaz mercenaries. With the help of a former SBS man Adam, who had worked with and against Spetsnaz forces, the friends survive and Lin Hang the Chinese leader suffers defeat.

Donny Weston & Abby Marshall # 3....

A Thrill A Minute

They are back! Fresh from their drama-filled action adventure excursion to the United States, Abby Marshall and Donny Weston look forward to once again taking up their studies at the University. Each of them is looking forward to the calm life of a University student without the threat of being murdered. Ah, the serene life.... that is the thing. But that doesn't last long. It is only a few weeks before our adventuresome young lovers find that the calm, quiet routine of University life is boring beyond belief and both are filled with yearning for the fast-paced action adventure of their prior experiences. It isn't long before trouble finds the couple and they welcome it with open arms, but perhaps this time they have underestimated the opposition. Feeling excitement once again, the two youths arm themselves and leapt into the fray. The fight was on and no holds barred!

Once again O'Neil takes us into the action filled world of mystery and suspense, action and adventure, romance and peril.

Donny Weston & Abby Marshall # 4....

It's Just One Thing After Another

Fresh from their victory over the European Mafia, our two young adults in love, Abby Marshall and Donny Weston, are rewarded with an all-expense-paid trip to the United States. But, as our young couple discover, there is no free lunch and the price they will have to pay for their "free" tour may be more than they can afford to pay, in this action adventure thriller. Even so, with the help of a few friends and some former enemies, the valiant young duo face danger once again with firm resolve and iron spirit, but will that be sufficient in face of the odds that are stacked against them?

And is their friend and benefactor actually a friend or is he on the other side? The two young adults look at this man of mystery and suspense with a bit of caution. Action, adventure and romance abound in this, the latest escapades of Britain's dynamic young couple.

Donny Weston & Abby Marshall # 5

What Goes Around...

Just when it seems that our two young heroes, Donny Weston and Abby Marshall are able to return to the University to complete their studies, fate decides to play another turn as once again the two young lovers come under attack, this time from a most unsuspected source. It appears that not even the majestic powers of the British Intelligence Service will be enough to rescue the beleaguered duo and they will have to survive through their own skills. In the continuing action adventure thriller, two young adults must solve the mystery that faces them to determine who is trying to kill them. The suspense is chilling, the action and adventure stimulating. Finding togetherness even among the onslaughts, Donny and Abby also find remarkable friends who offer their assistance; but will even that be enough to overcome the determined enemy?

Donny Weston & Abby Marshall # 6

Without Prejudice

Donny Weston and Abby Marshall, on their way to park their beloved boat *Swallow* in Malta to be ready for the summer, encounter the schooner *Speedwell* at La Rochelle, where problems arise for Commander Will and his wife Mary Pleasance. Tom Hardy and Lotte Compton, both from the

Speedwell join forces with Donny and Abby to oppose the threats to the Commander. From Valetta the four follow up the threat, only to find themselves faced with a plot to use a famous mercenary in an assassination that will rock the foundations of the Euro community, and the western world. Backed by Russia and with the tacit approval of the head of MI6, a rogue CIA operative has set things up for a public shooting at a Euro summit.

The four foil the plot and the assassination fails, but ironically the CIA agent, is credited with foiling the coup and promoted. He wants revenge, and comes after the four with blood in his eye and his guns loaded. The outcome is decided in a action-packed shoot-out in high speed boats in the cold waters of the Thames estuary.

Sea Adventures

Better The Day

From the W.E.B. Griffin of the United Kingdom, David O'Neil, a exciting saga of romance, action, adventure, mystery and suspense as Peter Murray and his brother officers in Coastal Forces face overwhelming odds fighting German E-boats, the German Navy and the Luftwaffe in action in the Channel, the Mediterranean, Norway and the Baltic – where there is conflict with the Soviet Allies. This action-packed story of daring and adventure finally follows Peter Murray to the Pacific where he faces Kamikaze action with the U.S. Fleet.

Distant Gunfire

"Boarder s Away!" Serving as an officer on a British frigate at the time of the French Emperor Napoleon is not the safest occupation, but could be a most profitable one. Robert Graham, rising from the ranks to become the Captain of a British battleship by virtue of his dauntless leadership, displayed under enemy fire, finds himself a wealthy man as the capture of enemy ships resulted in rich rewards. Action and adventure is the word of the day, as battle after battle rages across the turbulent waters and seas as the valiant British Royal Navy fights to stem the onslaught of the mighty French Army and Navy. Mystery and suspense abound as inserting and collecting spy agent after spy agent is executed. The threat of imminent death makes romance and romantic interludes all the sweeter, and the suspense of waiting for a love one to return even more traumatic. Captain Graham, with his loyal following of sailors and marines, takes prize ship after prize ship, thwart plot after diabolical plot, and finds romance when he least expects it. To his amazement and joy, he finds himself being knighted by the King of England. The good life is his, now all he has to do is to live long enough to enjoy it. A rollicking good tale of sea action and swashbuckling adventures.

Sailing Orders

For those awaiting another naval story of the 18/19th century, then this is it. Following the life of an abandoned 13 year old who by chance is instrumental in saving a family from robbery and worse. Taken in by the naval Captain Bowers he is placed as a midshipman in his benefactor's ship. From that time onward with the increasing demands of the conflict with France, Martin Forrest grows up fast. The relationship with his benefactors family is formalised when he is adopted by them and has a home once more. Romance with Jennifer the Captains ward links him ever closer to the family.

Meanwhile he serves in the West Indies where good fortune results in his gaining considerable wealth personally. With promotion and command he is able to marry and reclaim his birth-right, stolen from him by his step-mother and her lover.

The mysterious (call me merely Mr Smith) involves Martin in more activity in the shadowy world of the secret agents. Mainly a question of lifting and placing of people, his involvement becomes more complex as time goes on. A cruise to India consolidates his position and rank with the successful capture of prizes when returning convoying East-Indiamen. His rise to Post rank is followed by a series of events, that sadly culminate in family tragedy.

While still young Martin Forrest-Bowers faces and empty future, though merely Mr Smith has requested his services????

Quarterdeck

Following the highly successful introduction of Martin Forrest-Bowers into the Royal Navy in the best-selling sea adventure, ***Sailing Orders,*** David O'Neil, the UK's hottest selling author, presents another daring tale of Martin and his valiant men in a stirring story of war and sea, romance and action, valour and courage.

Now married and a decorated Captain himself, Martin returns home to find his wife Jennifer at death's door. Prompted by his safe return, her recovery is assured and is followed by the necessity of returning to work for 'plain Mr. Smith' with clandestine excursions and undercover trips to France. . At sea once more, he is involved not only with preventing treasure ships from falling into French hands, but also with events on the east coast of America in the run-up to the war of 1812.

Action, battle, romance, adventure and thrills abound in O'Neil's latest venture into the world of sea battles with France, Spain and American pirates.

Winning

Continuing the dynamic series of Captain Sir Martin Forest-Bowers RN and the unconquerable crew of the Royal Navy are once more in the thick of the action, with the task of upsetting the Maritime life of the Newly Independent Republic of America. The war of 1812 has been declared and combined with the French war it puts the Royal Navy into the position of possibly fighting on two fronts. Fortuitously the American navy is small and spread wide. The new ships are being built but are slow to come into service. In fact apart from one inconclusive action Martin fights most of his actions against pirates and the French. To his astonishment, the major action Martin fought was on land alongside Americans against a man setting up his own kingdom. Returning after a final sea battle with a renegade French flotilla and its prize, Martin finds that the war was over,

Part Two: With Admiral Bowers retiring, and the fleet shrinking rapidly, fewer commands are available. Martin finds himself on the beach. With his friend Antonio Ramos and many of his former officers and men, He forms a trading company and with two discarded frigates and an East-Indiaman, crewed by investors in the company they undertake a voyage to South America, with an undercover role to remove two renegade ships from the Pacific shores of Chile. Their travels take them around the world. The voyage is financially successful. But there are still no naval commands available, accustomed to winning, it seems this time it is Jennifer his wife who is winning this final battle.

Adventure thrillers

Making Waves

Nazi Germany and the Bomb!

Only a scant handful of highly placed people were aware that the German Nazi were in the process of developing an atomic bomb before the outbreak of WWII. A small group of agents recruited by British Naval Intelligence sets out to stop or at least slow down the development of the bomb and the missiles that would launch the deadly explosive that would vaporize London.

Not willing to pass their down time standing by idly, the band of assassins and saboteurs used every opportunity to disrupt the Nazi war effort. From 1938 to D Day, the Team operated undercover, fighting to keep the efforts of the Abwehr and the Gestapo at arm's length the entire time.

Failure didn't mean just capture, it meant vicious torture and excruciating painful death for the Team and absolute destruction for all of the United Kingdom. And—without doubt—the rest of the world

Minding the Store

O'Neil scores again! Often favourably compared to America's W.E.B. Griffin and to U.K.'s Ian Fleming, and fresh from his best-selling action adventure, "Distant Gunfire," O'Neil finds excitement and action in the New York garment district. The department store industry becomes the target of take-over by organized crime in their quest for money-laundering outlets. It would seem that no department store executive is a match for vicious criminals, however, David Freemantle, heir to the Freemantle fortune and Managing Director of America's most prestigious department store is no ordinary department store executive and the team of ex-military specialists he has assembled contains no ordinary store security personnel. Armed invasions are met with swift retaliation; kidnapping and rape attempts are met with fatal consequences as the Mafia and their foreign cohorts learn that not all ordinary citizens are helpless, and that evil force can be met with superior force in O'Neil's latest thriller of adventure and action, romance and suspense, mystery and mayhem that will have the reader on the edge of his seat until the last breath-taking word.

The Hunted

David O'Neal, UK's answer to W.E.B. Griffin and Dean Koontz strikes again with his newest suspense thriller filled with action, adventure, romance and danger. When the Russian Mafia joins forces with other European and Asian gangsters to take over a noted world-wide charity organization to smuggle guns and drugs into unsuspecting nations and begins to kill innocent people, one man – Tarquin Gilmore – Quin to his friends – declares war on the Mafia. To achieve his goal of total destruction of the criminal gangs, he surrounds himself with a few dangerous men and beautiful women. But don't be fooled by their beauty, the girls are easily as deadly as any man. On the other hand, there are a lot more gangsters than Quin and his friends and it's a battle to the finish. A stirring tale of crime and murder, mystery and suspense, passion and romance, guns and drugs... but that is war!

The Mercy Run

O'Neil's thrilling action adventure saga of Africa: the story of Tom Merrick, Charlie Hammond and Brenda Cox; a man and two women who fight and risk their lives to keep supplies rolling into the U.N. refugee camps in Ethiopia. Their adversaries: the scorching heat, the dirt roads and the ever present hazards of bandit gangs and corrupt government officials. Despite tragedy and treachery, mystery and suspense while combating the efforts of Colonel Gonbera, who hopes to turn the province into his personal domain, Merrick and his friends manage to block the diabolical Colonel at every turn.

Frustrated by Merrick's success against him, there seems to be no depths to which the Colonel would not descend to achieve his aim. The prospect of a lucrative diamond strike comes into the game, and so do the Russians and Chinese. But, as Merrick knows, there will be no peace while the Colonel remains the greatest threat to success and peace.

Romance

Seasons

Life and Death, Love and Hate in the Luscious Vineyards of France

Take one French Mademoiselle. Add one recently jilted English stone-mason. Put in a dash of a French one-legged ex-paratrooper. Stir in one inquisitive French priest. Blend in a crooked French businessman, a lawyer without a conscience

and several strong-arm Serbian gangsters willing to do anything if the price is right, and you have
the makings of a first-class brawl.

Top that with blatant attempts to steal valuable crops of grapes and olives and you will have the latest masterpiece from David O'Neil.

And More to Come

Printed in Great Britain
by Amazon

64532007R00173